THE YEMEN CONTRACT

ARTHUR KERNS

DIVERSIONBOOKS

Also by Arthur Kerns

Hayden Stone Thrillers
The Riviera Contract
The African Contract

Diversion Books
A Division of Diversion Publishing Corp.
443 Park Avenue South, Suite 1004
New York, New York 10016
www.DiversionBooks.com

For more information, email info@diversionbooks.com

First Diversion Books edition June 2016
Print ISBN: 978-1-68230-070-1
eBook ISBN: 978-1-68230-069-5

To Donna

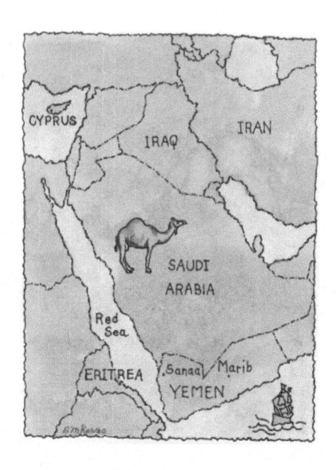

PRINCIPAL CHARACTERS

Hayden Stone: Former FBI agent, now CIA operative.

Sandra Harrington: CIA operative and Hayden Stone's partner.

Colonel Gustave Frederick: CIA official, a close friend of Stone.

Contessa Lucinda Avoscani: Love interest of Stone. They reunited after twenty years.

Abdul Wahab bin Khalid: A terrorist figure and Hayden Stone's nemesis.

Prince Mohammed al-Tabrizi: Saudi Arabian father-in-law of Abdul Wahab.

Ambassador Marshall Bunting: US ambassador to South Africa. A birder.

Patience St. John Smythe: Canadian intelligence and former love interest of Stone, now in a relationship with Ambassador Marshall Bunting.

Mark Reilly: CIA operative who works with Stone.

Jacob: Israeli Mossad agent and an old friend of Stone.

M.R.D. Houston: CIA station chief in Sana'a, Yemen.

Elizabeth Kerr: CIA intelligence analyst in Langley, Virginia.

Roberto Comacchi: Italian intelligence officer. Friend of Mark Reilly.

Vincente: Lucinda's cousin, head of Italy's intelligence service.

Ali al-Wasi: Yemeni intelligence chief, a friend of Stone.

Uthman: Lives in Sana'a. Knows Wahab's family and the Prince.

Kheibah: A native of the Hadhramaut. Strives to be an al Qaeda leader.

Dokka Zarov: Fugitive Chechen Muslim who flew Russian warplanes.

Paolo: Italian Intelligence agent sent by Lucinda to safeguard Stone.

Zaki: Hotel driver in Sayun.

Marcello: Lucinda's bodyguard in Asmara.

Yazzid: Bedouin who helped Stone and Sandra rescue the two CIA captives.

Nadheer: Stone's second driver in Marib, who is shot.

Mohammed: Stone's driver from the airport who took him to Marib.

Hakim: Tried to kill Stone and Sandra in Sicily.

CHAPTER ONE

SYRACUSE, SICILY—OCTOBER 6, 2002

Lying still. Eyes closed. Sandra Harrington listened to the lace curtain brush against the window frame. She smelled morning rain, a surprise for hot, dry Sicily, but then this was the stormy month. The rain would clear the air of ash drifting in from Mount Etna. She detected another odor. Blood.

Sandra's eyelids pushed open, and she focused on the ceiling's dusty light fixture. Her body felt strange, numb. Only after effort did her fingers move. Her left arm ached from where the fat man had jabbed the needle through the sleeve of her blouse. The sequence of events began to roll through her mind as she struggled to lift herself from the bed.

After arriving from Sana'a, Yemen and checking in to her hotel, she had phoned the agent she was to meet. The man had not appeared at the café at the appointed time. An hour later, after doing the required countersurveillance, she arrived at the alternate meeting place and waited for five minutes by the fountain in the quiet courtyard. He didn't show.

A fly buzzed in the window. Sandra managed to raise her right hand and saw blood. She dropped the hand down to her belly and thigh, which were bare and felt sticky.

She thought again about the previous afternoon. Failing to meet her source, she became anxious. Had al Qaeda discovered him? She had hurried back to her hotel. A block away, she turned a corner and bumped into the three men. They made no effort to disguise their intentions. The fat man stabbed her in the left arm with a hypodermic; the man with the lazy eye wrapped a scarf around her face; the young one, with severe acne, who didn't seem to know exactly what to do, held back. They walked her to her hotel, entered by the back door, and took her up to the room. They threw her onto the bathroom floor, where she stared at the small hexagon tiles. She slowly lost consciousness.

Raindrops flew in from the window and sprinkled her naked body. Sandra ran her hand across her skin, feeling gluey blood. Where did it come from? She felt for cuts or wounds. None. Inch by inch she raised herself. The wind had picked up and the curtain slapped at the window. In the distance, thunder rumbled. She stretched out her numb left hand and felt cold skin.

She turned her head and saw a young woman, not older than fifteen, lying half-covered with a bloody sheet. A long gash ran from the young woman's left ear across her throat and halfway up to her right ear. Her empty eyes turned backward toward the carved headboard. A small gold cross lay on a thin necklace between her breasts.

Again, she struggled to raise herself. The effect of the drug made movement almost impossible. She managed to slide her legs off the bed, and with her good arm pushed herself up to a sitting position. A siren wailed in the distance. Had al Qaeda alerted the police? Part of the plan? Two naked women in bed together, one with her throat slashed. She would be accused of murder. With her body not responding, Sandra knew escape was out of the question.

She reached over and pulled her cosmetic bag off the dresser. Then both she and the bag fell to the floor. The kit landed under the window. She inched toward it and stretched out her good hand. Outside the room, excited voices came from the staircase. She hadn't much time.

From the bag she removed an electric toothbrush. Her left hand still would not function, so with her right she put the bottom of the brush into her mouth, bit down, and turned the base a half-turn to activate the transmitter. Breathing heavily and hearing a pounding on her door, she switched on the electric toothbrush. It hummed.

The door to her room was about to be breached when, with one supreme effort, she grabbed the window ledge, pulled herself upright, and then tossed the humming brush into the alley below.

As the police entered the room shouting, Sandra collapsed, praying the signal from the emergency alert system inside the toothbrush had connected with the CIA satellite overhead.

SANA'A, YEMEN

The waiter carried a hamburger and french fries to the table where Colonel Gustave Frederick sat ramrod straight in a weathered outdoor stacking chair. Seated next to him, Al Goodman had elected to have the soup of the day, his reading glasses atop his thinning black hair.

Colonel Frederick studied his burger, then scraped off much of the condiment, which was either old salsa or bad chili. He took a bite. It wasn't as bad as it looked.

The two sat under a pale, cloudless sky at the U.S. Embassy's outdoor snack area, which served the staff during the milder months. From beyond the compound, in a distant minaret, a tape-recorded muezzin's call to prayer floated over the quiet, parched landscape. Frederick had arrived a month before to head a CIA special operations group. Jihadist terrorists were his targets. He studied Al Goodman's soup and wondered if it tasted better than his burger.

"How long will you inspectors be at the post?" he asked Goodman, who was on the Department of State's Inspector General's team inspecting the embassy's security operations.

"Two weeks. How about you?"

"I'll be here a lot longer, I suspect."

The CIA had sent Frederick's group to Yemen to investigate reports that al Qaeda and its sympathizers were planning to set up mirror terrorist operations similar to the ones in Afghanistan. Recent defeats by U.S. Special Operations had put the jihadists back on their heels, but not broken their spirit. Yemen was also the homeland of Osama bin Laden's family.

"This is an interesting country. Never been here. My last

post was Monrovia, Liberia," Goodman said as he spooned his soup. "Before I left, two of your people got into a shooting match with jihadists. The jihadists lost."

Frederick laughed. "You have to be referring to Sandra Harrington and Hayden Stone. Sandra is working for me now, and Stone has retired, for the time being."

Goodman nodded.

"Compared to Monrovia, this is a garden spot. Quite an interesting place." Frederick smiled. "Very tribal. Men walk around town with AK-47s slung over their shoulder. Daggers in their belts."

CIA Station Chief M.R.D. Houston approached, pulled a chair under the shade of the umbrella, and joined them. Houston, with an earnest face and jug ears, was also newly arrived, having been transferred in from Cape Town. Frederick had met him a few months before during the African operation.

"Colonel. We have a cable from headquarters that's Level: Immediate. Looks serious. Better come to the station to read it."

Frederick nodded and rose, then asked Goodman if he'd like the fries he hadn't touched. Shaking his head, Goodman said, "The kitchen probably used palm oil. My arteries are clogged enough."

On the third floor of the main embassy building, behind a vault door, Frederick stood and read the cable. The CIA at Langley, Virginia reported they had picked up an emergency signal originating from Syracuse, Sicily. It had Sandra Harrington's signature.

"Anything from Rome station?" Frederick asked Houston.

"No. All their people are north on a priority rendition."

"Anything interesting coming in on the terrorist communications traffic?"

Houston handed him three cables each dated days apart. "Seems some bad guys traveled from Beirut to Palermo a few days ago. The last cable mentioned something about a lot of volcanic ash in the air."

"What the hell does that mean?" Frederick asked. "Is it some kind of code?"

"No, Mount Etna's been spewing out smoke and lava for the past few days. Major eruption. The region around Syracuse has been covered with ash."

"Shit." Frederick threw down the cables. "Terrorists traveling to Sicily and I sent Sandra there without backup."

Mark Reilly, a CIA case officer, entered the secure space. Under cover as an Army officer, he wore silver lieutenant colonel's oak leaves on his shirt lapel. Frederick had specifically requested him for his team. The past spring they had worked on the French Riviera operation. Frederick found him tough and a seasoned veteran.

"Read this," Frederick said.

Reilly took the cable and paged through it. "Why didn't we know about this?"

Frederick threw off the question with a wave of his hand. "I need you to go to Sicily and find her. Learn what happened. Take the jet. Go as soon as you get your travel documents and operational gear together."

"I could use backup."

"We know someone who speaks Italian," Frederick said. "Hayden Stone."

"He retired," Reilly said.

Frederick grunted. "He'll meet you in Syracuse."

TUSCANY, ITALY

Hayden Stone traced the heavy dark wood of the dining table with his finger. The varying shades and patterns of the wood marquetry fascinated him. Contessa Lucinda had mentioned some time back that the wood for the table and accompanying china cabinet had come from a monastery north of Florence. Very old, she told him—centuries old, in fact. Unfortunately, the monastery had been renovated as a boutique hotel, and the panels from the chapel sold to collectors.

Lucinda, her brother Sebastian, and sister-in-law Margo chattered in Italian, some of which Stone understood, and most he found uninteresting. Lucinda's brother, a thin man with a thin moustache, was married to Margo, a Russian woman with a large mouth and a mole above her lip. Although she claimed some minor German title—Bavarian or Bohemian (it changed as she drank)—she had come into the marriage short of funds.

"Hayden. You're so quiet." Lucinda touched his arm and turned to the other two. "Let us speak in English for a while."

"Hayden does quite well in Italian," Margo said, smiling as if she had tasted something too sweet.

"Think I'll have a brandy and cigar on the porch." Stone rose from the table.

He felt Lucinda's eyes follow him as he went out through the French doors onto the terrace overlooking the gentle hills of the Casentino Valley. The evening light caught the autumn colors of the grape vines. On the hills, grass had made an appearance after the rains. The day had been warm and windy, but now the air was still, and the temperature dropped, bringing a chill.

A few moments later, Lucinda came out and joined him. "You need your jacket." She draped his sport coat over his shoulders. "And you probably forgot your matches. Here." Although tall, she had to rise on her toes to kiss his cheek. "Antonio will bring us cognac."

They leaned on the railing. He lit the cigar and handed it to her. She took a puff and gave it back. She wore the pants suit he had complimented her on many times—fine soft twill in olive green that complemented her auburn hair. A stylish Italian, she dressed for the season rather than the weather.

"Those two in there are driving me crazy," she huffed.

Antonio came with the drinks, and they enjoyed the sunset until their glasses were empty.

Lucinda was the Contessa Lucinda Avoscani, whom Stone had met twenty years before when he lived on the French Riviera. At the time he'd been a U.S. Naval officer assigned to Nice. After an intense summer affair, he was reassigned, and departed. He only answered one of her many letters. Eventually, they stopped coming.

The previous April, they had met again and gradually reestablished their relationship.

Lucinda's family seat was a palace in Villefranche, France. This villa was her grandmother's ancestral home, supposedly dating back to Roman times.

"My brother and that Russian want to take some of the unearthed artifacts and sell them to a Swiss dealer. You know as well as I there are legal implications to the sale of Italian antiquities."

"Why do they need the money? Your family's finances are back on an even keel."

"Some people just need more and more," she said.

"The last stay at the sanitarium appears to have helped your brother's nerves, but your sister-in-law is a real turkey."

"What is the meaning of turkey?"

Stone sighed. "She appears difficult."

Lucinda paused on the path and took his hand, raised his fingers, and brushed them against her lips. "No, my dear. She is a Russian bitch."

They continued on to the building that housed the relics. She unlocked the door and switched on the lights, illuminating an expansive room. Two wooden tables stretched the length of the room, stacked with tools of the archaeology trade: pans, picks, microscopes, and brushes. Interspersed among them stood the result of the exacting labor: terracotta vases, a bronze mirror, iron nails, statues, and assorted gold pendants.

"You have enough here to fill one floor of a museum." Stone remembered the upgraded alarms recently installed in the far wing that housed her private collection. "Any of these headed up to the villa?"

"This one." She took from the table a foot-high bronze chimaera, a mythical female beast combining the characteristics of a lion, a serpent, and a goat. Replacing it, she told him to come over and see a section of wall painting lying on the table. The top half of the picture showed Etruscans wearing bright colors, living the good life. The panel below showed the underworld, where blue demons dominated, and the dead languished.

She leaned against him. "Early in their civilization, the Etruscans thought the afterlife was a happy place. Toward the end of their era, their predictions were gloomier. What do you think, Hayden? What will be our afterlife?"

He enjoyed the thrill he got from her touching him, especially when she unexpectedly moved her body next to him. "I'm optimistic by nature," he answered.

"I need you here to help me. I know this friend of yours. Colonel Frederick wants you to come back and work for him."

"Fred called a month ago and hinted that I should return, but I'm still here."

"For how long?" She motioned that they should return to the villa. "As I said, I've come to rely on you."

"I intend to stay here with you." He took her hand. "If I ever did leave, it would only be for a few days."

She stiffened, annoyed, and hurried to turn off the lights.

When they returned to the main house, the brother and his wife were arguing in the dining room. Stone sensed that Lucinda was becoming ruffled, which meant she might start throwing things. He suggested they go to the living room and light a fire in the fireplace. The evening chill had crept into the house. He believed a fire in the hearth helped calm nerves.

Lucinda agreed and said she would meet him there in a few minutes. He decided to go to the computer room and check his e-mail. When he had finished and logged off, he found Lucinda sitting in front of a quiet fire sipping a Campari. She had placed a tumbler of Irish whiskey next to his chair.

"You have a frown," she said. "Did you receive a disturbing message?"

"My ex-wife answered my e-mail. As usual, she's up to her old tricks."

"I notice you always say, 'ex-wife,' and do not use her name."

Stone took a big swallow. Lucinda knew exactly how he liked his whiskey. He pondered her remark. "I noticed that too."

"Did she reply to your offer to have your two children come here to Italy for their breaks?"

"Oh, she's all for it now that she has her new position as the

SAC in San Francisco. Much too preoccupied with work to be bothered with the kids."

"What is this SAC?" Lucinda asked.

"Special Agent in Charge of the FBI office. She's a climber in the bureaucracy." Stone laid down his glass. "What she wants is a change in our divorce settlement, where she gets half of my pension and I get half of hers."

"She wants more?"

"No. She wants to eliminate it, and is willing to give up any claim to the house in Virginia." He looked for some reaction from Lucinda. "She's being very cooperative."

When Lucinda was about to render one of her judgments, her lip curled ever so slightly. Sometimes Stone enjoyed watching it, especially when he was not the one being judged.

"With this new position, your ex-wife's pension will be much larger. No?" Lucinda did not wait for the answer, but went on. "If she has a new love interest, she may be rearranging her financial situation."

Stone saw on Lucinda's face what looked like both relief and renewed confidence. "Yes, on both accounts," he said.

"I'm looking forward to meeting your children. Do they look alike?"

"Not that much. She has her mother's looks, dark and serious. He's athletic and has a sense of humor." He grinned. "Like me."

"You do, sweetheart. On occasion."

Stone finished off his drink. "Oh, Alice is coming without that boyfriend, or fiancé, Simon. As you know, their marriage plans were put off."

"The wedding, which your daughter asked you not attend because of her mother's animosity toward you?" Lucinda leaned closer to him.

Stone nodded.

"Ah, that is something that would hurt any father."

Stone waved the remark off.

"No darling, it upset you." She started to get up, but instead moved over and nudged her nose against his cheek. "Things have changed. For the present, your ex-wife has what she wants, so be agreeable and sign the papers. Soon you will see your children, and we all will have much fun." Lucinda thought a moment. "You have one of those white-suit lawyers, do you not?"

"It's called a 'white-shoe' law firm."

"Make sure he approves everything, before you put your name on the documents." She rose and pulled him up. "Bring your drink upstairs. I will make you forget your ex-wife."

• • •

She was true to her word and, when finished, rolled onto her stomach, exhausted. Stone reached over to the nightstand and switched off the light. His body, although sweaty, felt a chill, and he needed the covering of a sheet. Lucinda, lying next to him, moved against him each time he inched away.

He stared into the darkness. For the last six months they had been constant lovers. Even when he took the assignment in Africa, she had briefly joined him. He had begun to count on her being there. Why had she abandoned her twenty years before?

From somewhere in the room, he heard a faint beep every minute or so. He ignored it, thinking it one of the many electronic devices crowding their lives, like a radio, pager, or razor. A few minutes went by, and Lucinda sat up.

"Are you going to see what that is, or am I?" she said, annoyed.

Stone rolled out of bed, went to the bathroom, and got a glass of water. He searched the shelf and examined all the electronic gadgets and found none active.

Lucinda called from the bedroom, "It's your phone."

He returned and found her standing by the desk. She pushed it into his hand. "Your damn CIA phone. You may want to use it outside."

Stone went onto the balcony. The autumn wind had picked up, and he tightened the belt of his robe. The cellphone was the one he had failed to return to Colonel Frederick when he retired.

Frederick had called a month ago, advising he was on the way to Yemen and could use his services. Stone had declined.

The message light flashed dimly. He switched on the phone and saw that Frederick had called less than an hour before. He thought back to his conversation with Lucinda and her telling him she needed him. *Bad timing, Frederick.* He hit redial.

"Hi Fred."

"I'll get to the point. Sandra is in trouble. She was in Syracuse, Sicily to meet a source. Situation went bad. She's in jail for murder. Mark is on the way there and he needs support."

"Damn."

"I need you. We need you. A plane is waiting for you at the Florence airport."

CHAPTER TWO

SYRACUSE, SICILY—OCTOBER 7, 2002

Hayden Stone peered out the executive jet's narrow rectangular window. The plane had hit air pocket after air pocket since flying over Naples. Executive jet seemed a misnomer. No thick carpet or leather seats. No attendant offering free drinks. The interior was bare bones. Just a means of fast transportation for government employees hastening from one post to another.

The Straights of Messina passed below, the narrow passage between eastern Sicily and the Italian mainland. Years ago, when he was the officer of the deck on a navy destroyer, his ship had sailed through that waterway, gliding past the Greek mythological monsters—the whirlpools of Charybdis on the port side, the rocks of Scylla on the right. He'd left the navy, served in the FBI, and was now a CIA independent contractor—and here he was again.

Leaning back in his seat, he paged through the three-page intelligence summary Colonel Frederick had sent him. The information provided was vague, but Sandra Harrington, a professional CIA officer, a trusted associate of his, and a pal, had somehow gotten herself into a jam. He'd get her out of it, no matter what.

When a spy got arrested and jailed, you had to act fast. The first few hours were crucial in getting them released, one way or another. To extricate Sandra by force would be problematic since the captors were U.S. allies, the Italians.

He closed his eyes. At least he was working with the retired CIA officer, Mark Reilly. However, the two of them would need a lot of backup from CIA headquarters. He sat upright and took a drink from his water bottle. Sometimes fighting a government bureaucracy was scarier than going against the bad guys.

. . .

The plane set down at Catania Fontanarossa Airport, taxied through a steady drizzle, and then parked at the executive gate. Stone thanked the pilot and co-pilot and headed to the lounge. An unsmiling Mark Reilly waited at the door, accompanied by a younger man who was the same height as Reilly, six foot or so, with an athletic build. He wore a suit that looked tailored, like the one Lucinda had him buy. That and the assuredness Stone noted in the man's almond eyes hinted he was from SISMI, the *Servizio per le Informazioni e la Sicurezza Militare.* It was good to see Reilly had called in his chips with the Italian secret service.

"May I introduce Roberto Comacchi," Reilly said.

Stone exchanged a strong handshake. "Signore Comacchi. *Buon giorno.*"

"Please. Roberto."

Reilly told him a car was waiting. "We can talk on the way to Syracuse. It's an hour's drive."

Comacchi took the wheel of the Fiat sedan with Reilly sitting next to him. As they left the terminal, Stone checked for surveillance. A lone Fiat, identical in make and color to their car, pulled from the curb and followed. He caught Comacchi watching him in the rearview mirror. Roberto had a backup.

Stone spoke in English. "Mark. When did you arrive? Have you seen Sandra?"

"Came in yesterday, checked into the hotel—a small place that Roberto knows." He took a deep breath. "They won't let anyone see Sandra. She's recovering at a police medical facility. 'Still being questioned,' they said."

"Has the American consulate in Palermo sent anyone over?"

"Not yet—"

"My organization is making inquiries," Comacchi said, gesturing with his right hand. "There is more to all this affair, shall we say. You explain, Mark."

"We have two Italian bureaucracies at work here. The Justice side is the magistrate who's conducting a criminal investigation. He sees the murder as a juicy lesbian lovers' quarrel and is anxious to give a press release. He craves publicity and the locals will love it."

Comacchi said, "My organization, SISMI, has received reports of three al Qaeda members traveling to Syracuse for 'an operation.' If they were involved, we believe they would be gone now. Unless...."

Reilly turned around and faced Stone. "Unless they intend to wait around and see what we do."

"When can we see Sandra?" Stone asked. "How's she doing?"

Roberto Comacchi shrugged.

Stone thought a moment. "Roberto. Can you get a look at the police report? While we wait to see her, we might learn something that can help us find the killer or killers."

Comacchi rolled his right hand and continued to drive through the drizzle. Stone figured that Roberto was an intelligence officer posted to Sicily, a region foreign to his own province with no nearby relatives to put him in a compromising situation. J. Edgar Hoover had the same policy for his FBI special agents.

The passing cars were dirty with the mud and ash from Mount Etna's eruption. Stone asked how long the volcano was expected to be active. Again, a shrug and a hand wave.

Then Comacchi leaned his head back toward Stone. "The magistrate thinks Signora Harrington is just a tourist. He has no idea that she is one of your officers. At this time it is best not to tell him. What my connections have told me is that both women were drugged, but the authorities can't identify the drug. The magistrate assumes an illegal drug, of course. However, the police are not certain, except to say it was a paralyzing drug."

"Let's go to this medical facility and see if we can learn more," Stone said.

"We've got to be circumspect," Reilly said. "But Roberto, didn't you say you had a friend working there?"

"Signora Harrington is being held in the police wing of our

major hospital. The doctor who examined both Sandra and the dead girl," Comacchi said, and then with emphasis, "her name is Maddalena Galli. She and I are old friends. I wish it to stay that way."

Stone looked out the rain-streaked window. He couldn't see the countryside because of the heavy drizzle. "Let's get to this hospital and meet your Doctor Galli," he said.

. . .

Stone and Reilly let Roberto Comacchi lead the way up the marble steps into the hospital and past the disinterested reception personnel. The three made their way along a green corridor toward a set of double glass doors, their heels clicking on the marble floor. Stationed at the doors, two uniformed prison guards chatted with a member of the Carabinieri, Italy's military police.

Comacchi said he knew the policemen, yet he still offered a perfunctory show of his SISMI credentials to the three Italians. Stone remembered the times when he flashed his FBI badge to get that little extra attention. Sometimes it worked.

An involved discussion ensued while Stone and Reilly hung back. After a few minutes, Comacchi came back and led them to a window overlooking a dismal rain-soaked courtyard.

"What's up, Roberto?" Reilly asked.

"I can get past, but you can not. There is a question whether I'll be able to get into Signora Harrington's room. Definitely, you cannot."

"We can make ourselves busy and meet you in the lobby," Stone suggested.

"The timing may be good. My friend over there said that no one from the magistrate's office is expected for an hour or more." Comacchi whispered, "My friend is also getting me a look at the police report."

"You work wonders, Roberto," Stone said.

"The same friend knows a relative who wants to join my

organization when he graduates from university." Comacchi gave a look of resignation.

Stone said in a low voice, "If you get to see Sandra, tell her we're here and we'll get her out of this mess."

"We shall hope you are right."

• • •

Stone and Reilly walked back to the main hospital area and came to an elevator. They stopped and watched visitors bringing sacks stuffed to overflowing with meats, breads, and cheeses to their hospitalized loved ones.

"Mark, since we're alone, what about that agent Sandra was to meet? Any word on him, or from him?"

"Nothing from Langley, nor from Colonel Frederick."

Stone whispered, "How can we ask Roberto if they've recently found a dead Tunisian?"

"Can't." Reilly looked around to make sure no one was in earshot. "Look, Roberto may well know Sandra was to meet an agent, but we can't bring it up because we don't know he knows, and if he does know, we can't put him in a position where he has to lie about not knowing. Know what I mean?"

"I know," Stone grinned. "Working in the FBI was simpler."

Next to the elevator door, the hospital's directory extended almost from floor to ceiling. It appeared everyone who worked at the hospital had their name in white letters posted on the black background.

"Looking for our doctor?" Reilly asked.

"Yep, and there she is. Dr. Maddalena Galli. On the fourth floor."

The door opened. They stepped aside for exiting passengers and then, without speaking, entered the elevator. Stone smiled at the operator who pulled the grate closed with a clank. "*Quarto pavimento, per favore,*" Stone said.

On the fourth floor they made their way down a hallway looking for the number of Dr. Galli's office. Men and women in variously colored lab coats and smocks rushed by. They allowed a gurney carrying an elderly man to pass. The same sense of urgency found in hospitals throughout the world existed here. When they located the office, Stone reached for the doorknob, but the door flew open and a tall brunette bumped into him. Ignoring him, she called back to a colleague that she was going down to the cafeteria.

She turned back to Stone, studied his face for a second, and said, "Yes?"

"Dr. Galli?"

She looked up and down, as if examining him. "Yes. But I'm busy now."

Stone took an exaggerated breath and flashed a broad smile. "May we accompany you to the cafeteria? We've just arrived in town and we're famished."

"You are who?" she asked, and then nodded. "You are friends of the American girl."

"Yes," Reilly said.

Maddalena Galli closed her office door behind her, regarded both men, and then, with a tilt of the head indicating for them to follow, walked briskly to the elevator.

. . .

They sat at the end of a long table. Reilly had a beer and a ham and cheese sandwich, the Italian kind, with a fresh long roll stuffed with thin slices of prosciutto and a cheese Stone couldn't identify. He pointed and asked her what it was.

"You are not here to learn more about Sicilian cuisine, are you?"

"Not really."

Stone assessed Dr. Maddalena Galli. She was not Sicilian, nor southern Italian. No earthy presence, no honesty in her gaze, and a lack of warmth. She was slim and had high cheekbones, with long slender fingers that would help with bringing a baby into the world. He picked up aristocratic ancestry in her face.

He decided to come to the point. From this woman's

demeanor, she had no time to dawdle. "You examined Sandra Harrington. We are not allowed to see her. How is she?"

"How would you be in her circumstance?"

Stone grew impatient. "We know she is innocent of murder."

She continued to eat her lunch, tossing a salad with the dressing.

He pressed. "We came here to find out what happened. You can help Ms. Harrington and us. There are people. Bad people who want to…." At that point Stone didn't know what to say. Reilly jumped in.

"Doctor. Sandra is a good friend—"

"I didn't take you for family." Dr. Galli laid down her fork and lifted her face as if she were about to sniff the air. "You are friends of Roberto. No?"

Both Stone and Reilly nodded.

She waited a long time before continuing. When she did, she spoke through clenched teeth. "Signora Harrington…."

"Yes."

"She and the other girl were brutalized by fiends."

Again she paused, as if what she were about to say would be entered into a court of law. Stone realized that the doctor was one savvy woman. Suddenly, Roberto materialized. He wasn't smiling as he pulled out a chair and sat next to her.

"I see you two did not wait for me to introduce Maddalena."

"Would you believe we just happened to bump into each other?" Stone said.

"No," Comacchi drawled. "But do not let me interrupt. Please continue."

"Roberto," Maddalena said, touching his hand. "Please make the introductions. These gentlemen failed to give me their names."

Comacchi introduced the two and verified they were friends of Sandra Harrington. He added that they were colleagues of his from America.

Maddalena tore off a piece of bread and ate it with some cheese. She leaned back and looked at Stone. "As I said, the two women were brutalized. We have evidence that three men raped the girl before they cut her throat."

"DNA and semen?" Reilly asked.

Stone took a deep breath. He didn't want to ask if Sandra had been raped for fear of hearing she had. Maddalena spoke softly. "No, Mr. Stone. Your friend was not violated, which under the circumstances is odd."

Stone nodded. "How is she? Is she in much pain?"

"The drug her abductors administered may have done some neurological damage. In time we will know." She paused. "She is in deep depression. Knowing you two are here will help."

Stone turned to Roberto. "If we find these three thugs, we'll make them give us samples of DNA. One way or another. That'll clear Sandra."

Comacchi stiffened. "When we take them *alive* and question them, that will help also."

Stone got the message. "Let's go to the hotel where it happened. Do you have the address?"

"Yes. I've learned other things, but we can talk about it later in the car," Comacchi said.

Maddalena stood and touched Roberto's cheek as he rose. "I do not want to know what you three have planned. I must go. I have a busy schedule." She leaned over and whispered something in Comacchi's ear that made him smile.

CHAPTER THREE

Roberto Comacchi maneuvered the Fiat expertly down the flooded streets, where rivulets streamed along the gutters. Water flowed from pathways down the hills into the main thoroughfare. He told Stone and Reilly that if the rain didn't stop, some streets would become impassable. The hotel where Sandra had been assaulted was a ten-minute drive from the hospital and not far from the Greek ruins that overlooked the harbor. "It is in Ortygia. Quail Island," he said. "Very old district of Syracusa."

Stone asked, "Roberto, what did you learn from that police report you read at the hospital?"

"No witnesses saw the two women enter the hotel the previous night. The hotel staff claimed complete ignorance of what happened." Comacchi shrugged. "It is to be expected. Many of the employees working there have criminal records, so they would not be especially forthcoming."

Stone leaned toward Comacchi. "Any of the staff have ties with terrorists?"

"I saw nothing like that in the file. Also, I saw no reports from police informants. Too early in the investigation for that."

"What about the dead girl?" Reilly asked.

"Ahh. Very sad. She was fourteen years old, a student at a Catholic school. She finished classes at four in the afternoon, left for home, and never arrived. Parents went to the police, and we now know the rest." Comacchi slowed and stopped. The street ahead was flooded. He turned onto a side street and continued, "The parents and the neighbors are incensed. They cry for revenge."

"Any indication this may have been a mob hit?" Stone asked. "A mafia payback to the girl's family?"

"We do not believe so, but the police are double-checking with their informants. Indication is the local Mafioso has made a financial contribution to the grieving family."

"Great. The mafia is looking for justice," Stone said, and leaned back. "That doesn't help us time-wise. Back to Sandra, did they find anything in the room that could help us?"

"Signora Harrington checked in the hotel before noon, about eleven o'clock, left her room about two in the afternoon. The police found one suitcase, which contained only a woman's personal belongings."

Stone wondered if Sandra had carried any of the tools of the spy trade with her. Had she hidden them? Had the terrorists taken them?

Comacchi continued, "Her passport was recovered along with a wallet with her identification and three euros. No credit cards were found."

"I guess the killers helped themselves," Reilly said.

Or the police, Stone thought. "We'll put a watch on those credit cards. How did the police know to go to the hotel?"

"An anonymous call to the Carabinieri. Which is luck for us. They record all incoming calls to their headquarters."

"Someone called the military police, not the local cops," Reilly said. "I think they were counting on the publicity."

"Yeah," Stone said. "Thought was put into this abduction and murder. We're dealing with more than just a bunch of thugs having a good time."

The car slowed in front of a small hotel nestled in among other granite-faced buildings along the narrow street. Puddles reflected the soft light from the street lamps hung on the building facades. A gloomy rainy afternoon in Syracuse with smells of wet stone. There was no sign of a police presence. Comacchi pulled the car halfway up the sidewalk so other automobiles could pass.

He turned to Stone. "It may not be wise for the three of us to go inside the hotel right now. We do not want to overwhelm the staff, no? The police gave them long interrogations."

"You may be right," Stone said. "You two go in and find

out what you can. I think I'll stroll around and scope out the neighborhood. I'll be back in thirty minutes." The three checked their watches. An Italian wool cap lay on the seat next to Stone. "Roberto, mind if I borrow your hat? The rain is getting heavier."

"Don't lose it," Comacchi said as the three exited the car.

• • •

Stone began scrutinizing the area surrounding the hotel. First he circled the four-story building, studying the arches, the windows, and the roof. No fire escapes. The three al Qaeda operatives had to enter by one of the ground floor entrances. He walked into the alley behind the hotel. The usual debris, with stacked crates and weeds growing high. Nothing to get a grasp on, as far as evidence was concerned. Nothing he could discern as an investigator. Damn.

He left the alley, returned to the street, and took a right. The rain continued. Shops and offices lined the one-lane street consistent with what one would find in any semi-commercial district. It reminded Stone of old Paris neighborhoods. The rain shoved pedestrians indoors. No tables sat outside the fronts of the cafés.

Except for one open trattoria. From the street, Stone looked into the darkened bar. Men clustered at the back, talking in heavy accentuated Sicilian accompanied by animated gestures. A hunch that he might learn something prompted him to enter.

"Caffè," Stone said.

"Espresso?" the young man asked. He sported a surly smirk and long sideburns.

Stone knew he had entered a neighborhood bar that didn't need cash from strangers.

The bartender glanced at his patrons, who appeared interested in the stranger, then went to a coffee machine and began the process of brewing his drink.

Being in Sicily meant he had to accept the glares and resentment given to all non-regular patrons, not just Americans. Be cool, Stone told himself.

The coffee was presented in a discolored cup on a chipped saucer. It was dark, heavy, and good at the first taste. Stone leaned against the bar and looked out at the rain.

A few moments passed, and the young man, after looking once again at his companions at the end of the bar, asked, his voice almost guttural, "Are you a *turista?*"

"No. A travel writer."

"Americano?"

Stone couldn't tell if it was a question or statement, but answered, "*Irlandese.*"

"Americans are not welcome here." The barman made an appearance of wiping the top of the counter with a stained white towel. He pointed with his chin toward the open door. "Some bitch lesbian *Americana* killed one of our girls. At that hotel down the way." He waved his hand.

Stone steadied his hand as he raised the cup to his lips. "How do the police know she did it?"

"The *sbirra* say she murdered the girl. Raped her first, then slit her throat." The man slid his index finger across his neck. "What are you writing about?"

Stone cleared his throat. "Your ancient ruins and churches."

"Go see the cathedral. It is built on a Greek ruin."

The barman began waving his towel as he yelled out the door to a passerby. "Filippo. *Como si senti?*"

The young man stopped and approached the door. "*Bonu, grazii.*"

Stone didn't see any cheer in Filippo's eyes.

The barman asked him where he was going and Filippo said he was going to church. They spoke in Sicilian, which Stone found hard to follow.

"What's going on at the hotel?" the barman asked.

"Two *polizia* are asking more questions." Filippo said.

"What kind of questions?"

"They are looking for Arabs. I don't know what else. I'm going to the cathedral." He turned back into the rain.

Stone placed euros on the counter and waved a farewell that was ignored. On the street he saw Filippo, hunched against the raindrops, turn a corner. Stone waited for him to get a two-minute start, then followed.

After a few blocks, Stone had closed the distance. A block later they entered an expansive piazza. He followed Filippo's path, avoiding the puddles in the square. The cobblestones were slippery underfoot.

Stone went through the tall doors of the church moments after the young man entered. The smells of incense and candle wax greeted him. At the front row of pews he paused and removed his hat, shaking off the water. His eyes adjusted to the darkness. Tour books featured the building as one of Syracuse's highlights. The church had not so much been built on a Greek temple as it encompassed the ruins. The ancient Doric columns were integral to the structure. This had been consecrated ground long before the Greeks, then during the Greek reign, and now the Christians took on the obligation.

From a distance he saw that Filippo had gone to a side altar and knelt before a silver statue of some saint. He took his time approaching him, noting old women saying their rosaries, others motionless with their eyes closed. No one sat in the section where Filippo knelt.

Stone took a pew five rows away and studied him. Filippo looked intently at the altar, his wringing hands in constant motion. He shifted his weight from one knee to the other. The rain had spotted his blue suit coat.

Stone looked around, saw no one near, and approached Filippo, who was kneeling next to a metal stand holding an array of votive candles. He brushed his left hand on Filippo's shoulder.

"*Mi Scusassi.*" After excusing himself, Stone took his time lighting two candles.

Stone lingered before the candles and made an exaggerated sign of the cross. From his peripheral vision he saw the young man glare. Without turning, Stone asked, still in Sicilian, "*Parra inglisi?*"

"*Vattinni!*" As he told Stone to go away, he started to rise from the kneeler, but Stone with his left hand held him down and pressed his thumb hard into his neck. He repeated his question whether Filippo understood English. The man growled that he did.

Stone changed his approach. Filippo, although bothered by something, was not a wimp. "I need to talk with you, my friend. Let us sit in a pew." He waited for an answer, still pressing down with his thumb. "*Pi fauri*. Please. We must speak."

Filippo stood, then with both hands pushed Stone away. Surprised, Stone reacted by giving him a hard backhand, his ring cutting the young man's cheekbone. He then grabbed Filippo by the shoulders, walked him to a nearby pew, and pushed him down. He took the pew behind him. Filippo dabbed his cheek with his handkerchief.

"Turn around, Filippo. I want to ask you some questions about the murder at the hotel."

The young man sputtered, "How do you know my name?"

"Doesn't matter." Stone waited a moment. "Before you tell me what you know about the murder, tell me, why you are troubled? Why do you pray?"

Filippo held the bloodstained handkerchief to his cheek. "That is my business. I come to pray, not to be beaten up." His dark eyes held Stone's gaze. "Your accent is American."

Stone said each word slowly. "I am an American like the woman who is falsely accused of killing the girl in your hotel. I want to know what happened." Stone heard the clicks of a woman's shoes as she walked up the aisle to the center altar. He didn't have much time to get information from this man.

"I have spoken to the police. I don't know you. I now leave."

Stone opened his jacket exposing the Colt .45 automatic. "Look you little shit. This gun has big bullets that make a lot of noise. Can you imagine the echoes they would make in this church? Not to mention the big holes in your gut."

Filippo's mouth hung open.

"The American woman is my friend." He now switched to Italian. "She is falsely accused. We do not have much time. You know something. That's why you are troubled, yes?"

Filippo blinked a few times and looked toward the main altar. Stone needed an opening with this man. No time to offer him coffee, talk about his family, his love life, the usual prelude to an interview in an interrogation room. He looked back at the side altar.

"Who is that saint you were praying to?"

"Santa Lucia."

"You were praying for the girl who was murdered." Stone let his statement hang, and then it came to him. "You don't blame the American woman, do you? You know she didn't do it."

Filippo made a move to rise, but Stone patted his gun and placed his hand on Filippo's arm.

"I'm looking for three men from the Middle East. *Tre Arabi.*"

Stone watched the young man's shoulders shrink within his suit coat. "At the hotel the police asked me this morning about them." He put both hands to his face, quickly taking the hand from his swollen cheek.

"You talked with these three Arabs. You dealt with them. Now you are sorry."

Filippo nodded.

"I am waiting to hear your story." *Or better, your confession.*

"The police know you are here?"

"Yes," Stone said. He patted Filippo's shoulder.

"But you people are not police. You are—"

Stone searched for the word. "*Investigatore.*"

Filippo looked down and spoke so softly Stone had to move closer to hear.

"Three men with Arabic accents came to the hotel desk and asked for a room. I told them we had no rooms." He looked up at Stone. "My bosses say no Arabs in our hotel."

"Remember what they looked like?"

Filippo snorted. "The man with a goatee did the talking. He seemed the boss. He never smiled. There was a young one, my age. He never spoke. His face was all...." He dotted his face with his two index fingers.

"Acne. Pimples?"

"Yes. The third one was tall and had a funny eye. He had a gun tucked inside his belt."

"What happened then?"

"They left. Next day I am walking to the hotel and the boss comes out of a *pasticceria,* eating a cannoli. Cream dripping on the front of his jacket. He walks alongside me, and talks, but says nothing. I try to get away, but then he says, 'Would you like to earn a few euros?' I tell him what fool would not. He holds on to my sleeve and stops me. 'Tomorrow a blonde American woman will come to your hotel,' he says. 'You will call this number when she arrives.' I ask if that is all. He says, 'Yes.' He puts fifty euros in my hand and walks away."

Stone leaned back in the pew. Al Qaeda knew Sandra was coming to Syracuse. Knew the hotel where she was staying. What happened to the agent she was to meet? What was al Qaeda's motive in all this?

Filippo continued, "The next day the blonde signorina arrives at the hotel and goes to her room. I called the number and tell some man she arrives."

"Were you not suspicious of these men?"

The young man let out a long sigh.

"Do you still have the telephone number you called?"

Filippo fumbled in his pockets and pulled out a dirty slip of paper. He handed it to Stone, who examined it and recognized the Middle Eastern method of writing numbers.

Stone leaned closer. "Did you see them again? These men?"

He nodded and looked away. Stone saw tears forming.

"Go on."

"Later, when I came out of the toilet and saw the three men bring Signorina Harrington in the back door of the hotel and take her up to a room."

"You told no one about this?"

He shook his head. Stone wanted to pull out his gun and hit him over the head. He clenched his fists and asked, "Did you see anything else?"

Filippo looked down. "I saw the man with the evil eye take the young girl up the stairs. She was crying."

Stone's body stiffened; his muscles hardened, as when

he was ready to attack. This worthless prick saw what was happening and did nothing.

"That is why I come to pray. I feel guilt."

"A lot of good that does, asshole." Stone wondered if it was worth beating the crap out of this miserable piece of shit. He looked at his watch and saw that Comacchi and Reilly would be waiting for him. He stood. "Let's go back to the hotel." Then more as an afterthought, he asked, "Ever see those bastards again?"

"Yes."

Stone sat. "Where? When?"

"This morning. I saw the boss man leave the *pasticceria* and walk to his hotel. I was going to tell the police."

"You'll take me to the hotel. *Presto.*"

CHAPTER FOUR

SYRACUSE, SICILY

The rain had stopped, and Hayden Stone followed Filippo down the wet cobblestone street. Stone phoned Reilly on his cellphone, but only got a busy signal. Filippo paused at an intersection and whispered in Stone's ear. "It's the hotel around this corner, on the other side of the street."

Stone looked around and counted four storefronts down to a faded sign announcing the Flora Hotel. The structure stood three stories and looked tired. Drawn shades hung ragged at the bottom. The street was deserted.

"You saw the boss man, the man with the goatee, enter this hotel?"

"*Sì.*"

"Only him, not the other two?"

Filippo nodded and appeared anxious to leave. Stone took the man's arm and spoke in Italian. "Return to your hotel. You'll find the two policemen there. Tell them everything you told me and say that Finbarr wants them to come here to the hotel as soon as possible. Also, give them this telephone number you gave me. The one the Arab gave you."

Filippo took the piece of paper and as Stone watched him scurry off, questioning whether the man could be trusted to find Roberto Comacchi and Reilly. He was certain that if Filippo did return to his hotel and find Stone's companions, he wouldn't give them the full story. He tried phoning Reilly again. No answer.

The rain resumed, this time heavier than before. Stone pondered if he should stay in position or not,

The rain helped in making the decision. He crossed to the hotel side of the street. Anyone looking out the hotel's front windows would have a hard time seeing him approach. The marble steps and the wood doors to the entrance needed cleaning. Inside the dimly lit reception area, he recognized the place as one that would handle transients—perhaps workers and farmers in from the countryside.

The man behind the reception desk wore a gray sweater and had what looked like a buzz cut prison haircut. A pale pallor magnified the creases in his face. Stone looked at his watch as if he was meeting someone and drifted to a side room that had tables and chairs. Apparently the hotel breakfast room. He was about to take a chair when a Middle Eastern man in his early twenties entered the front door, hurried past him, and climbed the stairway to the upper floors. Fiery red pimples covered his face.

The receptionist answered the loudly ringing phone and turned away. Stone followed the man up the stairs.

At the top of the first landing, he watched the young man hurry down the hallway. Stone followed, keeping a distance.

As he followed, he sensed something was not quite right, and slowed his pace. The man continued walking to the end of the corridor.

Stone's hand gripped his .45 Colt. Then the man spun around with a gun in his hand. Stone's pistol was out and aimed at his midsection when the door to the room to his right side creaked open.

Stupid move.

Stone never saw who struck him.

• • •

Cold water splashed Stone's face. He sat naked in a metal chair, eyes closed. The water that drenched his body felt good. It ached from bruises on his arms and shins. A young man wound duct tap around his upper torso. Stone's feet were bound to the legs of the metal chair and each arm was taped separately to the back supports. All secure, except for his left wrist, which was loose. Nervous from being berated in harsh Arabic, the kid had probably been careless. Stone recognized the dialect as Iraqi.

Stone opened his eyes. A man with a close-cut goatee raged, shouting and gesturing to the young man. Next to him, a tough-looking, thuggish man with a bad eye repeatedly slapped a two-foot pipe in his hand. No doubt he'd had fun hitting Stone while he'd been unconscious.

The kid finished binding Stone and said to the goateed man, "He is bound tight, Hakim."

Stone scanned the room and was surprised to see that he wasn't in a hotel room. The expansive area had a concrete floor and narrow windows lining the high ceiling. The place resembled a warehouse. The smell of motor oil hung in the air.

A table was placed next to his chair. On it were pliers, an assortment of knives, and a hacksaw with a shiny new blade.

Hakim turned to the man holding the pipe and said in Arabic, "Get his attention. Not the face."

The thug came up and, with a yellow-toothed smile, stabbed Stone's genitals with the pipe. Stone yelled out, "Son-of-a bitch."

"Such language, Mr. Stone." Hakim laughed and then shouted to the kid to set up the camera equipment.

The young man hurriedly set a video camera on a tripod, ran a cable to a laptop computer sitting on the floor, and connected another one to a bulky satellite telephone.

Hakim took a microphone from the kid and began speaking distinctly in English. "Mr. Hayden Stone. Please speak up. It will help us move along." He placed the microphone directly in front of Stone. "Who is your immediate superior in the CIA?"

Stone pulled his throbbing head back from the instrument, and then took his time answering, "Pardon. There must be a misunderstanding. I'm a mere travel writer."

Hakim said, "Ahmed. Hit him."

The pipe came down hard on Stone's shoulder blade. Blood flowed, and pain radiated down Stone's side.

The other thug's name is Ahmed. Learned something.

Hakim appeared to enjoy the beating. "You, Hayden Stone are CIA. Yes?"

"I'm a Yankee Doodle Dandy. Yankee Doodle, do or die."

"Well put, Stone. You will die, but before you do, we must go through our performance." He motioned to Ahmed. "Cut the right hand loose. Hold it down on the tray."

"I have a question." Getting no response, Stone continued, "Which one of you perverts slit the little girl's throat? And did you get a hard on when you did it?"

"Hold his hand down!" Hakim shouted to Ahmed as he picked up the pliers and inspected them, snapping them open and shut. "Fool! Don't get in front of the camera. Our client wants to watch his face as it happens." He leaned his face next to Stone's, his breath reeking of garlic. "We must extract some information from you." At this, he laughed, closed the pliers on the fingernail of the little finger on Stone's right hand, and yanked.

Stone thought he had touched a high-velocity electrical line. His scream came involuntarily. His body, charged with an overflow of adrenalin, jerked the chair off the floor. Blood spurted from his finger.

Hakim laughed as he stuck the pliers holding the bloody fingernail in front of Stone's face. He looked over at the kid behind the video camera. "Get over here and help."

Stone pulled with the injured right hand, and both Hakim and Ahmed tightened their grip on his hand. The kid ran to Stone's left side and put an arm lock on his head.

As they all struggled, Stone realized his left arm had become free from the duct tape. His forearm burned from where the tape pulled off his skin. The kid's eyes fixated on Stone's bleeding finger and as he pressed against Stone's face, the gun stuck in his back pocket hit Stone's nose.

Stone couldn't make out the make of the cheap looking pistol, but guessed it Russian or Chinese. He just hoped that if it had a safety, it wasn't on.

"Hold the next finger out to the camera," shouted the fat man, and he tried to grasp Stone's ring finger with the pliers.

The three terrorists shouted at each other as they jostled Stone, making the metal chair scrape across the cement floor.

They were having difficulty getting the finger into the view of the camera lens.

Hakim yelled to the kid. "Go move the camera closer!"

As the kid released Stone's head and turned toward the camera, Stone pulled the gun from the kid's pocket, and barely caught it from falling on the floor. He grasped the pistol handle and found the trigger. Only his forearm was free, so twisting his body, with the gun next to his belly, he squeezed off a round.

Ahmed leaped, yelled, and holding his side, fell forward onto the floor. For a second Hakim looked at Stone in amazement— the pliers still attached to the fingernail of Stone's ring finger.

"If you drop the pliers, I won't shoot you," Stone said. The feel of the pistol was cheap. Recycled metal?

Hakim dropped the pliers.

In that instant, Stone thought of the girl these three thugs had murdered. Stone smiled as he squeezed the trigger and saw a pop of red flesh on Hakim's forehead. Then blood seeped from the hole centered just above the killer's eyes.

Ahmed lifted himself up onto his knees and studied the hole in Hakim's head. He then glanced up at Stone, eyes expressionless, and remained motionless, as if he expected to be next.

The kid ran across the room, slid open the corrugated door, and was exiting when Stone put a bullet into the back of his right thigh. The kid screamed and hobbled off, yelling in Arabic.

Stone looked back at Ahmed. "Well, he'll draw the attention of the police, wouldn't you say, asshole?"

Ahmed's calculating eyes looked at Stone's naked body and then at his finger. It had bled a pool on the tray. He was waiting for him to pass out. Time for a non-lethal shot to the gut.

Stone was aiming when uniformed men burst in the open door yelling, "Polizia!" Behind them came Roberto Comacchi and Reilly.

"Cover your faces," Stone shouted to his colleagues. "We're on camera."

CHAPTER FIVE

THE FOLLOWING MORNING

Hayden Stone winced as Dr. Galli applied antiseptic on the raw flesh where Stone had once had a fingernail. He sat on a low table in her office, a quiet oasis in the bustling hospital overseen by stern, white-robed nuns. She wrapped a bandage around the fingertip and instructed him to see his personal physician when he returned home.

"Will the fingernail grow back?" Stone asked.

"If the matrix—the root bed at the base of the nail—if that is not damaged, it will grow back. It could come back a bit disfigured." She stood back and looked him up and down. "It appears they tried to take out the nail on the ring finger also, but it will only blacken."

An interested Roberto Comacchi and Mark Reilly stood behind Dr. Galli. Reilly spoke up.

"How's he otherwise?"

"Bruises on the legs and arms. His muscles protected the bones. The collarbone may have a hairline fracture. We shall see from the X-rays." She went to wash her hands at the basin in the corner. "The genitals are swollen. You should use ice on them, Mr. Stone."

Roberto held back a laugh behind his hand. "Any damage there, Maddellana?"

She cut him a look that said he had crossed the line. A lot of sweet talk would be required before Roberto would get a kiss tonight.

Stone held up his right hand. "How soon will this hand be functional, Dr. Galli?"

"You can use it now."

"I mean, like shoot a gun?" Stone had already accepted he'd have to retire his .45 caliber Colt because of the recoil. Instead he'd carry the 9 mm Sig Sauer P226 the agency had been urging him to use.

She shrugged off the question.

Reilly said, "It didn't prevent you from using a gun at the warehouse."

"Using my weak hand." Stone stretched his back, then added, "FBI agents are trained to shoot pistols with both hands. You people aren't?"

"Of course we are," Reilly said quickly.

Roberto jumped in. "And my service, also."

"Are you all finished with this *machismo*?" Dr. Galli interrupted. Finished cleaning up, she came back and sat next to Stone. "Now that your wound is dressed, we will discuss the condition of Signorina Harrington." She looked at the other two men. "And this is for all of you." She took a deep breath and looked up at the ceiling. "She needs... Roberto, how do you say *simpatia*?"

"The American expression is 'tender loving care.'"

"*Sì.* That is the phrase." She paused, looked directly at Stone, and raised an eyebrow. "She has asked for you, Mr. Stone."

"I've wanted to see her since I arrived in Syracuse."

"The police are now allowing her to have visitors."

"Oh," Stone said. "When will the DNA and other tests come back, matching those thugs with the murdered girl?"

Roberto answered for her. "The tests take time, but that man Ahmed is going nowhere soon. The officials are very interested in prosecuting him. The press was given his name this morning."

Reilly accompanied Stone and Roberto down the busy corridor. The three stopped in a quiet alcove. Out the window, Stone saw that it had stopped raining and a bright, sharp sun lit the city. In the distance the sea lay calm.

Stone asked, "How did you find me at the warehouse?"

"My people used the phone number that the man from the

hotel, Filippo, gave us. It was a phone purchased here in *Syracusa*. We put a locator search on its chip."

"We recovered the camera and laptop computer," Reilly said. "Also the satellite phone. We should be able to retrieve some interesting information from the computer and maybe the phone. We may learn who was watching you in the warehouse."

Roberto coughed. "A few matters have come up. Some legalities that are peculiar to our justice system."

Stone got an uneasy feeling.

"One, the matter of your abduction, and the killing of that terrorist. The police and the courts will want to know the details. The police made a report that when we entered the warehouse you were found bound to a chair, in a semiconscious state. The report reasoned that the man was shot by one of his colleagues. So your presence at court may not be necessary, and I emphasize 'may not.'"

"Under the circumstances, that would be a reasonable conclusion," Stone said.

"That would mean the surviving man, Ahmed, will be charged with murder of the other man."

"Along with the murder of that young girl."

Roberto raised a finger. "A second matter. The magistrate in the case still looks for sensationalism. He knows Signorina Harrington will be cleared of murder, but he plans to use her in the trial. The press and the public are anxious to see her."

This news prompted Stone to rest on the bench next to the window. The pain in his legs and arms from the beating had become intense. He could barely use his right hand, and now the ribs on his left side ached.

Roberto said, "I will do all I can to prevent this."

Stone looked at Reilly and knew the two were thinking the same thing. Sandra could not appear in a Sicilian trial, because the CIA wouldn't allow it. He looked up at Roberto. "You have to interview this bastard Ahmed, before the police get to him."

"Too late for that. He's being questioned by the police now." Roberto whispered in Stone's ear, "However, that young man, the one with a bullet in his leg. My people found him. My organization officially invites the CIA to join in questioning him."

"While you visit with Sandra, I'll go with Roberto and get a look at this guy," Reilly said.

"This may work out," Stone said. "It would take time to crack Ahmed. He looked like a tough nut, but the kid appeared to be only a half-assed believer in al Qaeda." He looked at Roberto. "Where did your people find him?"

"He went to a pharmacy for bandages, and the owner became suspicious and called a friend at the police station. I was called, and had my people pick him up."

Stone thought a moment. "If the kid went to a drug store for help, it means he probably doesn't have any al Qaeda backup in town."

"A little less having to watch our back," Reilly said. "I'll be in touch. Say hello to Sandra."

. . .

Sandra's still eyes were fixed on the ceiling. The space was clean, Spartan, and quiet. The single bed was positioned between two windows that overlooked a parking lot. A door on the right led to a private bathroom. Sun coming through the window brightened the white curtains and bedsheets.

The moment she turned her head and saw him, her eyes filled with life. Gently, he sat on the edge of her bed and brushed her unkempt hair from her forehead, and then kissed her on the cheek. Her skin felt as cold as it looked, and her face lacked the strength he so admired. It was as if she had aged ten years.

He sat back and the two looked at each other for a long moment.

"Where the hell have you been?"

He figured she was trying to sound tough, but her voice cracked.

"Sightseeing. I'm a travel writer."

"Get me out of here."

Stone explained what the magistrate had planned for her—a

star performance in a Sicilian court of law. She looked away and uttered a slight moan.

"I won't let that happen," he said.

She looked back.

"Reilly and I are going to fly you out of here." He patted her arm. "Soon."

"What the hell happened to your hand?" She took it and touched the bandage on his finger. "They got to you, didn't they? What did they do to you?"

He told her. "Reilly and Roberto came and rescued me." Stone let her continue to hold his hand. "They lured me into a trap, and I fell for it."

"You're getting careless. Or maybe you're no good without a partner." Her brow creased. "So, it wasn't me they wanted. They used me to get to you."

"I feel bad about what you went through."

"Forget it, Hayden. I figure they were after both of us."

"Listen to this," Stone said. "While they were beating the shit out of me, I was being videotaped. No, actually recorded live, over satellite. Someone enjoyed the proceedings."

"You really pissed somebody off."

"Sorry I got you involved."

"You'd do the same for me."

A nursing sister came in and frowned when she saw Stone sitting on the bed next to Sandra, holding her hand. He rose, and as he gave the nun a slight bow, an idea came to him of how he and Reilly would extricate Sandra from Syracuse.

• • •

"You're leaving town. Here's your disguise." Stone slipped back into Sandra's room ten minutes later and tossed her a white nun's habit. "Are you able to put this on?"

She paused and, gaining her composure, said, "I'll change in the bathroom. Turn around and don't look at me getting out of bed."

The two men went to the window and gazed out at the

noon sunshine bringing out the aged beauty of the city. Reilly whispered, "Why not wait till dark? This seems so… fast."

"There's a CIA plane waiting for us. Right? Why wait? The best plan is a simple plan. Let's just walk out."

Reilly shrugged.

Sandra emerged from the bathroom wearing the white habit. "Where's the wimple?"

Stone and Reilly looked at each other.

"The white starched thing that goes around the neck and head. Under the veil."

"We didn't see one. Just pull the veil over your head. Hide your hair," Stone said. "You'll look like a novice."

Sandra's eyebrow arched.

"An older novice," he said. "Let's go."

. . .

Stone held Sandra's arm as they hurried across the tarmac toward the private jet. She stumbled on the hem of the habit a few times. It belonged to a taller woman.

Reilly, who was following them, called out, "Your plane is on the right. I'm taking the other one with our package."

Sandra stopped, almost tripping Stone. She turned around to Reilly. "Who's the package?"

Reilly shook his head in a noncommittal manner.

"Is he one of those bastards who killed the girl?"

Stone squeezed her arm. "Let it go, Sandra. Get on the plane."

A black Fiat sedan pulled up next to Reilly's plane, and two men emerged. They pulled out a hooded figure and marched him up the ladder into the jet.

"Which one is he?" she demanded.

"The kid with the bad complexion," Stone said.

She reached for the pistol in his shoulder holster. "Give me your gun. Let me shoot that shit in the balls."

Reilly spoke up. "Roberto and I are taking him to Cairo to meet our Egyptian colleagues."

Sandra took deep breaths. The veil slipped, and her blonde hair fell down against her cheek. Stone didn't know if she was going to cry, or break loose and run toward the terrorist.

"Hey pal." Stone pulled her to him. "After a few days of intense interrogation about his al Qaeda connections, that asshole will wish you had shot him. Besides, it wouldn't look good for a nun to whack some guy."

• • •

Sandra surprised him by not taking a seat next to him on the plane. She refused to speak to him or take the offer of drinks from one of the CIA crew. An hour into the flight, he watched her body shudder. She kept looking at her hands, turning them back and forth as if they felt dirty.

Her behavior reminded him of the pain in his little finger. Now the finger next to that one ached. The whole hand throbbed, and he jumped every time he touched anything with it.

As he rubbed it, Sandra surprised him by dropping into the seat next to him. She studied his face for a while, and then asked if he would join her in a drink. They both had vodka on ice.

"Want to talk about what happened?"

She shook her head.

"Let me know when you do."

They were on their second drink when she asked, "Any idea who hates you enough to have gone to all this trouble?"

"Only one person. Abdul Wahab bin Khalid."

Sandra leaned close. "I heard the Canadian Security Intelligence Service had him under wraps."

Stone nodded.

"By the way, where are we headed?" Sandra drained her drink. "Yemen?"

"Not yet." Stone gave her a gentle bump with his shoulder. "We're going to Cyprus."

CHAPTER SIX

THE RED SEA, OFF THE COAST OF YEMEN
—OCTOBER 9, 2002

Aboard the Red Scorpion, Abdul Wahab bin Khalid relaxed, watching the gulls dive for the fish churned up in the yacht's wake. Only a few of the birds were successful, and those flew off before others stole their catch. So much like life, thought Abdul Wahab. Someone always trying to take away one's successes.

He breathed in the salty air and told himself to enjoy the mild weather. This time of year, the temperature on the Red Sea hovered around eighty degrees at noon. Quite pleasant with a cloudless sky, and off on the starboard side there were interesting islands to study as they passed, the surf foaming over black rocks.

His fingers smoothed down his black moustache and goatee, trimmed that morning by the ship's barber. Across from him, sharing the view from the canvas-covered fantail, sat his father-in-law, Prince Mohammed al Tabrizi. The prince spent a considerable bit of his time living on his gleaming, white, three-hundred-foot vessel. Still, he maintained constant contact with his family in Saudi Arabia. Now he was traveling to Yemen to visit distant cousins, and Wahab had asked to join him. He had business there, Wahab explained.

That past summer Wahab had been a guest aboard the Red Scorpion while anchored at Nice, France, but that stay had been marred by one personal disaster after another. The whole matter was best forgotten, but he couldn't let it go. Nor could he stop thinking about the cause of his problems, the CIA operative, Hayden Stone. Two days ago, secreted in his cabin with his computer, he had delighted in watching Stone being tortured. Then, before his eyes, Stone had broken his bonds, and overcome those three idiots Wahab had sent to Syracuse to kill him. At least they pulled out one of his fingernails. But no matter. At that very moment, plans were in motion to bring about Hayden Stone's demise.

His attention was diverted by the sound of a jet overhead. Wahab pointed up. "Your Highness, it appears the F-15 is being relieved by another jet from the base in Taif."

The prince's white *thobe*, the robe draped from his neck to ankles, flapped in the gentle breeze. Even though he had lost weight, Wahab observed that he still presented a formable figure. The gray traces in his beard gave him a dignified presence. The prince tilted his head and looked up at the two planes.

"It is reassuring that we are being protected," Wahab said. Before coming aboard he had been told that a cousin of the prince, a general in the Royal Saudi Air Force, thought it wise to be cautious in these pirate-infested waters. The general ordered around-the-clock air cover for the ship. The crew had also been armed.

The prince turned to Wahab and continued to finger his prayer beads, his eyes and thoughts hidden behind dark glasses. "Abdul. What do you have planned for your visit to Yemen?"

"When I was a young man, I visited Sana'a, and I want to see if it has changed. Also, their museum has acquired some interesting artifacts from the Marib area of Yemen. Finds from the archaeological site of the Queen of Sheba. I am interested in the lost Sabaean civilization."

"Of course you are." The flowing red and white checked *gutra*, held in place by a black double-corded *igal*, covered the prince's head. The wind caught the cotton cloth, and he pushed it back from his cheek. "It is good to hear that you are returning your attention to scholastics. Your venture into politics and those radical matters has proven a problem for your family."

Wahab shifted in his seat. "Last year I had thought it prudent and wise to join our brothers in Afghanistan. At the time I believed helping the Taliban and their cause to be just. Besides, we of our tribe must not fall out of step with the jihadists."

The prince put his beads away. "Sometimes, my dear friend, you sound like a harangue from one of those Gulf state news broadcasts. All young men desire to go to war." He crossed his legs, revealing American-made boat shoes. "You are not young, yet you still have a blood lust."

"My Prince…." Abdul Wahab gripped the arm of his chair. He had to be careful with his father-in-law. "I only hold certain beliefs important."

"Abdul, you are a very interesting man. A bit of a mystery." The prince clapped his hands, and a Nubian servant appeared. "We will have tea."

Wahab demonstrated the required deference with a slight bow of the head. He then removed his Panama hat and wiped perspiration from his brow.

"Have you visited my daughter? Your wife living in Jeddah?" the prince asked. "Your principal wife, I might add."

"When I leave Yemen, I'll fly there and visit." His wife resided in a secret sanitarium reserved for nobility. Beautiful as she was, her mind had dissolved into fantasy, no longer recognizing reality. He glanced at his gold watch and saw that it was noon.

"And your other wife, Lady Beatrice Roscommon?"

"After visiting Canada for a short spell, she has returned to Cape Town," Wahab said, happy to see the servant returning with the tea service. The prince disapproved of Lady Beatrice, but she was his window to the West. He took a cigarette from his case, snapped it shut, and lit the cigarette with his gold lighter.

As the Nubian placed the silver tray on a nearby table, the yacht rolled, upsetting the china. The noise from the motors below deck grew louder and the ship's speed increased. The prince removed his dark glasses, rose, and searched the horizon.

"There." The prince pointed. "We have uninvited guests."

Abdul Wahab jumped up and saw that one of the speedboats towed by the mother ship had cut away and was now heading toward them at a high rate of speed. Although a good mile away, it was closing the distance fast. The second speedboat likewise had broken away from the ship and followed.

Men stood behind a machine gun mounted on the bow of the first speedboat. Others lined the side of the boat. He counted nine men, all carrying firearms.

He turned toward his father-in-law, who stroked his beard and whose eyes had attained the sharpness of the proverbial tethered falcon suddenly unhooded.

"Pirates!" an armed crewman yelled, running down from the bridge. "Sire. You must seek safety below deck."

"You will bring me a machine gun and a pistol," the prince ordered and then, looking at Wahab, "Bring the same for him."

"I suggest we go up to the bridge, Your Highness," Wahab said.

"We will stay here at the stern. The action will be most enjoyable, don't you think, Abdul?"

"True." Wahab watched the speedboat closing in. Members of a terrorist organization? Hardly. A band of pirates from the islands. Poor buggers. They were to meet with paradise sooner than they imagined. No treasure for them today.

Crewmembers handed the prince and Wahab M4 carbines and Browning HP 9mm pistols. Wahab saw that the prince's firearms were specially made, with polished stocks and grips and intricate Arabic scrolling on the chrome plating of each gun. Wahab's weapons were standard issue.

The speedboat had closed the distance to almost five hundred yards. He checked the pistol to make sure it was loaded, then removed the carbine's thirty round magazine to inspect it and slammed it back in place. He slipped the pistol under his belt and raised the M4 to eye level and selected the semiautomatic option.

"May I fire a warning shot, Your Highness?"

"I would suggest you do so before they open up with that machine gun."

Wahab fired one shot at the boat to test the range. The round fell short and he fired again. This time the bullet struck the boat's hull.

The men in the speedboat answered with a burst from their

machine gun, spraying the water next to the yacht. Direct hits pinged the side of the yacht. Wahab knelt next to the railing and selected the three round burst option on his carbine and fired. The prince remained standing and fired until his M4 emptied.

The yacht's captain ran up and asked the prince to take cover, but he refused, and yelled, "Radio the F-15 overhead to assist us. What is that fool up there waiting for?"

As the captain turned to return to the bridge, he tugged the prince's sleeve and pointed to the other side of the ship. The second speedboat had come around the stern and opened fire. It maneuvered to come along the other side of the yacht.

"Your Highness, go to the bridge with the captain," shouted Wahab. "I'll stay here with the crew."

The prince hurried inside the cabin with the captain, up to the bridge three decks above.

Wahab ordered one crewman to keep firing at the second speedboat, and told the other three to fire at the first speedboat, now only a hundred yards away.

The four fired in unison, and two of the raiders fell, but the pirates manning the long-barreled machine gun raked the yacht's superstructure. Wahab threw himself onto the deck as one by one the crewmen next to him went down.

He looked around and saw that he alone remained alive. Shoving a fresh magazine in the M4, he crawled from the open deck through the door of the ship's dining room. He looked back and watched the speedboat pull alongside. The machine gun trained at the crew on the two upper decks. Pirates in ragged clothing leapt from their boat onto the yacht and advanced toward him.

Wahab stepped forward to the open door and coolly fired at the closest men. Two buckled, clutching their stomachs.

Other pirates sprayed bullets from their AK-47s in his direction. As his targets fell before him, Wahab felt the exhilaration he remembered in Afghanistan when he had killed one American soldier after another. Then the killing was for jihad. Now it was for his own enjoyment.

His gun emptied at the same time he saw that the second

speedboat had positioned itself a few hundred yards behind the yacht. As three raiders advanced toward him, Abdul Wahab dropped the carbine and pulled out his Browning pistol.

His finger was on the trigger when the second pirate boat trailing the yacht exploded. The F-15 had hit it with a missile. The three pirates turned to watch a second missile hit the remains of the boat, exploding it in a bright orange burst. One of the pirates dropped his gun to place his hands over his ears. The acrid smell of nitrates and gasoline floated toward them.

The three pirates paused and stared at the smoke and falling wood of what was once a sleek, twenty-five-foot boat. As they did, Wahab rushed on deck and, with his pistol, placed one 9mm round in the back of each of the three men's heads.

The men fell forward, their bodies reacting with individual shakes and twitches. Wahab turned when he heard footsteps behind him. The prince, accompanied by armed guards, brushed past and went to the rail where the first speedboat had turned to flee. They fired their weapons at the retreating craft.

"Your Highness. You've been shot," Wahab said, touching the prince's shoulder.

The prince lowered his empty M4 carbine and stared at the speedboat heading for the mother ship. "As they say in those American Western movies, it is only a flesh wound." He looked up at the sky at the F-15, which had banked and now flew low at a decreased speed. "This should be interesting to watch."

The pirates on the escaping speedboat began firing at the plane with their AK-47s. No one fired the boat's machine gun. Perhaps they were out of ammunition.

At that, the water around the speedboat erupted, then the craft disintegrated in flame and smoke. The Gatling gun on the F-15 fired until the boat's form disappeared, then the plane accelerated with a loud blast from its twin engines, and pointed its nose toward the mother ship. The jet launched two missiles, which left thin white trails. The rusty ship's bow blew off and within five minutes no trace of the ship remained except for flotsam and an oil streak.

Wahab looked at the prince's bloody shoulder. "Your Highness, the doctor must attend to that."

"Abdul, you and the captain restore order on the Red Scorpion." The prince looked around at the once-polished teak deck, now covered in blood, spent shell casings, and dead bodies. "Have this cleaned up."

After the prince left, the captain and Wahab inspected the yacht. Many of the crew lay dead, others wounded.

"A royal naval frigate is on its way to help with the injured. I see it there on the horizon," the captain said. "Abdul Wahab. What do we do with these?" He pointed to the dead pirates.

"Throw them to the sharks."

"And the wounded pirates?"

"The same."

CHAPTER SEVEN

Sandra Harrington adjusted her seat back a notch so she could rest her head. Hayden Stone was driving the Fiat sedan, which came with the CIA villa. The house sat alone on a hillside within the British cantonment that housed military personnel. With the temperature in the seventies, the dry air coming in the open window felt refreshing. The countryside of Akrotiri, or the Western British Sovereign Base Area, reminded her of Prescott, Arizona, where her parents had retired. The air had that same dry, herbal smell. She gazed at the rolling hills of chalky soil dotted with clumps of green low-lying trees.

Following the medical examination, which found her physical injuries unthreatening, she went along with the physician's diagnosis that she suffered from depression resulting from her experience. As was CIA routine after an employee's traumatic experience, she had a long session with the CIA-contracted therapist flown in from McLean, Virginia. She'd had another session that morning.

The attractive, well-groomed woman with a slight Georgian accent had listened as Sandra spoke of her ordeal in Sicily. At the end of the morning session, they had touched on her negative feelings for men since her abduction. They would discuss it further the next day.

"What did you think about that castle called Kolossi?" Stone asked. "Goes back to the twelfth century, and all the knights were headquartered there. Even the Knights Templar. Amazing that the building still stands after all this time, even after the Ottoman occupation."

"Very nice." She managed a thin smile. Stone had become less morose when they landed in Cyprus—one of his favorite spots in the world, he told her. He'd convinced her to join him in sightseeing. The base was littered with historic ruins, and they spent almost an hour touring the classical site of Kourin, wandering around the open Greek theatre, and gazing at the Sanctuary of Apollo. They rested on a toppled Roman column and Stone slipped into philosophizing about history and religion. Although she found it a bit boring, she listened. When he let his guard down, as he did now, he reminded her of a boy she dated in high school. That fellow had had a touch of naïveté.

"I wonder if anyone still believes in the ancient Greek and Roman gods. You know, Apollo and Hermes? Can you imagine coming across some village here or in Greece where they still worship them? That would be quite a find."

As he chattered about the archeological sites they visited and passed, she only half listened, letting her mind float. She found it easy to relax with Stone. And, of course, great to work with him. Her negative feelings toward men did not extend to him.

Stone winced from his bruises when he moved too quickly. Now, as he drove the car, she saw that the bandage on his right little finger showed a touch of red.

"Getting hungry?" he asked. "I know a great place to eat. It's a few miles up the road in Pissouri Village. A family-run place tucked off the main square."

Sandra's stomach growled. While in Cyprus, they hadn't eaten off-base. "What's on the menu?"

"Sort of Greek and Turkish food, but unique in a Cyprian way."

They pulled into the village and parked off the main square. The Mediterranean Sea sparkled through the pine and cedar trees. She caught a whiff of ocean air. Off the mosaic-paved square, Stone led her down a narrow walk to the taverna. Pots filled with flowers and plants lined the five steps leading up to the entrance.

A young girl put them at a table next to a window. "I won't go heavy," Stone said. "We'll just get a taste of this and that."

She watched him explain to the owners that he wanted all portions on the same plate. "The lady has to enjoy seeing the colors of the dishes all together and take in all of the delicious smells."

At last the owners understood what Stone wanted. They insisted that the hummus and bread be served separately from the main course, which gave Sandra and Stone time to take in the restaurant's atmosphere. The place held only nine tables with straight-backed wooden chairs. A local artist's bright watercolors lined the whitewashed walls of the room. They were the only non-Cypriots having lunch.

In time their meals were brought to the table, the steaming food spilling over the sides of the plates. Stone pointed out the Cyprus potatoes, long and waxy with a distinct taste. There was also Cuttlefish in red wine and onions accompanied by peas, along with okra baked in the oven with tomato and the local olive oil.

She had a glass of wine, but Stone declined, which surprised her. She never knew Stone to turn down an opportunity to have a drink. "The roads here are tricky to manage," he explained. "Remember, we're driving on the wrong side of the road, and it takes a while to adjust. A custom left over from when the British ran the country. So, I need my wits about me."

As they ate, he continued his banter about the island where few Americans visited. "Most of the vacationers are Brits. The Swedes come in the summer, and you should see the girls on the beaches."

"How about the Swedish men?"

He laughed and changed the subject. She continued to allow him to jabber. Before they had left the villa, he told her that in a few days he'd be returning to Italy. His job was done. She leaned closer to him. "I'm moving from Paris back to Washington. I've been offered a position on the Intelligence Community staff."

Stone said nothing.

"I know. It's a desk job, but it's a promotion." She took a bite of the cuttlefish. "I need a break from fieldwork."

Finally, Stone said, "Me too."

• • •

As they departed the restaurant, Sandra remarked on the clarity of the air.

"I want to show you an interesting spot with a fantastic view," Stone said.

They drove about ten minutes along the coastal road and parked at a dirt parking lot atop a limestone cliff overlooking the sea. Around them, the arid landscape looked as clean as the air smelled. They got out and went up to the wooden railing and looked down at the transparent blue water.

"See that rock?" Stone pointed. "That's the Rock of Aphrodite. Legend has it that this is where she was born and rose from the waves. For centuries worshipers would come here to celebrate. Had some wild parties down there, they say."

Sandra thought about how many years that story had been told. Then she asked, "Ever take a swim down there?"

"No, but I always wondered how neat it would be to swim at night under a full moon."

"Hayden. I never realized you were such a romantic." Sandra smiled and breathed in the salt air. She wanted to touch his arm, but more than that, she wondered how it would be to join him down there in the little bay under the moonlight, feeling the warm water on her bare skin.

FLORENCE, ITALY—OCTOBER 14, 2002

The morning rain eased, and Contessa Lucinda pulled her Maserati sedan into the only available parking space at the Piazzale Michelangelo. She had suggested to Stone that they drive north from her villa in the Casentino Valley to Florence for lunch, and to do a little shopping.

When Stone had flown in from Cyprus, she had met him at the airport and was alarmed at his injuries. "You are in a terrible business," she told him after they had made love. Now and then he had jumped when she touched certain parts of his body, where bruises and cuts appeared. Then there was that damaged finger.

The two strolled across the large square to the balustrade from where she studied the city spread out before them. As they took in the panorama of Florence, she reached over and ran her finger down the scar on Stone's cheek. He took her hand and kissed it. The sun broke through the clouds, deepening the tone in the wet tile roofs of the city below. The cathedral, Il Duomo, glowed in the sunlight.

"I always like to come here first when I visit Florence," Stone said. "Like I always have an Irish coffee when I go to San Francisco."

Lucinda thought he acted more relaxed after spending a day with her. He had confided that he believed his days working for his government were coming to an end. She anticipated his permanent return.

"Shall we have lunch?" she asked, and turned up her collar against the damp chill. He hugged her. It was unusual for him to show any public display of affection. She held on to him a little longer than he wanted, then said, "Shall we go? I know the perfect place for lunch."

• • •

Lucinda drove down the hill and crossed a bridge over the Arno to the medieval section of Florence. Traffic was heavy even with the tourist season over.

"I love this restaurant," Lucinda said as they sat at the window, with a view of the Ponte Vecchio. "My father took me here many times when I was young. I am quite fond of this scene."

Staring at the famed bridge spanning the Arno River, Stone said, "The story has it that during World War Two the German commanding officer made a deal with the Americans. Against Hitler's orders, the general wouldn't blow it up if the Americans wouldn't cross it with their troops and tanks. We kept our word."

Lucinda nodded. "Somewhat like the German general who disobeyed Hitler and didn't burn Paris."

Stone tapped his fingers on the white linen tablecloth. "I guess not all the destroyers of civilization come from the East. Every culture has its share of barbarians."

The night before, Stone had told her about Sandra being abducted, and about his own capture. "No sense keeping secrets from you," he had said. "You know all the players. Al Qaeda and Abdul Wahab." Today, she decided to broach the subject again.

"Hayden, this Sandra has been your associate for a while?" She knew the answer, but wanted to know just how close he and this Sandra were. "Do you have a photograph of her?"

"No." Then after a long pause, while she felt him study her, said, "She's decided to leave field work and take a desk job in Washington. The terrorists gave her a rough time."

"They also gave you a rough time." She turned her wine glass. "Why did they?"

Stone didn't answer her until after they ordered lunch. He then leaned forward and whispered, "We think Abdul Wahab was behind it all. Theory is he's holding a grudge against me, because I spoiled his plans in Africa and the South of France."

The waiter served a rich *Ribollita*, the hearty Florentine soup made of cannellini beans, vegetables, and red cabbage, which brought back memories of her childhood during winter Tuscan afternoons.

Lucinda thought back to the previous spring. Wahab, working on behalf of the Saudi Prince Mohammed al Tabrizi, negotiated a lease on her palace in Villefranche. Her palace had ended up a ruin after the terrorists Wahab had invited held a shooting match. She harbored suspicions that Stone somehow had been responsible, but was afraid to tell her the details.

"I never trusted that man," she said. "Thank goodness the prince came through and paid for the repairs to my palace." She sipped her Orvieto, which she found to be a pleasantly dry, crisp wine. "I thought that after the affair in Cape Town Wahab was taken away by your secret service."

"The Canadians bundled him up and took him to a confinement center. That reminds me, have you heard from Patience St. Jean Symthe? She was the lead Canadian security person."

She shook her head. "How could Wahab do you harm if he is in custody of the Canadians and also your people, the CIA?"

"Don't know. I hope my colleagues are finding that out as we have lunch."

• • •

When Stone paid the bill, Lucinda saw his worn wallet. "Florence is the place to buy a new wallet," she said as they left the restaurant. "We will walk to a leather shop I know. It is on a side street, not far from here."

The sidewalks still had small puddles from the rain, which they avoided as they walked, her arm through his. Noise from passing cars and loud voices bounced off the stone-faced buildings and paved streets. Lucinda pointed to a side street, and as they turned into it, a haggard-faced man bumped into Stone, then continued walking.

Stone took her arm and moved briskly a few steps, then stopped and looked back.

"Hayden. What is it?"

"That was an old friend, Jacob."

"Why didn't he stop?"

She watched Stone check both ends of the deserted alley. "He's a Mossad agent I worked with in Africa." Stone's hand squeezed her arm, and she pulled away. "Jacob was giving me a message," he whispered. "Something is about to happen."

Lucinda looked down the alley and spotted the leather shop a few doors away. "There is the shop. We can go there and wait to see what happens."

As she spoke, two men emerged from a nearby doorway. Both carried pistols fashioned with silencers. Stone pushed her aside and leapt forward two steps, jumped, and kicked the man in the stomach. The man fell back and groaned when he hit the street.

With a sharp blow with the side of his left hand, Stone broke the gun arm of the second man, sending the gun clattering across the cobblestone pavement. He knelt on one knee, clutching his arm.

She watched as Stone slipped on the wet surface and struggled to regain his footing. The man he had kicked rose, and raised his gun. Stone snatched the barrel. As the two struggled, Broken Arm got up and began kicking Stone's legs, trying to knock him down.

Lucinda ran to pick up the gun lying on the pavement. As she bent down, a blow to the side of the head dazed her. She fell to her knees. The second man had struck her with his good hand. She watched him run back toward Stone, who continued struggling with the other man.

Her face ached, and her new designer pants had a rip in the knee. Worse than that, her lover was about to be killed. In a rage, she scrambled over to her purse lying on the ground, opened it, and limped toward the three men.

In Italian, she yelled, "Stop! Or I shoot!" She pressed her .25 caliber Berretta pistol to the back of the head of the man with the broken arm. An urge to kill overcame her. "*Bastardo!*"

"Take the gun from her," the other thug shouted, and elbowed her away.

Stone kneed him in the groin and twisted the gun from his hand. Both Lucinda and Stone pulled back, leveling their guns at the two assailants.

"I am going to shoot the one who ruined my new slacks."

"We want them alive!" The surprised shout came from the Mossad agent, Jacob, as he brushed past her with four other men.

Lucinda watched as Jacob's men seized the two thugs and threw them into waiting cars. After his men sped off, Jacob returned, and said, "Let's go someplace where we can talk."

• • •

In the tavern, Lucinda sat in the booth across from Stone and Jacob. Jacob ordered café for all three of them. She found the Mossad agent to be a blunt man, not quite crude. Definitely Jewish. He had Middle Eastern features. Eastern Sephardic? The man did not look well and had a very sallow complexion.

He had brushed back his hair. *Mio Dio*! The top portion of his right ear was missing.

"We can talk here. I know the owners," Jacob said. "Are you on pills now?"

Stone had thrown two yellow pills in his mouth and taken a long drink from his water glass. He slammed the glass down. "For the pain in my ribs. Those bastards gave me a few body blows."

"Sorry I didn't get to you sooner. Had to find my boys." Jacob inspected the bandage. "How's the finger?"

"No problem. I figure my next manicure will cost ten percent less." He smiled at Lucinda, and she rolled her eyes. "How come you were there?" Stone said. "You were tailing those two thugs, right?"

Jacob looked hard at Lucinda, and was about to speak when she said, "I know Abdul Wahab, his father-in-law the Saudi prince, and their connections to al Qaeda. You must have heard what happened on the Riviera this summer?"

Jacob tilted his head. "Tell me, Contessa, would you have pulled the trigger?"

Lucinda leaned across the table and said, "Why did you stop me?"

Jacob smiled, which surprised her. She surmised that he was not a man who smiled often.

"The two men who you met today came from Yemen. The port of Aden, to be exact." Jacob pointed to Stone. "They were here to kill you on the orders of, we believe, Abdul Wahab."

Even though she wasn't touching him, Lucinda knew Hayden's body had tightened. The scar on his cheek became more pronounced.

"In Sicily, Wahab led me into a trap," Stone said. "He used Sandra Harrington as bait. Now, he found me through Lucinda."

Jacob asked, "Stone, why did the CIA and the Canadians set

Wahab free? After the Africa job, I thought he was to be kept under wraps."

"Wahab should have been shot, or at least taken to trial in the U.S. for the murder of two CIA case officers in France. I had the impression that the brass thought he could be turned against the jihadists for our benefit."

Jacob shrugged. "Perhaps we do not have all the facts."

Lucinda watched Stone's face and guessed what he was about to say.

"The only fact I know is that Wahab wants me dead, and will use people around me to get to me, even the closest people." At that, Stone touched her leg. "I have to take him out."

Lucinda stiffened and looked back at Jacob, who shot her a glance.

"He's right, Contessa, except for the 'I' part. It's *we* who will take him out."

• • •

Lucinda drove through a soft rain south toward her villa, the windshield wipers slapping a steady rhythm. The automobile responded to her commands like any well-tuned machine with a high-powered engine under its hood.

"We'll take a hot whirlpool bath when we get back to the villa," she advised.

"I've got to go to Yemen, you know," Stone said. "I'm tired. I really don't want to go this time."

"I wished I still smoked," Lucinda said. "I could use a cigarette right about now." She drove a while, then said, "We cannot run the rest of our lives, nor hide. My family, the Avoscanis, never ran from the Moors, nor from anyone, for that matter. My father opposed Mussolini and the fascists. We were accused of being communists. Many in Italy still will not have anything to do with us, because of those days."

She looked over and saw that he had fallen asleep. A few moments later, she heard him snore. As the windshield wipers continued their beat, she thought back to when she had first met Hayden. He was a handsome young man in a dashing navy uniform, who asked her to dance at that holiday party. Two months later, they made love. She had been twenty, and he was her first.

Then Stone abandoned her. Never wrote, never made contact for close to twenty years. Now he had returned, and she intended the reunion be permanent.

She glanced at the clock on the dashboard. In an hour, they would be back at the villa.

. . .

They arrived at the villa and immediately went upstairs to the bedroom. When Lucinda went into the spa, she found Stone sitting in the bubbling water.

She let her robe drop to the floor and took her time climbing over the edge. She slipped slowly into the churning water, letting her breasts float free. He always enjoyed examining her body.

She entwined her legs in his and felt his foot begin rubbing against the inside of her thigh. Her legs closed tight, and she smiled when he wiggled his toes.

"When you travel to Yemen, will this *woman*, Sandra, be there?"

He cleared his throat. "Last time I saw her, she intended to stay in Washington." He reached over and caressed her arms. "You are positively exquisite."

"But you rescued her." She crooned and moved closer to him and opened her legs. "I hope you are not in Yemen long. I don't like taking baths alone."

"So I gather."

When his finger circled the nipple on her breast, it began to tighten. Underwater, she lifted herself onto her knees and slid forward, straddling him. She kissed his open mouth, and then licked his ear.

When he brought her down on him it was though electricity charged through her body, as if water swirled around them.

She folded into him. The glow lingered. He buried his

face in the hollow of her neck and kissed her. A few minutes passed, and she lifted off him. One day soon, she would insist he cease his wanderings. She must be prepared for that day of confrontation.

Tomorrow she would phone her cousin, Vincente, the head of the Italian secret service, the one who had given her the Berretta and taught her to use it. He would be interested in what had happened in Florence that day and to learn that Hayden would be heading for Yemen. He might be in a position to help him find Abdul Wahab.

When Hayden did depart, she would contact Prince Mohammed al Tabrizi and negotiate the additional expenses for the repair of her palace in Villefranche. Then she would bring up the matter of Abdul Wahab, the attack on her and Stone in Florence by what she believed were Wahab's men, and what the prince could do to prevent a reoccurrence. That would add oil to the fire.

Would she ever find herself in a position to lure Wahab into a situation where she could use her Berretta on him? Perhaps then Hayden would cease going on these adventures.

CHAPTER EIGHT

TUSCANY, ITALY—OCTOBER 16, 2002

A *sirocco*, the periodic wind from the Sahara, pushed against the glass-enclosed breakfast room, now warmed by the morning sun and the small fire in the room's corner hearth. Hayden Stone felt at ease living at Lucinda's villa. Her *maggiordomo* approached and announced a visitor. "A gentleman wishes to speak with you, Signore Stone."

In the library Stone found the visitor before a bookcase, admiring the collection of eighteenth century leather-bound books. A man of about thirty, he turned as Stone entered and, with a lift of his chin, introduced himself. "Roscoe Snodgrass. Rome instructed me to come and speak with you. You are Hayden Stone, the gentleman in this photo?"

Snodgrass handed Stone an Irish passport. Within he found the name Finbarr Costanza and a photograph with his likeness. A current visa for Yemen was attached inside. He closed the passport and returned it. No question, the CIA station in Rome had sent Snodgrass to provide him his bona fides for the trip.

"No, please keep it. And these." The man opened a light tan, Italian-looking portfolio, and fumbled with other identifications and papers.

"Let's sit and look them over." Stone led him to the couch, then said, "Pardon my manners." He offered a handshake. Snodgrass's hand was cold and dry.

On the coffee table, the man displayed an array of credit and identification cards, Yemeni currency, and a business-class ticket on Lufthansa from Frankfurt to Sana'a. The ticket was for the next day.

"Doesn't give me much time," Stone observed.

"Colonel Frederick advised via cable the following…." Snodgrass paused and shut his eyes, as if trying to read the words in the cable as he remembered them.

Stone sized up the man before him. From the cut of his suit, he'd apparently bought it in Milan, and the shirt and bow tie definitely came from Florence. Shoes, surprisingly, looked English. Snodgrass had to be single. A woman would not have put his color combinations together—at least not a woman who cared.

"Are you based in Florence?" Stone asked.

Appearing annoyed by the interruption, Snodgrass said, "You needn't know where I'm based." He looked Stone up and down, then continued, "The Colonel advised that Abdul Wahab has disembarked from the yacht named Red Scorpion at the Yemeni Red Sea port, Al-Hudayda, and was last tracked heading inland. Time is of the essence that you travel to Yemen. You will be picked up at the Sana'a airport terminal and taken to a hotel you have frequented in the past." Snodgrass took a deep breath and again tilted his chin upward.

Stone always found it difficult to take seriously a man wearing a bow tie, unless, of course, it was a black tie. He knew his request would irritate the man, so he asked Snodgrass to repeat the instructions. Snodgrass obliged with forced restraint and, when finished, announced that he must be off.

While Stone led him to the door, he engaged in small talk, and then asked, "Don't you think the oysters at Harry's Bar are a bit sour lately? Think it's the pollution in the Grand Canal?"

Snodgrass stopped. "Harry's oysters are always top notch." As he said it, his face hardened. Stone had tricked him into revealing he was the CIA base chief in Venice.

"Cheerio," Stone said.

. . .

Stone returned and found Lucinda going into the library.

"May I look at these?" she asked, settling herself in the same spot on the couch where Snodgrass had sat.

Stone pushed the documentation on the table over to her.

After examining the items she leaned forward, elbows resting on her knees, and bit her lip. She always did that when she was about to broach a subject she considered important. A habit that stemmed even from the time he had first met her, twenty years before.

"Last night, I spoke with Vincente about your trip to Yemen. My cousin thinks it is a dangerous endeavor. I am having second thoughts about you going."

"We discussed it. Abdul Wahab is after me and will use you or harm you to get to me."

"My cousin said that he would put us in what you Americans call 'protective custody.'"

"I won't live that way. And if you thought about it, you'd know you couldn't either."

Lucinda raised her hands in resignation. With an exaggerated sigh, she said, "If you don't return to me, I may become a wanton woman, sleeping with any man that vaguely looks like you."

Stone grinned. "That comes as a surprise. I would expect you to do the right thing and retreat into a convent and pray for my eternal soul."

She gathered the passport and credit cards and tossed them at Stone. Then rising regally, she marched to the library door, closed it, and locked it. She spun around and approached, swinging her hips, all the while unfastening her blouse button by button.

"Something for me to remember every morning while I'm away?" Stone said, kicking off his shoes and stretching out on the couch.

SANA'A YEMEN—OCTOBER 17, 2002

The Lufthansa jet made a slow approach to the Sana'a International Airport. A familiar gray haze hung in the thin air over the arid landscape. Gradually, as the plane descended, the white cube-shaped buildings typical of Yemen architecture became visible. Here and there clusters of dusty green trees and bushes broke up the brown monotony. He began to smell Yemen, its cooking fires and the dust.

The airport handled both commercial and military aircraft. Off the runway sat vintage Russian MIG fighters, droopy-winged, four-engine Ilyushin transports, and derelict helicopters lined up in rows, more for a toothless show than ready combat.

Stone leaned back as the flight attendant provided information in English and Arabic. He took a deep breath, and could already taste the land. "Back to Yemen. Back to the Middle Ages," he muttered to himself.

• • •

Stone showed his passport to the immigration officials and passed through customs without difficulty. He paid a man in a blue uniform to retrieve his bags and headed out of the terminal, waving off a number of taxi hustlers hovering at the entrance saying, no thank you, he had his own transportation.

The late afternoon sun brought a hint of color to the sky. He walked along the sidewalk, searching for his contact. Fumes from the diesel powered trucks caught in his throat.

"Professor Finbarr Costanza?" a craggy-faced man asked, standing with his arms crossed over his chest at the open door of a dusty black van. The lettering on the vehicle's door read, YEMEN EXOTIC TRAVEL. He wore the traditional *futa*, the long white Yemeni garment, underneath a faded blue suit coat. An ornate tribal dagger, the *jambiya*, was wedged inside his belt.

Stone nodded, and said, "*Marhaban.*"

"*Ahlaan,*" the man responded to Stone's greeting, took his two suitcases, and slid them on the floor of the van's passenger compartment as Stone jumped into the passenger seat.

"We go to Sana'a, to the hotel Taj Sheba," the man said after getting behind the wheel.

Stone unzipped his leather jacket and asked, knowing the answer, "How long will it take?"

"One hour. *Inshallah.*"

The drive to the hotel took a little less on a good day, one without traffic jams or police checks. Stone never enjoyed the ride from the airport to Sana'a; it didn't match his romanticized image of Yemen. Garages, machine shops, and ramshackle eateries lined the tarred road littered with trash. Some of the buildings they passed had been interesting to look at years ago, but had fallen into a form of suburban decay. Dust and diesel oil hung in the air.

"First time in Yemen?" the driver asked in English.

"I have been here many times."

"You like?"

Stone nodded. "The country is beautiful." He then added the tiresome false phrase he heard other visitors repeat, "And the people are so very nice." Then he asked the man's name.

"Mohammed," he said, and then slowed and sounded his horn, at the same time rolling down his window. He waved to the driver of an SUV traveling in the opposite direction. The other driver also leaned on his car horn.

"My cousin," he explained to Stone.

"Is Sana'a your home?"

"My family lives in Kawkaban. You know where that is?"

"In the mountains, west of here. It is beautiful." Stone spoke truly. Every trip to Yemen, he made it a point to visit the mountainside village. Accessible only by vehicles with four-wheel drive, it had served in history as the fortress for the farming communities in the valley it overlooked.

Stone remembered the time in 1992 when, standing outside the Kawkaban hotel, the retired Algerian revolutionary, Ben Bella, came out of the restaurant with his bodyguards to a waiting SUV. One of the men, a Yemeni official, pointed to Stone. Ben Bella came over to him and offered a smile and a handshake. The old political revolutionaries were much more agreeable to meet than the present day religious fanatics.

"Do you speak Arabic?" the driver asked.

"*Qalilan*. A little." Stone's Arabic was the Modern Standard Arabic he had studied. It closely resembled the classical Arabic.

He could manage the language in Sana'a but not in the outer provinces, where they spoke the ancient dialects.

"Not many English speak Arabic."

"I picked it up as a pastime." Stone also figured this man, a local employee of the CIA station, wanted some information to feed his Yemeni intelligence bosses. He assumed the man had an income from two sources. Life was good for Mohammed, the poor boy from Kawkaban.

· · ·

The Taj Sheba had not changed since the last time Stone stayed there. Mohammed parked in front and a uniformed bellman took Stone's luggage up to the reception desk. Stone thanked his driver and offered him a tip, but it was refused.

"I will see you again, Sayyed Costanza," he said, then departed.

Stone climbed the stairs, paused at the top, and looked around. The city looked busy, was not too loud, and sat surrounded by beautiful buildings. A calm, tawny setting brushed by dusty, wood-burning smells. In the street before him, women passed fully covered in black robes, men in tribal attire, daggers tucked in their belts, some with Kalashnikovs slung across their backs. This was the Sana'a he knew.

At the reception desk the well-trained staff took his passport and credit card, then instructed the bellman to lead him to his accommodations. The room faced the street, but with the window closed, little outside noise came in. The view was worth any noise. The old city of Sana'a stretched out to the mountain range in the distance. The sun had set and lights began to appear from the windows in the buildings below. A muezzin called the faithful to prayer from a distant minaret.

In his room he found that an envelope had been slipped under the door. It was addressed to Professor Finbarr Costanza. Inside, the typed message read:

> *At 9:00 a.m. tomorrow visit the National Museum, proceed upstairs to the first floor, and study the exhibit on the Kingdom of Marib.*

The note was signed F. His boss and mentor, Colonel Gustave Frederick, had made contact. What was in store for Stone was unclear, but it didn't matter. One thing was certain: the target was Abdul Wahab. The fun had begun.

CHAPTER NINE

SANA'A, YEMEN—OCTOBER 18, 2002

Hayden Stone woke up to a hard knocking on his door. He swung out of bed, his 9 mm Sig Sauer in hand.

"Breakfast, sir." A clipped East Indian accent came from the hallway.

Stone went over and peered out the door's peephole. The man, whom Stone knew to be a relative of the manager, held a breakfast tray.

"Stay there," he instructed, and slipped the gun into his robe pocket. He retrieved a few riyal coins from the dresser, opened the door, tipped the man, and took the tray.

Breakfast consisted of coffee, processed orange juice, three non-descript hard rolls, and a small jar of strawberry jam. As he ate his meager breakfast, he studied the Sana'a city map to reacquaint himself with the directions to the National Museum, about a ten-minute walk from the hotel down Ali Abdul Mogni Street.

At eight thirty he left the hotel, took a left turn, and made his way through the throng along the busy street. Trucks and taxis inched both ways, but surprisingly few drivers blew their horns. Vendors had opened their wide storefronts to the public, some displaying meats, spices, and vegetables. Others sold hardware, appliances, and pirated CDs. All the wares appeared to be for local consumption; Stone recognized nothing specific for tourists, and there were few non-Yemenis walking the street.

What he enjoyed about Yemen was the apparent lack of interest the people on the street took in strangers, at least men. European women did elicit a degree of curiosity, if not amusement, especially if they wore revealing clothing.

He caught up with a group heading in the same direction, slowed his pace, and followed close, wanting to blend in. That morning he had dressed in a faded blazer, jeans, and a crumpled tan bucket hat. Horn-rimmed glasses with non-prescription lenses completed his professor's masquerade.

As he walked, he reviewed his situation. Either a sharp Yemeni intelligence analyst reviewing his visa application would have alerted superiors to keep a watch on him, or Mohammed, the driver who took him to the hotel, would have reported Stone's arrival to the local intelligence service. Being followed by the local service didn't bother Stone; surveillance by Abdul Wahab's people or other jihadists did.

Twice he doubled back and stopped at a shop and chatted with a vendor. Both times, he spotted the same pinched-faced man in a soiled *thobe*. But somehow the man didn't strike Stone as being a professional security man—much too sloppy, in both dress and technique.

Stone approached the museum. Housed in the deposed Iman's palace, it stood four stories high, with stained glass windows framed by white decorative scrollwork. The entrance to the museum was closed, so he pounded repeatedly with a closed fist on the heavy wooden door. Eventually, the door creaked open and a gray-haired man stood barring the way. In a dark business suit and equally somber tie, he took in Stone's attire and asked, "English?"

"Irish." Stone handed the man a business card. He studied it, turning it, examining both sides. "I've come to see the Marib exhibit," Stone explained.

"Our museum is closed to the public, Professor Costanza. I am the curator." He handed back Stone's card. "Did you write to us requesting a showing?" Stone detected German inflections in his Arabic accent.

"I'm certain my assistant did."

"Well then professor, do enter, before people out there think our museum is open." Stone stepped through the gate; the man stretched his head outside the doorway and looked up and down the street, then pushed the heavy door closed. Using a large old metal key, he engaged the equally ancient lock, then motioned for Stone to follow him across the dirt courtyard to the main building.

Inside, the man leaned close and spoke in a low voice. "The Marib exhibit is on the second floor." He pointed to a stairway. "The exhibits have signage in Arabic and some English." Eyebrows lifted, he gave Stone a skeptical glance. "If you need assistance in identifying the objects, go to the staff office and talk with an employee." With that, the curator disappeared around a corner.

The dim ceiling bulbs provided little light. The musty smell reinforced his feeling that he had traveled back centuries. However, all of Yemen seemed frozen in time, and that fascinated him. At the end of the hallway, a rickety spiral staircase led up to the second floor. The floors had the same numbering found in Europe; a second floor in America was called the first floor here.

He took the stairs and found himself treading softly. He met no other visitors.

Hundreds of artifacts lined the walls, some in glass cases, not many labeled in English. Stone had difficulty reading the signs and the exhibits in the dark room. Those he could see dated from the Sabaean era, 1000 BC. It had been a few years since Stone had visited Marib, the ancient capitol of the Sabaeans, but he recognized the distinctive eagle and snake motifs on the figurines.

A familiar voice came from the other end of the room. "I've been searching for an image of the Queen of Sheba on these sculptures. Didn't see any beauties that King Solomon would fall for." Colonel Gustave Frederick stood before a row of stone statues with his hands folded behind his back. He wore a stained safari jacket and rumpled khaki pants, which from past experience Stone knew was Frederick's way of blending in with the surroundings.

"Good morning, Fred."

"How's your Bible history?" Without waiting for an answer, Frederick proceeded to give him an abbreviated history of the Queen of Sheba's visit with King Solomon, which Stone already knew. Finished, Frederick asked, "You've visited Yemen before, am I correct?"

"Many times, Fred. What I wonder is, what mission is it this time."

Frederick folded his arms, as he did when about to say something profound, and then relaxed. "Before we get to that, I meant to tell you, thanks for helping Sandra in that predicament in Sicily."

After a brief pause, Stone said, "Always enjoyed Syracuse in the autumn."

"So I've heard." Frederick stiffened in a classic military manner. "Appreciate what you did. Thanks so much for helping one of our staffers. How's the finger mending?" He reached out and took Stone's wrist. "Hmm. Not very attractive." He dropped the hand. "Let's get to why I asked you to come here, shall we?"

"I bet it has to do with Abdul Wahab."

"Wahab set up the Sicily scheme to lure Sandra there because he knew you'd come to rescue her. You were his target. He wanted to finish you off and get on to whatever his big plans are."

"In a way I'm flattered by Wahab's attention. I haven't been anyone's obsession in quite a while."

Frederick's nose twitched as it did when he became annoyed.

"What you're getting at is," Stone continued, "I'm bait for Wahab. You want me here to find out where he is, learn the identities of his fellow conspirators, and then nail him before he gets me."

"Also, we hope to get an idea what he's planning."

"How did Wahab escape from the Canadians? Or did he?"

Frederick frowned. "I'm looking into that."

"I'm surprised you don't know. You're heading up the U.S. counterterrorist operation here in Yemen. Is Langley being forthcoming on all the details?"

"Of course not. We're a sideshow to the main performance about to premier in Iraq."

Stone knew that was what Frederick wanted—in on the Iraqi operation. The sooner he got results here in Yemen, the sooner he'd be back on the seventh floor at the CIA and involved in the preparations for the invasion of Iraq, where the real action would be.

"What do you want me to do?"

"Go east to Marib, Professor, and study the ruins there," Frederick said. "That's Sunni Muslim country and the breeding ground for al Qaeda. You've traveled there in the past?"

"Two years ago. I know some locals who may help me."

"Good. You'll leave tomorrow by land. Set up your own travel arrangements through some people we trust." Frederick walked over to a glass case filled with small black statuettes of gods and kings. "Fascinating civilization, these Sabaeans. Someday, when all this strife ends, perhaps they'll be able to do some quality archaeological work out there."

"Don't hold your breath."

• • •

Stone took the staircase down to the ground floor and looked for the exit. From the shadows emerged a gnome-like creature, with a hunchback and a broken front tooth. The man carried a flashlight on his belt. He took Stone's sleeve and pulled him into a side room and over to a window overlooking the main street.

In Arabic he explained that he was the museum's watchman.

"What is your name?" Stone asked.

The man shook his head and, instead of answering, pointed out the window. When Stone shrugged, he squeezed Stone's arm gently, and pulled him downward so that their eyes were on the same level and could look at the same thing. Again he pointed and said, "Two men wait for you."

One of the men was the pinched-faced man Stone had seen when he walked to the museum. "Police?" he asked.

Again the gnome shook his head. He then led Stone out of the room, through dark corridors to an exit on the other side of the building.

At the door, Stone asked, "Are those two men jihadists?"

"*Mumken*. Possible." The man cracked open the door,

looked out for a few moments, then said, "A person wants to show you an idol. You may find it interesting."

Stone cautiously followed the watchman onto the quiet backstreet, absent the bustling commerce found only a block away. He unsnapped the holster strap holding his Sig Sauer.

A dirty white sky hung above the two-story buildings on either side of the street. The man kept a quick, steady pace, and took a series of turns into trash-laden alleys. They went deeper, into neighborhoods where the few people they passed regarded them with suspicion. Stone made a mental note each time they turned onto a new street to remember something distinctive in case he had to make the return trip alone.

At last they stopped in front of an unexceptional three-story building, and the watchman knocked on the door. A voice came from the other side, and after Stone's companion gave a greeting, the door opened. Past a courtyard, the watchman took him to a smoke-hazed room, where a man in a well-tailored blue suit sat in a straight-backed wooden chair.

Stone knew the man as Ali al-Wasi. Behind him two large, unsmiling men stood against the wall. Ali ordered the watchman to leave, then took his time standing, and offered only a quick handshake. "Hayden Stone, you have returned to Yemen. What brings you back, my friend?" He motioned for Stone to take a seat.

Ali's eyes lacked the warm, open nature Stone had known. He had grown a close-cropped beard, darker than his light brown skin. A few gray hairs sprinkled his thinning black hair.

In past years the two had established a proper friendship, when Ali had worked as a local hire for the U.S. embassy's regional security officer. No longer an employee of the U.S. government, he had dropped all semblance of subservience and now considered himself on equal footing with Stone.

After exchanging pleasantries, but not offering tea, Ali said, "I still don't know the nature of your visit to my country."

Stone inspected his fingernails. Caution was in order. This man knew his true name and who he had worked for the last time they had met—the FBI. Did Ali realize he now worked for the CIA? "Would you believe that I've come here to study ancient civilizations?"

"*La.* No, my friend, you are not here to study pre-Islamic history." Still no smile from Ali. "It has been a year since al Qaeda wreaked havoc in New York City. You are on a hunt for the leaders of al Qaeda, and your people have sent you here." He took his time removing a cigarette and lit it with a long wooden match.

"You know my business is to find and arrest killers."

"This is Yemen, not America. You do not arrest my fellow citizens. We arrest them and take them to court."

"I misspoke. I only want to find the killers who belong to al Qaeda," Stone said. "Don't we all?"

Ali shook his head. "I doubt that you are on a personal mission. Your government sent you, but you did not check in with the police or the intelligence people. You entered my country under an assumed name and pretended to be a professor. Really, Hayden." He looked away, and then returned a hard gaze. "Twenty men from the Middle East came together, planned, and executed an incredible feat in attacking your New York center of capitalism. Why, with all your wealth and power, were you not aware of what they were going to do? We who have held your country in high regard all this time are now… disappointed, shall we say, by your incompetence."

"You retired from the U.S. embassy's security office. When I visited in the past, you and I became friends. You know my line of work." Stone assumed that Ali had joined or rejoined the Yemen police or intelligence service. "Was it your people who followed me from the hotel to the museum?"

Ali jaw's clenched, and he shot a glance at the man behind him. Could it be that, in addition to the two jihadists the gnome had pointed out to Stone, Ali's men had also tailed him?

"Mr. Stone, you will not find what you are looking for here in Sana'a. This is a republican region. The Sunni monarchists who applaud al Qaeda are farther east in the country."

"In Marib and the Hadhramaut."

"Where you plan to travel, no?"

Stone was thirsty and could use a drink of water. As if reading his mind, Ali produced a commercial water bottle and poured water into two glasses. He offered one to Stone, then toasted. "*Li'sahatikum*. To your health."

"You have no objections to my traveling to those regions?"

Ali shook his head. "You realize that we can offer you little protection in that area of our country. My government is at odds with the local sheik over oil revenues, with what he considers an unfair split from the Hunt Oil Company."

Stone said he enjoyed meeting with an old friend. He said he had places to go and began to rise.

"Before you leave, Hayden, I have a gift for you." He snapped his fingers, and one of the men behind him produced a newspaper-wrapped parcel. Ali handed it to Stone. "You are interested in Yemen's archaeology. This may interest you."

Stone unwrapped the heavy package and discovered a black stone bust about a foot high. The carving looked very old, and the features on the face barely distinguishable. Words appeared on the base in ancient Greek. He recognized one word, Χριστός. Christ.

"We found this in the museum. The possession of such idols is frowned upon in our religion," Ali said. "Best you take it away."

• • •

The watchman stood at the front gate waiting for Stone. The man led him back to his hotel. They chatted, and Stone tried to learn who this little man worked for, Ali, or perhaps the CIA station? He had no luck. Probably everyone and no one. No matter, the two of them got along.

Approaching the Taj Sheba hotel, Stone wondered if Ali had Colonel Frederick under surveillance and knew of his meeting with him in the museum.

At the hotel entrance the watchman asked in Arabic, "Are you enjoying your stay in Yemen?"

Stone turned. "*Ya saddiqi*, my friend. Your country is a constant surprise."

CHAPTER TEN

OLD CITY OF SANA'A—THE SAME DAY

Abdul Wahab and three men sprawled on cushions in the *mafraj*, the top floor of the tower house, customarily a place for socializing and chewing *khat*. He relaxed in the sleepy atmosphere, absorbing the Yemeni time and place, but still images returned of pleasant cocktail hours at a villa in the South of France. He missed the cheerful French sidewalk cafés and the first-rate cuisine.

He declined the third offer of *khat*. Assured his guests had sufficient sweets, and that fragrant tea steamed in the silver pot, the host, Uthman, excused himself. He returned to the floor below, where he and his immediate family maintained their quarters in three rooms of the narrow building. His extended family occupied the middle two floors. The ground floor of the four-story stone tower housed the animals and bulk storage.

Wahab closed his eyes for a moment, and thought of the failed attempt to kill Hayden Stone in Florence. Another botched job by his trusted people from Marseille. Could he no longer count on them? Now more of his men were in the custody of the Italian secret service. What would they tell the Italians? Worse, Hayden Stone remained alive.

Kheibah interrupted Wahab's musings. "Your mission in Africa did not end well?"

The man with the pinched face and close-set black eyes spoke with inflections and words from the far east of Yemen, in the governorate of the Hadhramaut. Years before, Wahab had traveled to the extended verdant valley south of the great desert of Saudi Arabia, the Rub' al-Khali. He had found for the most part that the people there had not been as belligerent as this man who reclined with him now.

His name, Kheibah, was one sometimes given by concerned Yemeni parents to ward off the 'evil eye,' and meant 'ugly.'" Wahab smiled, thinking how fitting the name was.

"Unfortunately," Wahab said. "Circumstances prevented the al Qaeda brothers from using the nuclear weapon against the infidels. I felt my obtaining the weapon was a major accomplishment. What our jihadist brothers did with it after I delivered it to them… well, we know. Stupid people do stupid things."

One of Kheibah's associates offered him a handful of *khat*, which Kheibah pushed away. "I do not use that." He turned back to Wahab. "Before the African adventure, you were not successful aiding our sick al Qaeda brother in Nice, France. He died, as well as many of our comrades. Your last two missions were failures."

Wahab bristled. Good God. He was expected to prove himself to this riff-raff. Maybe he should have stayed in Canada. "I conceived the plans and was successful in the part I played for both missions. Others failed in their tasks, not me." He reached over and poured himself tea. "Enlighten me of your successes in the cause."

"You came to us. I am not the one selling services."

"I do not sell. I *offer* my services." Wahab became uneasy. He had been assured of a welcome from these people. "It may be the wrong time to travel here. Perhaps the brothers in Afghanistan will welcome me back." He set the cup down and began to rise.

"Where do you go?" Kheibah asked, looking over at his two friends.

"I will take a walk and find a place to eat."

"That is unwise. You will stay with us."

Wahab's jaw set. *Am I a prisoner?* As he slipped his hand under his jacket, feeling for his Beretta, Uthman came into the room and announced that food would soon be coming. The owner of the house must have been listening at one of the air vents found throughout these tower houses, and used by Yemenis for eavesdropping.

Kheibah placed his hand on his heart as if in supplication. "Sayyed Abdul Wahab, do not misunderstand. I may have misspoken. You are our honored guest here in Yemen. We feel responsible for your safety, so we do not want you walking our streets alone."

"Of course, I took no offense." *Ibn himar. Son of a donkey.* Wahab turned to Uthman. "Thank you for your generosity with your offer of a meal."

Unbeknownst to Kheibah and his two cronies, Uthman was an old wartime friend of Wahab's father. They had fought in the British army together during World War II. Uthman's Sunni family had lived as minorities in Sana'a for three hundred years and had business connections with prominent Saudi sheiks. My ace in the hole, thought Wahab.

Soon four members of Uthman's family appeared, carrying hot trays of kebabs, hummus, and *saltah*, a spicy stew of mutton, garlic, and potatoes covered with a green sauce that filled the room with mouth-watering aromas. Kheibah and his two companions huddled together off to the side, gobbling their meal, while Wahab made social conversation with Uthman's relatives. He could talk nonsense with Uthman's people; he had to be careful with Kheibah and his two followers. They were dangerous.

Uthman left a cousin and came across the room and asked Wahab about his father-in-law, Prince al-Tabrizi.

"Ah, the prince. I left his yacht two days ago. He has business in Yemen, but I was not clear what sort of business." His host needn't know that the prince's yacht was headed across the Red Sea to Eritrea, for what purpose Wahab couldn't fathom. The prince had become very secretive in his dealings.

"You look tired, my friend. After the meal, I will show you where you sleep tonight."

Wahab watched Kheibah look over in his direction. The man had sharp ears. How would this ugly man keep tabs on him throughout the night?

Kheibah called across the room "Get a good night's sleep. Tomorrow we travel to the Hadhramaut. To the town of Tarim."

Wahab tightened his fist. He decided to surprise the ferret-faced man. "Uthman has arranged for me to travel to Marib tomorrow."

His host showed only a trace of surprise. "Yes." Uthman hesitated, then said, "Sayyed Wahab and I will discuss our trip downstairs in my quarters."

"I will meet you and your people in Tarim in a few days," Wahab said, "You must tell me how to contact you there."

Confused, Kheibah's eyes flickered. Delighted that he had disrupted Kheibah's plans, Wahab knew the ugly man had to honor the wishes of the host, the much-respected Uthman.

Finally, Kheibah muttered, "As you wish, Sayyed Abdul Wahab."

Wahab nodded, and wondered when the last time he had met such a loathsome person was. Disgusting, yet dangerous.

• • •

Uthman led Wahab down the steep spiral staircase to his quarters. The two women they passed in the hallway quickly covered their heads, and scurried into one of the three rooms on the floor. Wahab was shown to what resembled a sitting room, and the two sat in cushioned armchairs.

"You may smoke if you wish," Uthman said.

Wahab produced a pack of cigarettes and offered one to his host, which he first declined, then accepted. They sat quietly while a relative came in and served coffee. When he left, Wahab said, "Thank you for your hospitality and for helping me with those people."

Uthman's face stayed expressionless. "Kheibah has a questionable reputation. I do not know the other two, although I heard mentioned that this was the first time they have been away from their villages." He glanced at Wahab's clothes. "My understanding is you normally deal with more important people."

"I was referred to Kheibah's people by others involved in

the struggle. As you may have heard, I am involved in the cause of jihad."

Uthman sniffed. "Everyone today is involved with jihad, or say they are. The men upstairs," his eyes looked upward, "they are treacherous. They will set events in motion and know not how to control them."

"I will keep that in mind."

"I do not worry about you, my friend. You can handle yourself." Uthman crushed out his cigarette. "I worry about the innocents who will suffer because fools will blunder into what they consider some noble cause—or one they do not understand."

• • •

The next morning, before sunrise, a nephew of Uthman brought a basin of hot water and patterned face towels to Wahab's room. After changing into fresh clothes, Wahab went up to the top floor and joined the other men for breakfast. He sat on a cushion next to Uthman, maintaining a distance from Kheibah and his partners.

No sooner had Wahab started up a conversation with his host than Kheibah jumped up, sat on the other side of him, and interrupted, "We wish you a safe trip to Marib. Take warm clothes, for the night wind is strong this time of year."

"*Shukran.* Thank you for your kind thoughts." Wahab spooned his yogurt onto a warm piece of bread. "Are you heading for Tarim?"

Kheibah shook his head and bit into a peach. "We will stay a few more days in Sana'a and practice surveillance of the foreign infidel. I am teaching these two village boys how to follow Westerners."

Uthman snorted and, out of Kheibah's sight, gave Wahab's leg a knowing tap. He then got up and joined his cousins.

Kheibah following Westerners? This was of interest to Wahab. "How, may I ask, do you do this surveillance?"

Kheibah's mouth melted into what Wahab recognized as

a classical unctuous smile. "For the preparation of things to come, I am teaching these two men the art of surveillance. We go to the hotels where tourists stay, select interesting targets, then follow them."

"Any results?"

Kheibah dipped a torn piece of bread into the bowl of yogurt. "We have seen some choice candidates for kidnapping. Especially at the Sheraton and the Taj Sheba."

"Kidnapping? The sheiks in the outlining provinces have been doing that for years. It is a national pastime." Wahab laughed. "They seize tourists and then demand money or new roads from the central government. Speak with them about how to do it."

Kheibah sneered. "Soon they will be coming to us for guidance."

"Where do you go today?" Wahab threw out the question not really interested in the answer. He wanted to talk with Uthman about their trip to Marib.

"Back to the Taj. Yesterday we saw Germans, Dutch, and Japanese. All interesting targets, all rich."

The young man who enjoyed chewing *khat* the day before spoke up. "We followed an English yesterday."

Wahab became interested. "Any Americans?"

Kheibah shook his head. "The one he speaks of was not English. Our contact at the hotel front desk said he was Irish. A professor. We followed him to the museum, stayed a while, then left when he didn't come out."

"He didn't leave?"

"It was time for lunch, so we left."

"What did the man look like?"

The young man pointed to Wahab. "Tall, like you. Dark hair. Blue coat."

"He wore glasses," Kheibah said. "Why do you ask?"

"Curious," Wahab said. "It is interesting to know how well you do your surveillance. For instance, what color eyes did he have?"

"I don't know," Kheibah said.

"Ah," the young man added. "I saw his eyes behind the glasses. They were like a hawk's, moving back and forth as he walked down the street. And he had been in an accident."

"How do you know that?" Wahab asked. "Did he limp?"

"No. He had a scar on his cheek."

"Like this?" Wahab asked, tracing his finger four inches down his left cheek.

CHAPTER ELEVEN

BARAQISH, YEMEN—OCTOBER 19, 2014

Hayden Stone pitched his bags into the back of the Toyota Land Cruiser. Mohammed, the driver from Yemen Exotic Travel, had arrived at the Taj Sheba at precisely nine in the morning. For the trip to Marib, Mohammed had attached two diesel Jerri cans to the back of the SUV. He also brought a cooler holding bread, water, juice, and sandwiches. Canned meals resembling military food packs were stuffed at the bottom of a container.

The trip normally took three hours, but travel in Yemen could be unpredictable. Military check points and stops ordered by local sheiks to extract tolls added to the travel time. Stone had obtained from the hotel front desk a large wad of riyals for such delays.

Mohammed pulled away from the hotel and drove until he found the highway heading east. The well-maintained blacktopped road hummed under the Land Cruiser's tires. He maintained a steady forty-mile-an-hour pace, weaving in and out of traffic. After an hour, they left the mountain region of Sana'a and descended onto the flat brown expanse that extended to the edge of the Rub' al Kahli, the empty desert of Saudi Arabia. Trucks and military vehicles passed, and Stone spotted a number of camel trains and villagers riding donkeys. The checkpoint stops were uneventful, managed by bored soldiers and local tribesmen who accepted the *baksheesh*. They appreciated a little extra money.

By noon, hot air was blowing in the vehicle's open windows. Stone studied a map and found that the ancient site of Baraqish was on their way to Marib. He told Mohammed they should stop there and have lunch. Stone knew from his study of Yemen history that successive generations had lived at Baraqish for three thousand years, and that it had only been abandoned thirty years before.

Stone admired the view of the city, tower houses surrounded by a twenty-five-foot wall of huge, chiseled blocks. The complex sat on a hill, the earth-colored buildings framed by an intense blue sky. Two soldiers in dusty uniforms guarded the extensive site. From the window of the SUV, Mohammed bought two entry tickets from the men, then drove on and parked on a level area marked off by rocks. Blocking the dirt path into the site, three Bedouins sat on a boulder, each of them cradling an AK-47.

"They want money," Mohammed said. "Then they will offer to take us on a tour."

"Give them this money and tell them we'll find our own way."

The three accepted the riyals, talked a bit with Mohammed in an Arabic dialect Stone had trouble understanding, and then motioned them to pass and enter the deserted town.

They climbed into the empty, sand-colored site, dust rising from their footsteps. All around them lay the brown structures of a once-living city, melted over the course of time like sandcastles after a gentle ocean wave had washed up, and then retreated.

Stone selected an inviting spot in the shade of a crumbling wall, with a good view of the buildings and the surrounding flat land outside the ruins. "We'll eat here."

Mohammed took quick sips of water and tore a few pieces of bread from the loaf, then sighed and looked off into the distance.

The flat Arabic bread had the soft feel of having been cooked that morning. Stone opened a can of prepared roast beef that came from France, and noted the rich smell and taste of the meat and gravy. He guessed it was a French military field ration, and wondered how it had managed to find its way to Yemen. The French military ate better than American troops.

During the trip, road noise from the open windows of the SUV had limited conversation. Now the two chatted, saying nothing important, just exchanging idle pleasantries. Stone found the driver interesting and wanted to ask him how long it took for him to fashion his striped headdress in the morning.

He knew Mohammed worked for the CIA station, but he also had to report to the local authorities. Otherwise, he'd soon lose his work permit, end up unemployed, and back in his hilltop village of Kawkaban. Was a pistol secreted beneath his *futa*, the long, flowing, skirt-like garment worn by Yemeni men? Probably. Many Yemeni men wore guns.

Stone surveyed the surroundings. The ruins of Baraqish sat on a tell, a mound of earth formed over the course of fifteen hundred years of successive habitation—one civilization layered on top of the other.

"Many people have lived here," Stone said, waving his hand across the landscape. "Many stories could be told by their ghosts."

Mohammed stopped eating and turned away. He stayed silent for a while, returned to his meal, and finally said, "Spirits wander here. I would never come alone."

Stone thought about how the place would look at night under a full moon. "How about at night?" he asked.

"Never."

They stayed quiet, and Stone realized that he hadn't seen or heard a plane fly overhead since they arrived. In the distance, across the plain, a procession of camels moved in a line tended by what looked like four men and two veiled women. A small, finch-like bird with golden flecks on its breast broke the silence by landing on a nearby wall and chirping.

"This peach is good," Stone said. "Where did it come from?"

"From the Tihama region in the west." Mohammed had become less engaged in their conversation. He watched the same three Bedouins from the checkpoint meander among the ruins, occasionally sitting on the ground, then getting up, staying beyond hearing distance.

"They're watching us," Stone said, becoming uneasy.

"They are curious. Not many people come here, so they become bored."

The vast landscape stretched north beyond the irrigated

fields and date groves to the great desert, Rub' al Khali. "Do they come from there?" Stone asked.

Mohammed nodded. "The Bedu are hard people. Hard on themselves, on their families, on the women." He turned to Stone. "They practice their religion the same way."

"Not like Yemenis?"

"We are more reasonable," Mohammed said, and at that stiffened, as the three men abruptly rose. "I do not trust the Bedu. We go now." He threw the water bottles and food containers into the basket, and got up.

Stone rose and trailed him down the path toward the Land Cruiser. At first the three Bedouin looked confused, and then, talking among themselves, followed. Stone reached his hand inside his coat and released the safety on his gun.

They had almost reached the final turn that led to the parking lot, when Stone heard a series of *crack, crack* and little plumes of dust jumped on their right a few yards away. He saw a series of sand puffs on the left side. The bullets came from the Bedouins' AK-47s.

Stone and Mohammed drew their guns simultaneously and aimed at the three men, whose jaws and guns lowered.

Stone growled, "Spray the ground around their feet."

"If you say so, sir," Mohammed said, his eyes unconvinced that this was the best course of action. "They did not hit us. Shooting at us is their way of play."

"I play the same way. Fire!"

Both placed four rounds around the feet of the Arabs. They jumped, and then waved their guns above their heads. The three men glowered, then one by one began to laugh.

"It is best we continue to the parking area, but they must not see us run." Mohammed said, and they headed down the path. Their strong strides became a run when they turned the corner and were out of sight of the Arabs. Both leaped into the Land Cruiser, wheels spinning as Stone shut his door.

As they drove back past the two soldiers, Stone turned around and watched the three Bedouins standing in the parking lot, shaking their fists.

After a mile Mohammed said, "That doesn't usually happen at Baraqish."

Stone reloaded four rounds into his pistol's magazine. "No problem. The Bedouin provided a bit of entertainment." *Just wait until the real fun starts.*

MARIB, YEMEN

Stone took another swallow of water from the bottle, and then wiped his face with his checkered bandana. They headed east along the black strip of road, the afternoon sun behind them. The scene had become monotonous with sand-colored terrain and black rock mountains, similar to the Arizona desert.

Soon the Land Cruiser came upon scattered settlements next to green irrigated fields, then they entered the new town of Marib. Few people walked the streets. Some buildings built with rock appeared substantial, while others were constructed of clay blocks. Brightly colored metal doors broke the monotone setting, and Stone thought it resembled a Mexican border town. They left the town, and after a mile or so found the Bilqish Hotel and turned in through the double gateway.

Stone had stayed there before and knew the management tried to make their guests comfortable. The hotel even had a swimming pool, uncommon in this region, but it was often, as now, empty. It had been built for the foreign oil workers who came to Marib and, although new, had the feel of nineteen-fifties America.

Mohammed dropped him off and said that he would stay overnight "somewhere out of town" with relatives, then take "someone" back to Sana'a the next day. As usual, he was vague with the details.

The high marble lobby glowed with soft light from recessed filigreed fixtures overhead. A huge crystal chandelier hung from the ceiling. Stone saw that a tour group of five Europeans had just finished checking in and were now heading for their rooms. At the front desk, a man with a close-cut beard wearing a clean white shirt greeted him, took his passport, flipped to the visa page, studied it, then made a few notations in a green register. He looked up at Stone and inspected him.

"You have traveled from Sana'a," the man said in English, as did most Yemenis employed in the tourist industry. "Did you encounter difficulties on the road?"

"No. Why do you ask?"

"It is late in the day. We expected you to arrive earlier."

"We stopped at Baraqish," Stone said.

"You are interested in the ruins there?"

"Yes. I'm a professor and I study old things."

"Of course." The man turned and studied the slots in the wooden cabinet behind him. He selected a key and handed it to Stone. "It is strange. You are interested in archeology and our Yemeni history, yet it is oil men who made your reservation."

Stone knew his answer would be reported to a number of people: the authorities from the central government who were stationed here, the local sheik's people, and—as the CIA hoped—to the local jihadists.

"I am fortunate to have many friends in many places."

Stone thought the man smiled, but wasn't certain. "We have a restaurant here," the man said. "Unless one of your friends comes here to meet you, I suggest you use it. Otherwise, at night, it is best to have an armed guard take you to other restaurants, which, I assure you, are not as splendid as ours."

"I'll eat here."

At that the man snapped his fingers, and an unsmiling, pockmark-faced man with a huge wad of *khat* in his left cheek ran up and took Stone's bags. Stone followed the porter to his room.

He found twin beds without headboards. A small lamp, the shade askew, sat on the two-drawer table separating them. The flowery smell of disinfectant was not altogether unpleasant. Stone found his room clean, and although the tub had a lengthwise crack along the top, it would hold enough hot water to have a good soak. He could find only one washcloth and a single thin towel. After drawing a bath with warm water, he poured an Irish whiskey, neat. As he relaxed in the tub, gun within easy reach, he pondered who would contact him and when. His thoughts then went to Lucinda back in her Tuscan villa, and he smiled. She would consider these digs to be roughing it.

After changing into clean clothes, he headed for the restaurant. Surprisingly, the large room was crowded with tourists. Stone caught the smells of grilled meats and stews. At least five tour groups clustered together around tables in the room. Evidently, tensions between the sheik and the government had eased to allow travel from Sana'a. That would help him. He wouldn't be the only foreigner roaming the countryside.

A waiter who spoke decent English directed Stone to a table in the middle of the room, but he requested a table in the back next to the wall. He didn't want to be surrounded by tables of Germans and Swiss, who appeared to be trying to outshout each other. Besides, he liked a wall behind him.

Stone ordered *shurba wasabi,* a thick lamb soup, served with thin Arabic bread, brushed with a paste made from coriander and fenugreek. The latter gave the sauce a slightly sweet, nutty taste. The waiter poured freshly steeped tea into a glass full of ice, then offered Stone mint leaves, which he declined. They may not have been washed. A plate with a peeled peach, cut melon, and a banana accompanied the meal, and all looked and tasted fresh.

When he finished, the waiter asked if he would like dessert. At first he turned down the offer, but upon learning *bint al sahn,* sweet bread dipped in butter and honey, was on the menu, he changed his mind. As the dessert arrived, Mark Reilly appeared at the entrance and came to his table.

"Join me, won't you?" Stone asked, relieved to know that Reilly was a member of the CIA team in Marib.

"Already ate, but I'll have some coffee." Reilly pointed at Stone's dessert. "What's that?"

Stone told him, and he waved off the offer. "God, my teeth ache just looking at it. How are your accommodations?"

"Neat and clean." Stone saw a mining engineering company patch on Reilly's jacket.

"See you've found gainful employment."

Reilly grinned. "Yeah." Then he leaned closer. "Your buddy and target, Wahab, just arrived. He's staying with relatives of a guy from Sana'a, whose name is Uthman. We thought Wahab was headed for Tarim in the Hadhramaut, but he came here."

From the tone of Reilly's voice, this turn of events had not been welcomed. "How come you people aren't in Tarim?"

"The Hadhramaut area is a tough place to get a foothold. You've been there; you know that. The place is a few centuries earlier than the damn Middle Ages."

Stone nodded. "The people there are less suspicious than the people here in Marib, but they don't welcome foreigners. They tolerate tourists, but only if they don't stay too long."

The waiter came with two cups of coffee, and when the waiter left Stone asked, "So how do you expect to cover Wahab in Tarim, if he goes there? How many people do you have?"

"Six operatives. Also, we have drone coverage from here, but that's a problem," Reilly said. "Notice there aren't many planes flying overhead? We've been attracting attention. As a matter of fact, our drone took a couple of shots from Yemeni rifles. We fly at night, although we just received a drone that resembles a big buzzard. Lots of buzzards around here."

"That's all you got?" Stone said.

"We have satellite phone intercepts. That's how all this came about. Headquarters learned an al Qaeda cell had formed here and were planning something big."

"So you have a drone and telephone intercepts," Stone said. "What else? Any live sources?"

"Can't say." What Reilly said was that he couldn't tell him.

Stone now knew the CIA had one or more human sources on the ground. "So, that's all you have?" he asked.

"Nope." Reilly smiled. "We have you."

Stone found his dessert had become too sweet, and pushed it away. He took a swallow of the bitter coffee to take the taste away. "Tell me more," he said.

"I'm sure Colonel Frederick explained that you were here to bait Abdul Wahab and the people he meets. We're really interested in the people Wahab deals with. They're the bad guys we want. To identify and stop them."

"Wahab didn't escape from the Canadians, did he."

"Before you come to any conclusions about his status, keep this in mind," Reilly said. "The Canadians interrogated Wahab and did a psychological study. He has it in for you. He thinks you are the cause of all his problems. He wants to kill you before you do him any more damage."

Stone thought a moment. "The agency hopes that he will connect with the jihadists, then learn I'm in town, and hire them to kill me. Before they do, you'll identify them."

"Sort of like that."

"That's really a shit plan," Stone said.

"Hey, it's not my idea."

Stone finished his coffee and said he had to turn in. He then asked what he was supposed to do the next day.

"Your cover is a professor interested in the Sabaean civilization. In the morning, hire a guide and visit the 'Arsh Bilqis. Familiar with it?"

"The Throne of Bilqis," Stone said. "Bilqis is the Yemeni name for the Queen of Sheba. What do I do there?"

"Walk around for about an hour, pick up some shards, act like you're having a good time."

Stone knocked his knuckles twice on the table. "Listen Reilly, that particular site is wide open and has very little cover. I'll be an easy target."

"We'll try to back you up."

"Great."

CHAPTER TWELVE

EARLY THE NEXT MORNING

Stone rose early, and by seven o'clock had washed and dressed. At the hotel front desk he arranged for a guide and transportation to the Throne of Bilqis that the Yemeni government purported to be dated from the Queen of Sheba's time. A middle-aged man, named Nadheer, was summoned. He told Stone he'd wait for him outside and then shuffled back to a tired-looking van. The way the guide had interacted with the manager, Stone assumed he was a relative. It seemed everyone in this country was related to each other.

Stone went to the restaurant and found that only the coffee was hot. The attendant informed him that the breakfast buffet had been prepared at three o'clock in the morning for the tourists headed to the Hadhramaut. Stone settled for bread and peeled fruit.

The morning drive was pleasant. The air was cool, scented with spice. Sharp morning shadows from the palms and bent green trees presented a welcome contrast to the coming midday heat and glare from the sun-baked ground. The driver headed south through the new town of Marib and continued past the adobe ruins of Old Marib which, like Baraqish the day before, lay deserted and decaying. After crossing over the Wadi as-Sudd, swollen from a recent rain, they turned left through patches of cultivated fields and groves of date palms. The water for these crops came from a new dam, built by the government. Only the sluice gates of the Great Dam, built three thousand years before, remained. The dam had provided water for the Sabaeans for over a thousand years.

At last they arrived and parked at the archaeological site,

which the Yemenis attributed to the Queen of Sheba. Scholars debated that claim and called it the Temple of the Moon.

"I see the sand has been cleared away," Stone said to Nadheer, who nodded, his beard bobbing with his head. It contained at least four different colors: red, brown, gray, and white. Since arriving, Stone had ceased shaving in an effort to appear less Western, although not all Yemeni men grew beards. That morning he'd seen a stray gray hair in his new beard, which made him smile—his grandmother had told him she'd turned completely gray at age thirty.

"The government hires us to keep this place clear for the tourists. Always the sand dunes march in with the wind." Nadheer looked perplexed, and kept glancing around.

"What's wrong?"

Nadheer shrugged. "There are no soldiers at the gate."

The "gate" consisted of a metal frame covered with chicken wire. From his last visit, Stone knew that the two green folding chairs placed on either side of the gate were for the soldiers, who collected a token entry fee in return for a small square of paper stamped with the official seal of Yemen.

"We can pay them when they return," Stone said, and hopped out of the van. He pushed aside the gate and entered. Nadheer trailed behind.

At one point in time, a five-foot wall had circled the temple site. Within the confines stood limestone mounds. Six thin square pillars about twenty feet high stood on an elevated platform and provided the main focal point. One of the pillars was broken. The area was clean, well maintained, and deadly quiet.

Nadheer went over to a far wall and leaned against it, seeking shade. He fidgeted with a cigarette. Stone climbed the stairs leading to the pillars and sat on the top step. Taking a long swallow from his water bottle, he adjusted his brimmed hat to block the sun. The temperature had also risen. The only movement Stone saw was a lone buzzard soaring above.

"Well," Stone muttered, "Here I am, Abdul Wahab. Come out, come out, wherever you are."

At that, a piece of the step next to his right hand burst.

The sound of the shot immediately followed. It came from the direction of a bush on the hill directly ahead.

Stone scrambled down the stairs and ran toward Nadheer. Two more rifle projectiles cracked on nearby walls. By the time Stone reached the spot where Nadheer had been standing, the other man had jumped a short wall and was racing toward the van.

The sniper zeroed in on Stone, now crouched behind an ancient fire pit. He looked up and saw two faces peering over the hill, one behind a telescopic sight attached to a rifle. The distance was well over a hundred yards, too far to get an accurate shot from his pistol, but close enough to scatter some rounds in their direction.

He elevated the barrel to account for the distance and squeezed off four shots. After a pause, the next rifle shot landed far off the mark—Stone's shots had broken the shooter's concentration. Stone scrambled to the wall and rolled over the top. A bullet struck an inch behind him. The sniper had regained his composure.

Stone ran hard toward the van and saw that Nadheer had gone through the gate. Still no soldiers on duty.

He came to the entry, and a man popped out from behind a bush on his right. He pointed an AK-47 at Stone, who slid in the dust. Stone aimed his Sig Sauer at the attacker's midsection and fired two rapid shots. The man bent forward and rolled to the ground.

Stone seized the assault rifle from the man, who was twitching and groaning. Shots came from the direction of the temple, pinging the gate and wire fence. The two original attackers approached, crouching as they ran. Stone raised the AK-47 and fired in five-shot salvos until the magazine emptied. The man with the rifle fell, holding his side and crying to his companion. Stone recognized the man with the shooter. Abdul Wahab.

Nadheer cried out, writhing on the ground, holding his leg. Stone hurried over and dragged him to the van, one eye on Wahab.

By the time Stone got Nadheer into the van, Wahab and the

sniper had crossed over the hill toward a car. The man Stone had shot still lay on the ground, convulsing.

Stone helped Nadheer into the back seat, blood squirting from his driver's thigh. Stone stripped off Nadheer's headdress, and quickly wound it around the leg. Nadheer glared at him, as if he weren't sure he liked his turban used as a bandage. Stone ordered, "Give me the car keys."

Stone drove in the direction they had come and, when he turned onto the main road, saw Wahab's car five car lengths ahead of him heading in the same direction. He pressed the accelerator to the floor.

"A clinic is in Marib," Nadheer groaned. "I show you."

Stone closed the distance and tapped Wahab's bumper. Both cars crossed the bridge over the wadi and passed ancient Marib. Traffic increased, and their two vehicles weaved in and out of the line of trucks.

They entered the outskirts of the new town, and Nadheer yelled from the back seat that they should take a left turn. Stone ignored him, and continued straight.

"You should have turned left!"

"I'm taking a shortcut," Stone said, coming up to the bumper of Wahab's car and banging it again. His cellphone rang.

"I am bleeding! I am bleeding!"

"Close your eyes and relax," Stone shouted. He pulled out his pistol with his left hand and stuck it out the window. He put four shots through Wahab's back window, shattering it. The car jerked back and forth, hitting the sides of two cars passing in the opposite direction.

"Who is shooting?" Nadheer yelled.

"They're shooting at us. Close your eyes." Stone's cellphone rang again.

"Blood is all over. Get me to the clinic."

Stone looked back into the pleading eyes of his driver. "Shit!"

He braked, slid into a quick U-turn, and headed back for the clinic. His mobile continued to ring.

"What?" Stone yelled into the phone.

"Don't kill Wahab." The woman's voice sounded very familiar.

"I'm going to a clinic to get help for my driver."

After a moment, the woman said, "We're watching. I'll meet you." The call ended.

"There! Over there!" Nadheer yelled, pointing to a storefront.

Stone pulled in front of the clinic, jumped out, and yelled to a group of men smoking outside the front door. They rushed over, and amidst a great deal of shouting and gesturing, carried Nadheer into the clinic. It resembled an American drugstore. A young doctor emerged from the back room and demanded quiet.

Outside, Stone sat on a bench and watched a Land Cruiser pull up. From the front passenger side the slender figure of a woman dressed in a khaki pants suit emerged. She wore oversized sunglasses and a dark blue scarf covered her head and lower face. Even covered up, Stone recognized her by the way her hips swayed, strolling toward him. Sandra Harrington had come to Yemen.

"Hi, sport." She removed her sunglasses and looked him over with her green eyes. "Did you end up with any punctures?"

"No, but my driver's got a slug in his leg."

"Let's get you out of here." She motioned him back to the SUV.

"Not until I know my man is okay."

Five minutes later, a pickup truck pulled next to them, a single red light attached to the roof and flashing. Two men hopped out carrying a stretcher. A few moments later, they and the doctor came out with Nadheer. As they slid him into the back of the pickup, Nadheer waved at Stone.

The ambulance drove off, and Stone got into the SUV with Sandra. "I'll have to remember to tip him next time I see him."

Sandra said, "You're not going to be in town that long."

. . .

Two hours later, Stone found himself in the three-room, clay-brick house surrounded by low-lying trees that served as the CIA operations post. Built into a hillside, the house had a great view of the valley. The place offered few creature comforts. The floor was earthen, windows had broken glass panes, and tenants included local fauna, particularly vermin. Stone sat at a table with Mark Reilly and Sandra.

"Did I accomplish what you wanted me to do?" Stone asked.

"Both men you shot are in the hospital," Sandra said.

"Both? The one with the AK-47 had two slugs in him."

Sandra and Mark shrugged.

"I want a .40 caliber Sig, not this 9 mm version," Stone said, taking the gun out of his shoulder holster. "It doesn't have the stopping power I need."

"I'll give you some of the new 9 mm ammo we received. They're hot rounds the Office of Technical Services developed." Reilly went to the next room.

Stone moved his chair closer to Sandra. "How come you're back in the field? Washington politics too tough?"

"You could say that," she said. "I feel a lot better and I miss the action. Plus, I need to keep you out of trouble." She looked around, and then whispered, "I don't think it was a good idea to use you as bait. Today could have been a disaster."

"Whose idea was it?"

"Don't know. One thing I do know, it wasn't Mark's idea." She thought for a moment. "We had you under observation from the drone, but the operator didn't spot Wahab and his henchmen until they started shooting at you."

"From that turkey vulture I saw in the sky?"

"It's supposed to look like a long-legged buzzard. The drone has good range. We'll take it to the Hadhramaut."

Stone heard Reilly returning to the room. He touched Sandra's knee. "Glad you're back."

Reilly came back in and handed Stone two boxes of ammunition. The other operatives rushed in and began packing up the equipment.

"We're moving?" Stone asked.

Reilly nodded. "The shoot-up has caught the attention of the government security people. We've got to relocate. It's just as well; we have to get you to the Hadhramaut."

"I'm going with him," Sandra insisted.

"Don't know if Colonel Frederick will approve," Reilly said. "Besides, we haven't worked out your cover."

"She can be my academic protégé," Stone offered, smiling.

"Excuse me?" Sandra raised her eyebrows. "How about you being *my* assistant?"

"Children, let's not fight," Reilly said. "Seriously, we have to come up with something that will work."

"Sandra and I will go together as fellow scholars. Me looking for ruins, Sandra researching the local honey industry."

"Honey industry?" Reilly said.

"Honey. Arabs love honey. They're connoisseurs of it," Stone explained. "Some of the most prized varieties of honey come from the Hadhramaut, from a remote area called the Wadi Du'an. The people in Saudi Arabia especially prize this honey and will pay top dollar for it."

"I take it you've visited this place?" Reilly asked.

Stone smiled. "It's a world unto its own. I'm friendly with some beekeepers there."

"Why do I think that place sounds familiar?" Sandra asked.

"I'm sure both of you have heard of the place from a briefing or two," Stone said. "It's the ancestral home of Osama bin Laden."

CHAPTER THIRTEEN

Abdul Wahab rose from his cushion and leaned over the banister that circled the roof of Uthman's cousin's house. The gentle night breeze brought the scent of jasmine. Wahab liked that particular scent, for it brought back memories of when he and his first wife, the prince's daughter, were still in love.

"More tea, Abdul?" Uthman clapped for a servant to take Wahab's cup and refill it, then the two leaned on the railing, looking out at the night. "A beautiful time, the evening is, no? The poets write about the twinkling lights from homes," Uthman said, raising his face to the sky, "and the bright moon lighting the landscape, shining on the palm trees. The ancients who lived here in Queen Sheba's time worshipped the moon." Uthman's voice changed and became harsh. "I know what happened today at the Temple of the Moon, Abdul."

Wahab preferred the conversation stay on the scene before them. "The moon is most beautiful."

The two men stayed quiet when the servant returned and poured Wahab's tea. During the evening meal, Wahab had noted tension in Uthman's face after he had a long phone call from a relative, and then again when Uthman returned from conferring with a businessman, who had come to the house requesting a private audience.

"Would you care for a cigar, Abdul?"

"Thank you, no."

"My cousin's brother-in-law, the one who was shot in the stomach, has died."

Wahab recited a short prayer, then added, "My regrets and condolences to his family."

"I wish that were enough." Uthman turned away from the

moonlit landscape and whispered, "Abdul Wahab, I am in a very awkward position. In assisting you to eliminate that man, Hayden Stone, a relative is lame and another, unfortunately, is dead. Their families here in Marib are demanding recompense."

"Whatever it takes, I will provide."

"It is not that easy," Uthman's voice rose higher. "It must be seen that my immediate family experiences some payment as amends. Your money will not satisfy them."

Wahab balanced his teacup on the banister. He waited a moment, then said, "I do not know why, or how it could have happened. I provided the one cousin a very good rifle with a telescopic sight, and the other had his own AK-47."

"You misjudged your opponent."

"For God's sake, everyone in Yemen has an AK-47! Was he the only man in Yemen who couldn't use it?"

"Do not use God's name like that in this house," Uthman said between clenched teeth. He started to walk away, then came back and pulled Wahab to the far end of the roof, away from the other members of his family. "What is wrong with you? You make foolish mistakes. You make dangerous enemies.

"To complicate matters, the guide who worked for Stone works for me as well. He is the one who took Stone to the temple site, and he was the one who was shot by my cousins! Irony of ironies. He would be dead if not for Stone." Uthman threw up his hands. "Now I must make amends to my business partner, which is more complicated than dealing with relatives."

Wahab became uneasy. Uthman was not only his father's friend, but he was essential to his plans to enlist jihadists in the Hadhramaut. "I am truly sorry I have put you in this position. Anything I can do to help, ask it."

Uthman looked into the darkness.

"Leave Yemen." Uthman pulled out a cigarette and lit it, blowing the smoke out into the night air. "Why are you here, and why this vendetta against this man Hayden Stone, who from my inquiries appears to be a nobody?"

Wahab wished he had taken Uthman up on the offer of a cigar, but what he really wanted was a full glass of double malt scotch. "As I told you in your wonderful home in Sana'a when you had been such an agreeable host—"

"Get to the point, Abdul."

"May we sit?"

Uthman clapped for a servant and told him to bring over two chairs. As they waited, Wahab mentally rehearsed what he would say.

Seated, he began. "My family, although not of direct royal blood, comes as you know from a prominent tribe in Saudi Arabia. In fact, it was only because of circumstance, or perhaps the will of Allah, that my ancestors didn't become the rulers. Many of my family are married to royals. I married into the family of Prince Mohammed al Tabrizi, so my people have connections."

Uthman began tapping his foot. "Bring some more tea here," he shouted to the servant.

"The Kingdom is in turmoil. Its great ally, America, does not trust the country after the Twin Towers attack. Demand for a change in government is coming from many directions: liberals, secularists, but mainly the jihadists. When the change comes, I want my family to not only survive, but prevail."

Uthman looked Wahab up and down. Finally, he said, "And you, Abdul Wahab, see yourself in a position of power in this new realm to come?"

"Not me," Wahab said. "My family and tribe."

"Of course."

Wahab continued, "The jihadists, al Qaeda, all of them are striving for leadership in the Muslim world. That is why I must be part of the new struggle, the new path. The zealots from Yemen will be my army."

Uthman struggled for words. Then in a measured cadence, he said, "You will not find taking this path easy. Not all Yemenis like being told what to do by a rich Saudi."

"I hope to persuade them to my cause," Wahab said. "You know I fought against the atheistic Soviet regime who tried to conquer our brothers in Afghanistan."

Uthman sighed and looked away. "Do you still have contacts with the opium growers there?"

Wahab raised his hands. "That was a misadventure. The purpose was to bring opium into the Western societies and make them weak."

"And to make money."

Wahab let his teacup bang on the table. "Money to finance my organization. It didn't work as planned."

"Many of your plans go awry, my friend. You see why some people are hesitant to work with you."

Wahab wanted to ask him if he was speaking for himself. "When do I travel to Hadhramaut?" Wahab expected him to say he was not going there, an answer he didn't want to hear, but was surprised when Uthman said he had made plans for his departure the next day.

"There is the matter of this man, Hayden Stone," Uthman said. "I am interested in knowing about him. Who is he? Why do you consider him a threat?"

"He is American. He is CIA."

Uthman merely nodded twice.

Wahab showed a fist. "This man thwarted my plans in France and then in Africa."

"Thwarted, you say?" Uthman's voice rose. "In France, one of the major leaders of al Qaeda was killed. Was Hayden Stone responsible?"

"I really do not know," Wahab answered. "That entire mission, as they say, unraveled. I still wonder who was responsible." The recurring thought passed through Wahab's mind. Did the prince have anything to do with that?

"Abdul?"

"Yes. To answer your question, Hayden Stone engineered situations that prevented us from achieving our noble goals."

"*Neek Hallak!*"

Uthman just told him to screw himself. That crossed the line. Would he have to kill this friend, ally of his family? He took a deep breath. Uthman, fortunately, saved him from making the decision.

"*Ana assif.* I am sorry for saying that."

"Do not trouble yourself, my friend. I understand."

Uthman sighed. "I will arrange for your travel to the Hadhramaut. There you will go to the town of Tarim, where many of your zealots study at the religious schools, but...." Uthman leaned back in his chair. "Another matter. We hear rumors, and these questions about your activities may have reached the people at Tarim." He waited a moment before continuing. "After the failure in Africa to obtain the nuclear weapon, you disappeared for a time."

"I fled to Canada."

Now Uthman leaned forward. "Since al Qaeda destroyed those two towers in New York City, the Americans have lashed out. As one would expect they would. They have gone to Afghanistan and searched for al Qaeda with their planes and soldiers, but something else is happening. Jihadists are being killed."

"I know."

"Some of them are just disappearing. Important members of the jihadist movement."

"Their bodies are not found, or they become prisoners," Wahab added.

"When the jihadists—your people, Abdul—capture a Westerner, you hold that person for ransom or for propaganda in those television videos shown in the West."

"A successful tactic used for years by our brothers."

"On the other hand, the Western intelligence people use their prisoners to gain information, or to recruit them to their cause, no?" Uthman asked.

"I have heard that is so." Wahab said, becoming guarded. This man Uthman presented one problem after another.

"I will be blunt, Abdul."

Wahab motioned for him to continue.

"The rumors are that perhaps you were captured and then recruited by the CIA."

Wahab said softly, "Will what I say to you help dispel those rumors?"

"I know these rumors are false, but swear to me, so I may tell others."

Wahab thought carefully, and then said, "The CIA holds me directly responsible for the deaths of two of their spies in France. You have heard of their deaths?"

Uthman gave a non-committal gesture.

"The CIA does not forgive. Hayden Stone has been sent by the CIA to kill me in revenge." Wahab snorted. "It is doubtful I would work for the people who want me dead."

Uthman took a deep breath. "Abdul, we have all seen those Hollywood films where they show how devious the CIA is. Those who spread these rumors will say this is one of the CIA satanic tricks."

"I will prove to you I am not their spy, and you are the person whose belief is most important to me."

"How?"

"I will personally kill that genie, that *djinn*, Hayden Stone."

Uthman stared at him, and then took the leather cigar case off the table decorated in Arabic marquetry. "Have one, Abdul," he said, with a frown, "They say the Queen of Sheba's mother was a *djinn*," Uthman whispered. "Be careful what you tell those people in the Hadhramaut about the man Stone being a spirit. They may believe you."

Wahab leaned forward. "Stone will be there. I will look him in the eye and kill him."

CHAPTER FOURTEEN

HADHRAMAUT, YEMEN—OCTOBER 21, 2002

The Yemeni Air Boeing 727 stayed on the Marib runway for only ten minutes, leaving its engines roaring. Passengers had helped push the movable stairway across the cracked asphalt to the plane's door. Stone wondered if it would collapse when they used it to board.

He offered Sandra the window seat, telling her she'd enjoy the view, which she did. The plane rose and banked over the new Marib dam, and she remarked that the reservoir contained considerable water and looked out of place in the arid land below.

"The water should help the local farmers," Stone said, leaning across Sandra to get a better view. "You would think that along with the oil, the economy would be improving."

"Do you suppose it ever will?"

After catching a whiff of her floral cologne, he sat back and shrugged. "*Insha'Allah*. God willing."

They had left Mark Reilly and the rest of the team at Marib to pack their gear and head overland to the Hadhramaut, a trip Stone had taken a number of times. He advised Reilly to keep an eye on the guards, take a lot of cash for payoffs, and have their weapons loaded and handy. He was glad to take the plane instead of sitting in an SUV for hours.

On the left side on the cabin, grouped together, thirteen Arabs dressed in white robes sat intently reading little black books. Some wore glasses. All wore white skullcaps, most of them embroidered.

Sandra elbowed him, and whispered, "Who are they?"

"Probably from one of the schools in Tarim. The city's been

an Islamic religious center for centuries." The group resembled a group of pious seminarians heading for Rome.

One of the men, seated in the last row, began chanting a religious phrase. The others repeated the words in unison. The praying continued, louder and stronger. Sandra grasped Stone's hand.

"It's okay. Prayer time," Stone said.

The plane left the arid, desert plateaus and glided into the miles-long, spacious gorge called the Wadi Hadhramaut. As the plane descended into the valley, the men ceased chanting. Through the window Stone saw the bare, dirt-colored canyon walls and, below that, a fertile strip of palm trees and irrigated fields.

"Wow!" Sandra said. "It's like one long oasis."

"Wait until you see the six- and seven-story houses built of mud bricks. You'll really believe you've been transported back in time."

Sandra leaned against him, her Hermes scarf tied over her hair. "You really like this place, don't you?"

"Sort of like being taken to the world of *The Arabian Nights*, along with Sinbad the sailor and the genie."

"Hayden Stone, the hopeless romantic." She turned back to the window and watched the scene unfold below. As the plane approached the runway, she said, "Hadhramaut is a strange sounding name. Know what it means?"

"Comes from an Arabic phrase, 'to welcome death.'"

"You're making that up, right?"

"Wish I was."

At that, the Boeing 727 slammed down on the asphalt runway. Luggage tumbled out of the overhead bins, hitting passengers and landing in the aisle. People shouted, looking around confusedly. Oxygen masks dropped from above, striking others on the head.

"Holy shit," Sandra said, clutching Stone's forearm.

As the plane taxied in, Stone saw a new executive jet sitting just off from the terminal, next to a single-story corrugated building. The unusual antennae array atop the building caught his interest. The Sayun airport served the cities of the Hadhramaut and the terminal served as ticket office, waiting room, and maintenance hanger for small aircraft. A four-story control tower looked over the single landing strip.

The plane came to a halt and they disembarked. Stone was surprised by how quickly the baggage handlers unloaded the plane and pushed the overloaded cart to the waiting passengers.

Two tall men approached from the direction of the private jet.

"We have a reception committee," he said to Sandra. "The *Mukhabarat*, or the PSO, the Political Security Organization. The secret police. If they want a talk, let them take me. You go to the hotel."

"No. We're sticking together."

The men wore no headdresses. Creased trousers showed under their long *futas*. Their strides carried authority. Stone picked up his bag and pretended to be unaware of them. When he and Sandra turned to enter the terminal, the two men blocked his way.

"Mr. Hayden Stone, your passport, please." The man, who had blue eyes, was not asking.

"Pardon? Who are you?"

"Police."

"Of course," Stone said, handing over his identification.

The blue-eyed man looked at the photograph in the passport and then looked at Stone. He handed it back and ordered, "Also, this woman's."

Stone sensed hostile energy radiating from Sandra. She lowered the scarf from her face, presented a big smile, and handed him her passport.

The policeman repeated the inspection routine with Sandra's identification, and then gave it back. He looked down at their bags and said to his companion, "Place their belongings next to the building." He addressed Sandra next. "You, stay with your belongings." Pointing to Stone, he ordered, "Follow me."

"Excuse me, sir," Sandra cooed. "I go with him."

"No. Stay."

"She goes with me," Stone said, crossing his arms over his chest.

Blue-eyes hesitated, pulled a radio from his pocket, and walked off. His gestures were as overstated as his voice. At last came the affirmative statement, *na'am*, then he took a deep breath, put the radio back in his pocket, abruptly turned, and signaled. "Both come."

The two followed the policemen in the direction of the executive jet. Stone put on his sunglasses against the bright noonday sun.

"I'm hot," Sandra said.

"It's a dry heat," Stone said, smelling the dusty air that had a slight floral scent. "We'll have a nice cool evening."

Stone assumed that the person who wanted to speak to them was waiting in the jet. Instead, the policeman directed them to the cube-shaped hut with antennae displayed on the roof.

Inside the two-room structure, Stone's old embassy acquaintance, Ali al-Wasi, greeted them, this time with a friendly handshake, only now he was wearing a uniform with a general's designation on the shoulders. He told them to sit and offered them soft drinks. The air conditioner on the building's wall threw out a refreshing breeze.

"I see you've joined the army since we last met," Stone said. "New career?"

Al-Wasi ignored the question, and then said, "I understand some people didn't appreciate your archaeological research in Marib. Have you considered a new career?"

"May have to. Seems I've lost some of my charm."

Looking at Sandra, Ali said, "Perhaps you have not, Hayden. Please, introduce me to your colleague."

Sandra rose, extended her hand, and produced an exaggerated smile, and then, with head tilted, gave him her name, adding, "Such a pleasure to meet you, sir." Stone always enjoyed Sandra's performances.

"Of course, you are Sandra Harrington," Ali said. "We meet at last." He waited for Sandra to return to her chair and then, crossing his legs, began, "You are fortunate that I am here negotiating with local sheiks on behalf of the republic. Unlike with the citizens of Marib, my government has a better relationship with the people along the Wadi Hadhramaut."

"Interesting," Stone muttered.

"In Sana'a we talked about your presence in my country and your interest in al Qaeda." Ali uncrossed his legs. "I doubt you will find anyone here who does not support al Qaeda, or who will say he does not. You are, as they say, in the lion's den."

"You would like us to leave?" Stone asked, looking over at Sandra.

Al-Wasi smiled. "As a matter of fact, I would appreciate it if you stayed." He let this statement sit for a second, and then went on, "Our sources tell us a certain man by the name of Abdul Wahab bin Khalid, a Saudi citizen, is here to organize a terrorist cell."

Stone smiled, then gave a hand wave indicating that he had heard the same.

"This same individual, Wahab, reportedly seeks to kill you. For what reason I do not know, nor care."

"Where is Wahab?"

"We do not know. That is why we want you to stay here and do your… archeology or history or whatever."

Stone shook his head and laughed. "You want me to flush Wahab out of the bushes."

Al-Wasi looked away.

"You and others want me to lure Wahab into the open and see who he contacts?"

"Yes." He frowned. "Is Miss Harrington aware of the danger you've put her in?"

"I volunteered to accompany Stone," Sandra said, straightening in the chair.

Al-Wasi raised an eyebrow. "Of course."

The beginnings of a blush appeared on Sandra's cheeks. "We've worked together in the past," she added.

To Stone, he said, "You two must be cautious. Be alert. I am not telling you anything you do not already know."

Al-Wasi rose, signaling the end of the meeting. As they

moved to the door, he said he hoped they enjoyed their accommodations at the Al Hawta. "It is a former palace, now quite a pleasant resort."

Outside the building, Stone thanked him for the warning. "Appreciate your advice. By the way, what is your position with the government?"

"I advise our president on all matters of security," he answered. "As a courtesy I will assure that all your movements are followed."

• • •

On the way to the terminal to retrieve their bags, Sandra asked, "You know that guy from the past?"

"We were acquaintances when he worked as an employee for the American embassy here," Stone said. "Now it appears he's head of Yemeni intelligence."

Sandra said, "He seems to be on top of the situation."

"That's because one of his sources is probably the CIA. And certainly one of his contacts is our friend, Colonel Gustave Frederick."

• • •

Stone and Sandra arrived at the Al Hawta Palace Hotel. They took their time walking along a path through the gardens. The place was as Stone remembered. The two-story main building of the former sultan's palace, built of mud brick, shone bright white against the cloudless blue sky. The plaster on the walls probably came from the limestone kiln they had passed on the road. The workmen had traced uneven waves across its facade. Arabesque decorations lined the top of the roof and filigreed borders marked the doors. Late afternoon shadows brought a cool, soft quiet, broken only by birds beginning their evening songs.

The porters dropped their bags by the reception desk, and the two registered without incident. Stone and Sandra would have adjoining rooms on the second floor overlooking the gardens. Dinner was at seven, the deskman informed them, and handed their room keys to the porters.

"Wow!" Sandra said. "Who would expect something like this in the middle of nowhere?"

"This place is one of my mental images when I recite my mantra that Tibetan nun taught me."

Sandra gave him a skeptical look as they followed the porters. Passing the glass-enclosed coffee shop, Stone spotted a large man get up from a table. He wasn't tall, just muscular. The other feature that set him apart was his dress. He wore a black tank top and shorts. The man's eyes followed Stone.

At their respective doors, Sandra called over, "See you at a little before seven. Going to take a little time off."

Stone went inside his room and found a spacious room with a high ceiling. All the wall surfaces were covered with the same rippling, soothing plaster as the outside of the building. The single ceiling fan stirred the fresh, cool air. Maroon bedspreads covered the twin beds, both fashioned with dark wood headboards. The twin beds and the red, geometric-patterned throw rugs were a stark contrast to the cream-colored walls.

Stone undressed, showered, and, wearing only a bath towel, lay down on one of the beds. He stared at the ceiling and let his thoughts flow.

He didn't know all the details on how they would bait Abdul Wahab, or identify the people Wahab recruited as terrorists. The CIA's or Colonel Frederick's grand plan probably evolved on the hour. Stone only needed to know his part, and would be informed if there were changes. Being party to all the details would be a burden. If captured, and if he couldn't trick his opponents into killing him first, he'd eventually spill the beans.

What interested him was the cooperation between Colonel Frederick and General Ali al-Wasi. Evidently, both considered Wahab's actions a major threat. Perhaps the seeds of militant jihad already had been sown in Yemen.

As for Abdul Wahab, he had failed to have Stone killed in Sicily and Florence, and had put Lucinda's and Sandra's lives in danger. Then he tried to do the job himself in Marib, but again failed. He'd had to recruit local Yemenis to his jihadist cause, so for the time being Stone would be put on a lower priority. Maybe that's why he hadn't picked up any unusual surveillance, besides the muscle man in the coffee shop.

• • •

Stone and Sandra met outside their rooms and walked out to the open terrace where dinner was served. The night air had a chill and felt crisp. Stone looked around for Muscle Man, but didn't see him seated among the twenty or so diners.

"My God, Hayden. Look at the stars. Even with the candle lights, they shine so bright."

Stone looked up at the mass of pin lights, then back at Sandra, whose face was still raised. Her throat and neck glowed in the golden light; her blonde hair had a slight glisten. She looked down, catching his gaze.

"Penny for your thoughts," she said in a low voice.

Stone became flustered but was saved by the waiter asking for their drink order. The man told them he'd have no trouble getting a negroni for Sandra, and a vodka martini for him.

"Who were you with the last time you had dinner here?" she asked.

"I dined alone. Almost right here. At the time, I thought it a waste not to be with someone."

They looked at each other for a few moments, neither averting their eyes.

"Ever hear from that South African intelligence agent?" Stone asked.

"He stood me up. Never came to Paris."

Stone rested an elbow on the table. "What about that guy… what was his name—Farley something?"

"What's this all about?" Sandra stiffened. "Farley's been history since I caught him in my bed with my friend."

"You know me. I'm the nosey kind."

She laughed. "When did you last hear from Lucinda?"

"I called her yesterday." Stone thought a moment. "She's had it with me going off on these adventures."

"What does she think about you being with me?" Sandra said, looking up and accepting her negroni from the waiter. "I know I wouldn't like it." The hint of a lisp returned, as it did when she relaxed.

Stone sipped his martini. After a few sips and trying to avoid looking at each other, Stone said, "Sandra, we've worked together since France. We work together quite well. I enjoy your company, but we're professionals and we trust each other."

She raised her glass for a toast.

The glasses clicked, and she said, "Here's to good hunting."

• • •

The dinner was fair, but somewhat disappointing. Stone said he had looked forward to Yemeni cuisine, and Sandra agreed. The management believed their guests wanted westernized food. Lamb cooked liked steak, but overdone, and no local vegetables or legumes. For dessert, they provided excellent Belgium chocolates.

After dinner, the two walked through the gardens under the starlight, then climbed the stairs to the second floor, and headed toward their rooms.

"Let's go to the roof," Stone suggested.

Sandra hesitated.

"You'll see a view of the night sky you've never seen."

On the roof, it was as Stone had remembered: stars flooded the sky above, and a dazzling Milky Way crossed overhead. The overwhelming starlight cast a silver sheen on the pale buildings, palm trees, and nearby cliffs. All around them, house lamps defined the horizon. As he did years before when he looked up from this roof, Stone realized his insignificance.

Sandra remained quiet, came close to Stone with her arms held tightly around her chest. He couldn't see her eyes, but saw her nod once, take a deep breath, then walk toward the stairs.

• • •

Stone went back to his room and sat on the edge of the bed. As he started to remove his shoes, he heard a heavy rap on the door. The heavy pounding continued. Stone rushed to the door, gun in hand. He carefully opened the door.

Before him stood Muscle Man, his expression bordering on rage. Behind him, Sandra held her automatic pistol to the back of his head.

"Back up into the room, Stone," she said. "We've got a visitor."

Inside, Sandra growled, "Sit, or whatever you say in Italian!"

"Italian?" Stone kicked the wooden chair in the man's direction.

"Yeah. So he says." Sandra stood blocking the door with her Glock held in a ready position. "I found him sitting on my bed, smoking a cigarette. Now my room stinks."

In Italian, Stone asked the man who he was and what he was doing in Sandra's room. He shrugged and said he thought it was Stone's room.

"My name is Paulo. I work for Roberto Comacchi. You know him from Syracusa, Sicily." He pointed to Sandra. "When this lady was rescued."

Stone translated for Sandra and added that the man worked with Comacchi, the Italian intelligence man, who helped get her out of Syracuse.

"I got the gist of that," she said, still aiming her gun. "What's he doing here?"

Stone asked Sandra's question. Paulo answered in accented English, "Vincente, the big boss, instructed Comacchi to send me to watch over you." He looked at Stone.

Sandra lowered her gun. "The more the merrier."

"I don't know Vincente," Stone said.

Paulo shrugged. "He doesn't know you either, but his cousin does. Some contessa."

"Oh, that's great, Stone," Sandra said, "Your squeeze is keeping an eye on you."

CHAPTER FIFTEEN

HADHRAMAUT, YEMEN

The ceiling fan in Hayden Stone's hotel room clicked a steady beat, pushing down cool air. Paolo sat before him, his expression switching from glum to defiant. Stone offered him a whiskey, but he declined with a wave of his hand. In a way, Stone sympathized. After all, here was a tough Italian agent, subdued by a good-looking American woman. What if his buddies back in Rome caught wind of that?

"Do you have any identification proving you're with Italian intelligence?" Stone demanded.

Paolo glared. "Do you carry CIA identification?"

Stone held back a chuckle. This guy had chutzpah. "When did you get here?"

"Yesterday, by plane. I came from Sana'a."

"How many came with you?"

"Only I came. My boss Comacchi sent me from Asmara."

"You're solo. No backup or support?"

Paolo shook his head, as if the conversation was beginning to bore him. "Why do I need support? All I have to do is keep you from getting shot by these *provinciali*."

"These country hicks know how to kill," Stone said. "You say Roberto Comacchi is in Asmara. The country of Eritrea?"

"Vincente sent a team from Rome to check on some Saudi prince whose yacht is anchored at Massawa, the port down from Asmara," Paolo said, wearily. "The prince is related to this Saudi, Abdul Wahab. The one who wants to kill you."

Stone slipped his pistol inside his waistband behind his back, and took a seat. The prince this agent referred to had to be Prince Mohammed al Tabrizi, who months before had rented

Lucinda's palace on the Riviera for an al Qaeda functionary. The same al Qaeda individual Prince al Tabrizi was suspected of having killed.

Stone asked, "What's this prince up to in Asmara?"

"I cannot say."

Can't or won't, Stone wondered. *The prince is probably in cahoots with the Italians.* Stone asked, "Are any of my people there in Asmara?"

"You will have to ask them." With that, Paolo stood. "Since we have made our introductions, we have nothing more to discuss."

Stone almost laughed. "What's your plan of operation?"

"My plan is to stand off and watch," Paolo said, moving toward the door. "If someone tries to kill you, I kill them. *Buona notte.*" Paolo closed the door behind him.

The next morning, Stone walked within earshot of an espresso-drinking Paolo and made arrangements at the front desk for a car and driver. Stone told the driver that he and Sandra wished to visit the Sultan's Palace in Sayun. Afterward, he wanted to travel a couple of miles east to the town of Tarim to the Al-Ahqaf Library, and then wander through the *souks* that sold honey. If Paolo was going to follow them, he may as well have their itinerary.

Walking toward the parking lot, Stone and Sandra crossed the hotel gardens. When she stopped to admire the flowering pink bushes, he pointed up to the football-shaped nests hanging from branches in the high trees. "They belong to those yellow weaverbirds. You see a lot of them over in East Africa. The only way into the nest is from the bottom. Keeps the birds' eggs out of the reach of snakes and rats."

"What kinds of snakes are here in Yemen?"

"Some deadly ones you don't want to meet."

"We're going to visit another palace this morning?" Sandra asked. "I thought this hotel was the sultan's palace?"

"The sultans built many mansions along the valley, but the one we're going to visit is a huge one. A couple of stories high and now a museum. Quite impressive."

The driver gave his name as Zaki, but indicated he didn't

speak English—which Stone found hard to believe, but he played along. They drove along the paved two-lane road toward Sayun. Along both sides of the road, where the flat wadi wasn't irrigated, the soil consisted of the same hard clay as the thousand-foot cliffs on either side of the wadi. The cliffs had been crumbling for centuries, breaking away and piling up along the foot of the ridge.

"Everything is so old." Sandra made the remark casually, as if falling under the spell of the surroundings. "It's so quiet, even in the daytime."

"Enjoy the place," Stone said. "But don't let it lull you into becoming careless."

She turned and stared at him, then raised her scarf and covered her blonde hair.

They entered the town of Sayun, passing a string of shops and garages. Men stood talking in front of four-wheel drive vehicles. A lot of activity, for so little noise.

Zaki parked the car in front of the immense palace, which stood almost ten stories high and gleamed in the sunlight. The rounded turrets fashioned at the four corners made it resemble a wedding cake. Close up, it became apparent that the building needed maintenance. The facade appeared to be melting from the wind and rain.

"All these mud-brick buildings in Yemen require constant plastering and patching, or they end up like the abandoned derelicts we passed on the road," Stone said as they paid the entrance fee.

They joined a group of five tourists waiting to be led through the building. The guide took them past archeological exhibits on the ground floor. Then they climbed a number of floors to view a display of local folklore and crafts.

Stone periodically slipped off from the tour group and peered out a window to see if Paolo was waiting below on the street. Stone knew he was there somewhere, but he never spotted the big man. He did see General Ali Al-Wasi's two security men leaning against a black sedan, smoking cigarettes. They made no effort to conceal themselves.

. . .

On the road to Tarim they passed more crumbling forts, formed from the dirt fallen over the centuries from the cliffs above. Like the palace in Sayun, the fortresses had rounded battlements at each of their four corners. The structures blended in with the dun-colored dirt, starkly contrasting against the cloudless cobalt sky.

"I take it they were used for protection from enemies," Sandra said.

"Yes. As peaceful as this place appears, someone may be out to get you." Stone turned around and looked out the rear window. The same black sedan he'd seen from the palace window now followed them. Some distance behind them, a dusty SUV followed. Paolo, he guessed.

"So what do we do in Tarim?" Sandra asked.

"Tourist stuff." Stone turned and through the windshield saw the city in the distance. "Maybe we'll skip the palace in Tarim and head straight for the Al-Ahqaf Library. It's worth seeing if you appreciate calligraphy. Like the Celtic manuscripts, I can't understand what's written, but they're beautiful to look at."

"Then what do we do?"

"Visit the *souk* and check out the honey market."

"Are we still being tailed by Al-Wasi's men?" she whispered.

Stone looked out the back window. "Yes."

"What about Paolo?"

"Looks like it."

Sandra paged through her guidebook, and said quietly, "Wonder what we can expect today."

. . .

At the Al-Ahqaf library, Zaki introduced them to a guide, whom Stone suspected was either a relative or a close friend. The man's English had a hint of a British accent. They didn't stay long, but did manage to view one of the oldest copies of the

Quran. Sandra appeared uninterested in the exhibit, and Stone suggested they go to the marketplace.

"Is this market any different from the one in Sana'a?" she asked as they got back into the car.

"They all have their own flavor," Stone said, finally catching a glimpse of Paolo. He stood across the street next to several parked motorcycles, in plain view. Stone wondered if it was a signal.

Zaki drove through the town and in a few minutes parked off the street next to overloaded trash dumpsters. A slight breeze blew dust over the market area. They got out and headed for the *souk*. Zaki insisted he accompany them.

"What do you want to buy?" Sandra asked.

"Nothing specific, but you can find neat things."

They wandered past large bins of spices of varying colors—yellow saffron, rusty cinnamon, golden turmeric, and bright red chili powders. Brown hemp bags stuffed with Mocha coffee beans lay to the side. They overheard a great deal of bargaining, but little attention was directed toward them. The smell of incense floated in the air.

"Smell that incense," Stone said. "Incense and myrrh were the big exports to Rome two thousand years ago," Stone stopped before a makeshift stand displaying ornamental knives and swords. "The region became quite wealthy, then the market collapsed when the Roman emperors adopted Christianity in the fourth century. Incense was seen as a pagan trapping."

"Really," Sandra said, holding up a silver Marie Theresa Thaler. Stone bargained with the tradesman and, when he thought he'd reached an acceptable price, handed over the riyals for the coin. He put it in her hand.

The wind had increased, and the tarps covering the merchants' goods flapped, making sharp cracking sounds. Traders began covering their wares. Stone could taste the dust.

Sandra adjusted her scarf, her eyes hidden behind sunglasses. She placed the coin in her bag. She whispered, "I'm surprised the men aren't leering or staring at me."

"You've had the good sense to cover up," he said, then added with a grin, "and look submissive."

She pretended a docile look. "Screw you, Stone."

They wandered awhile and came across the Abufaraj Honey Center. The blue-door entrance was shoehorned between two clothes merchant stands. The lopsided building had significant cracks running down its front. Inside, florescent lights illuminated a warehouse-size room with disorderly rows of wooden tables, all holding jars of honey.

Zaki, their driver, led them to a table on the right side and introduced them to another cousin. In classical Arabic, the cousin told Stone that here was the best honey in Hadhramaut and it came from Wadi Du'an. "Taste it," he said, and offered them spoons of the thick, mahogany-colored liquid.

"This is what the Arabs call *bariyah*, the best," Stone said. "Comes from the flowers of the buckthorn tree, which makes it buttery and gives it a pleasant aroma. Jars of this are given as wedding presents to the bride."

"Delicious," Sandra exclaimed. "I'll take two jars."

They left and went back out into the *souk*. As he turned toward the stands displaying rugs, he saw Paolo on the right side inspecting coffee beans, and down to the left the two security men with cigarettes standing in the way of passing shoppers.

In a whisper, Stone asked if she spotted their surveillants.

She did, and then said, "Everyone's at the party except Abdul Wahab and his goons."

"By the way, have you checked in with Colonel Frederick or Mark Reilly?"

"Satellite's been down," she said. "Let me check now."

"Hold it!" Stone said. He stared as a man in Western dress accompanied by four men in Yemeni attire entered a *hammam*. "Look at the front door of that bathhouse. There's Abdul Wahab with four others."

"I'll tell Frederick or Reilly we've spotted them."

"No time," Stone said. "Let's follow them inside."

CHAPTER SIXTEEN

TARIM, YEMEN

Stone and Sandra hurried toward the entrance to the *hammam*. Stone paused before entering. "I don't like these places," he said. "They're not like our gyms at home. They're dark and dirty."

"Hayden, slow down. Let's wait outside. We'll get photographs of these people leaving, then get their identities from General Al-Wasi." Sandra tugged Stone's sleeve. "That's what you want to do, right? Identify the men Wahab is recruiting?"

Stone pulled away.

"You're not interested in getting pictures, are you, Stone? You want to kill Abdul Wahab."

"You stay at the entrance. They won't let you in anyway. Keep Zaki occupied."

"We have no plan, no backup," Sandra exclaimed. "And you don't have the authority from Frederick to take Abdul Wahab out."

"Wahab has tried to kill us both. Now it's our turn."

Sandra pulled his sleeve hard this time. "Don't you get it? Wahab is our double agent."

"No. He's your double agent. I have a score to settle with him."

"I'm going in too," Sandra said. "Tell Zaki to go get the car and bring it here."

Stone walked over and gave the instructions to a bewildered Zaki. Stone stalked back to the *hamman* and was greeted by an overweight, glaring attendant. He told the man he wanted to take a look at the facility before using it. The man vigorously shook his head, saying the bathhouse was closed for a private party.

Stone whispered to Sandra, "Keep this guy occupied." He then elbowed past the attendant and went into the reception area and looked for the door to the baths. Sandra removed her scarf, shook out her blonde hair, and smiled at the attendant, who was now very confused.

The *hammam* was dimly lit by bare lightbulbs attached to the damp walls. Burnt incense mixed with steamy air. From another room came the soft strumming of an *oud.*

He entered the next room, where a young attendant with a puzzled look on his face accepted a few riyals, showed Stone a locker, and handed him a checkered *pestemal.* Neither Wahab nor his men were in the locker room.

When the boy turned the other way, Stone threw the robe aside and proceeded into the steam room. He found it vacant. Next he carefully made his way through the shower area, but again no one was there. The next door led to the pool. He pulled out his Sig Sauer and eased open the door.

He stopped. Creamy light streamed down from small octagonal windows set in the vaulted ceiling. Thick pillars lined the sides of the room. Brilliant blue tiles formed intricate patterns on the walls and on the bottom of the Olympic-sized pool. Somewhere the sound from a low waterfall echoed. The cool air was a welcome contrast to the humid heat back in the steam room.

Stone advanced one step, and immediately had a warning flash. Except for the sound of trickling water, he sensed an unnatural silence. He was not alone.

Pistol thrust forward in a two-handed grip, he crouched, then carefully stepped back into the barrel of a gun.

In front of him, behind the marble pillars, midway across the pool came the deep, cultivated voice of Abdul Wahab. "What an exquisite setting to die in. Don't you agree, Mr. Hayden Stone?"

Wahab stepped out, as did three other men. A voice behind Stone ordered, "Throw down your gun."

Maintaining eye contact with his captor, Stone tossed his Sig Sauer into the pool. The action was unexpected. The big man's eyes flicked toward the gun sinking in the pool.

In one movement, Stone shifted his body, lifted his right arm, swung around, and came down on his assailant's gun hand. Wrestling with the gun, Stone turned the big man's body around so it acted as a shield against Wahab and his henchmen.

"Surrender, Stone!" Wahab yelled, moving forward along the edge of the pool toward him. "It is all over."

Both hands on the big man's gun, Stone twisted it out of his grasp, and then slashed the butt across his face. The big man cursed and punched Stone, slamming him back against the wall. The gun fell and banged across the marble floor.

Wahab along with the other men rushed forward. Stone kneed the big man in the groin and chopped his nose with his hand. His opponent staggered, blood streaming down his face. Their feet tangled, and both tumbled forward into the pool.

Wahab shouted a curse. Splashing in the water, the big man took repeated swings at Stone's face. Stone took two deep breaths, grasped his assailant's hair, and dove down, dragging the big man with him. Bullets sprayed the surface of the water around them as they submerged.

When they hit bottom, the big man yanked his jambiya from his belt and slashed Stone's left forearm. Stone thrust out his right forefinger and gouged his attacker's eye, then seized the knife and twisted it away from him.

The big man gagged on a bubbly cough, swallowing water. He looked up toward the surface as if pleading for air. With one slice, Stone slit his throat, and pink plumes of blood rushed into the water.

Stone watched the big man flail, his hands holding his neck. As he kicked for the surface, Stone looked around and spied the gun he had thrown into the pool. It lay only three feet away.

The air in his lungs exhausted, he grasped the Sig Sauer and looked up. At that moment he saw a bullet tracing bubbles whirl down and strike his right calf. He felt no pain.

No matter. His lungs cried for air.

If this was the end, he intended to make it very costly for Abdul Wahab.

Bracing his feet on the bottom of the pool, he pushed hard

for the surface. As he burst from the water, he began shooting. One of the two men in front of him crumbled, his pistol clanging on the marble floor.

As Stone sank below the surface, Wahab and the remaining thugs sought cover behind the row of pillars. The Italian operative Paolo was positioned at the far end of the pool and exchanging fire with Wahab and his men.

Stone surfaced in time to watch Wahab and one man reach the exit door. Stone emptied his gun in their direction and managed to place a bullet in Wahab's back. Although yelling in pain, Wahab, along with his accomplice, struggled out of the building.

Paolo ran over from the far side of the pool, took Stone's hand, and pulled him out of the pool. Without speaking, they looked at three dead men. One floated in the bloody pool, two lay next to the marble columns.

Something was wrong. Stone had a bad feeling. "Sandra. We've got to check on Sandra!"

The two dashed back through the door to the showers, through the steam room, and halted at the lockers. Sandra slumped on a bench, looking down at a bloody towel pressed under her left breast.

"Sandra!"

"That attendant was working for Wahab. He attacked me." She shut her eyes and bent forward. "Hayden. I'm bleeding like a pig. For God's sake, get me out of this dump."

Stone found fresh towels and replaced the bloody one, holding it to the wound.

Paolo moved off, looked behind the row of lockers, and yelled, "Stone, there's a body here. The neck is very, very broken."

"That's the fat shit who tried to kill me," Sandra said.

Shouting came from the *Hammam* entrance. General Ali al-Wasi burst into the locker room and, seeing Sandra, shouted, "From the street we heard shots."

Stone quickly explained that Sandra had been stabbed. "We have to get her to a hospital."

"Of course," Al-Wasi said, "but the gunshots?"

Stone looked behind him for Paolo, but he had disappeared. "Look in the pool," Stone said to al-Wasi. "You'll find some dead men."

Al-Wasi said, "We must get Sandra medical attention. My people will take you. I will see you at the hospital after I learn what has happened here." He pointed to his lieutenant and, in Arabic, ordered the two be driven to a clinic.

Stone and Sandra rode in the backseat of al-Wasi's sedan. In a few minutes the car pulled up in front of a medical center.

While they hurried through the entrance door, the police driver pointed to Stone's bloody pant leg. "You also need attention."

• • •

Stone lay on a table while a serious-looking physician sewed five stitches in his left forearm. A bullet remained in his right calf. Al-Wasi arrived and asked Stone about the three dead men in the *hammam*.

"Wahab's men," he said. "But he got away."

"It figures Abdul Wahab was involved," al-Wasi said, punching numbers on his cellphone.

Stone closed his eyes and listened to him on the phone with the local authorities. Afterward, he gave orders to his men, and then consulted with the hospital staff about Sandra's condition.

At last, he turned to Stone. "Miss Harrington will be fine. The doctors say it is a very deep knife slash between two ribs, but it will not be life threatening."

Stone winced as the doctor dug under the skin of his leg. "Good thing I was in the pool when this bullet hit me," Stone said. "It lost a lot of energy after entering the water."

The doctor held up a bullet clamped in his forceps for both of them to examine. "There was minimal muscle damage. The bullet traveled under the skin and stopped."

"Nine millimeter," al-Wasi said.

"Yeah," Stone agreed, and took it from the doctor. "I'll add it to my collection."

Al-Wasi pointed to Stone's hand. "I meant to ask you about that missing fingernail."

"The work of Abdul Wahab's goons."

The general made himself comfortable on a stool. "Abdul Wahab and a particularly ugly man by the name of Kheibah were last seen in a car passing through Sayun, where your hotel is located. They were driving east, toward Shibam."

"Good place to hide. It's a vast complex of buildings like skyscrapers." Stone fingered the bullet. "Think that's where he'll hide out?"

Al-Wasi shook his head. "Remember years ago, when the two of us traveled there? They are a tight-knit community. Any stranger's visit is noted by the people."

"Unless this man Kheibah is from there."

Al-Wasi leaned down, and said, "Your Italian friend has disappeared. Just like a *djinn*, a spirit."

"That Italian genie," Stone laughed, "helped save my life."

"Someone has recently told me that Abdul Wahab thinks you are a *djinn*, Mr. Hayden Stone." Al-Wasi straightened. "He fears you and will attempt to kill you again. We will use that to our advantage."

* * *

General al-Wasi's men drove Stone and Sandra the twenty miles back to their hotel in Sayun. Zaki, the hotel's driver, followed them in the rental vehicle. Stone asked how she felt.

"Let's wait till we get to the hotel to chat." Then she laid her head back on the seat and closed her eyes.

When they reached the hotel, they thanked al-Wasi and headed for Sandra's room. Both went in, and she lay down on one of the two beds. Silently, she stared at the ceiling. He asked if it was okay to rest on the other bed.

"Help yourself."

"We've got to call Colonel Frederick and report," Stone said. "You or me."

She tossed her phone over to him. "Before you call,

Hayden—you know what happened to me. Now what happened to you in the pool?"

Stone related the sequence of events, Paolo's involvement, and the shootout with Abdul Wahab.

"So you winged that prick. Better luck next time." She let out a long sigh. "What we did was stupid. Follow orders." She stared. "I know that's hard for you to do."

Stone groaned. He rose and punched in Colonel Frederick's number on her phone. "I'm calling Frederick. What should I tell him?"

"That we're having a swell time. Wish he were here."

Colonel Frederick answered on the second ring. His voice had that military timbre he used with subordinates when he was either angry or worried about them. Stone sat up in the bed, put a pillow behind his back, and switched to speakerphone.

"Spare me the details of both your adventures today," Frederick said. "I've been fully briefed by our Yemeni intelligence counterpart."

"Yes sir."

"How's Sandra feeling?" Frederick asked.

Stone watched her vigorously shake her head indicating she didn't want to speak with him. "She was stabbed in the chest. Has a deep wound."

"We'll get both of you out of there in a few hours. A helicopter from Mark Reilly's base camp will come and get you." Frederick talked with someone next to him about the extraction status. He came back on the line and said, "Stone, I understand you got yourself shot again."

"It's become annoying."

"To you or me?"

Stone ignored his sarcasm. "Where the hell are Reilly and his people?"

"Doing what they're tasked to do. Sitting on the plateau overlooking that wadi, what's its name, Doran?"

"Wadi Du'an. Ancestral home of Osama bin Laden." Stone paused and looked at Sandra. "Wadi Du'an is hot and dry and has a short flowering season, but produces a rich, aromatic honey."

"Stone, I don't give a flying fart about honey."

Stone saw that Sandra had sat upright at the foot of the bed. She mouthed the words, "Please, shut up."

"What do we do next, Colonel?"

"Sandra goes to a decent medical facility in Cairo and you go to Asmara, Eritrea."

"What's in Asmara?" Stone asked.

"Me," Frederick said. "And Roberto Comacchi of the Italian secret service. Last, but not least, our mutual Mossad buddy, Jacob, is sitting in front of me."

"Are the restaurants still good there?" Stone asked.

"Wouldn't know," Frederick said. "Oh. Tell Sandra, who's sitting there next to you, listening, that when she feels up to it, she can join us in Asmara." The line went dead.

Sandra rose, went to the bathroom, returned, and lay down. After a deep sigh, she closed her eyes.

He waited a while, and then asked her, "Need a blanket?"

"Thanks. I'm okay," she said, her hands covering her face. "Don't you have anything better to do than sit there and look at me?"

"No."

CHAPTER SEVENTEEN

SHIBAM, YEMEN—OCTOBER 22, 2002

Every time the car lurched or hit a bump in the road, Abdul Wahab grimaced. He lay sideways on the back seat, to elevate his butt cheek. Blood oozed along the leg of his gabardine trousers. The pain he could endure, but the thirst made swallowing difficult.

"Why don't you have water bottles?" Wahab yelled to Kheibah at the wheel of the dilapidated Fiat.

The man glanced back and answered in the same tone, "Why did you get my three men killed? It will take time to replace them." He looked ahead and swerved around two donkeys loaded with firewood.

Neither spoke for a while. Wahab moaned, then asked, "You said we are going to Shibam?"

Kheibah cursed under his breath.

"There are hundreds of people living there," Wahab said. "We'll be seen."

Kheibah raised one hand, explaining as if to a child or a student, "Everyone sees everyone here in the Hadhramaut, especially if you stay somewhere you do not belong. We will hide among people I know. For a while."

Wahab rested his head on the armrest of the car door and closed his eyes. He heard Kheibah call a relative and tell him to locate a doctor who knew about gunshot wounds.

"My friend shot himself accidently," Kheibah explained. "It is not serious."

When he added that his friend in the car likely would not die from the wound, Wahab detected a hint of regret.

Kheibah finished the call. "I see the city in the distance.

We cannot drive beyond the walls; no cars are allowed. We must park outside the Gate of Shibam."

"I need to wear a *futa* to cover the blood on my pants," Wahab said.

"You will stay in the car, and I will get help."

"Also, bring water," Wahab said. *Bloody fool.*

• • •

The car approached Shibam, which sat on a rise in the middle of the mile-wide wadi. Date palms surrounded the town. The town's eight-story buildings huddled together behind a fifteen-foot wall. Kheibah parked the car and said he would return soon. He slammed the car door and hurried through the open city gate, disappearing down an alley.

Wahab rested in the backseat, pressing his hand to his wound. He knew it wasn't severe—he had received much worse fighting in Afghanistan. Through the open window, he heard an occasional car arrive and leave from the parking lot; otherwise it was quiet. No breeze stirred the air.

The plan had almost worked. Wahab and Kheibah had tailed Hayden Stone and that blonde woman from the Al-Ahqaf library. Earlier that day, the old merchant at the front entrance of the palace in Sayun had called Kheibah and said he overheard them say they would visit the library. Wahab was impressed with Kheibah's network in the Hadhramaut.

The shoot out at the *hammam* was a disaster. Unexplainable. How could it not have succeeded? Five men against one?

Wahab reviewed the sequence at the pool. He stopped at the image of Stone bursting from the water, gun in hand. The man should have been mortally wounded yet, like a phantom, he still lived. A chill made Wahab shudder for a second. Was Stone really a *djinn*?

After what seemed an hour, he heard Kheibah's voice. He was speaking with other Yemenis. The door opened, and Wahab looked out at two strange faces. One man had blondish hair.

Kheibah handed Wahab a *futa*. "Hurry," he ordered. "The doctor has arrived."

Wahab struggled into the *futa*, and then limped with the assistance of the two strangers through the gate and across the small square to a narrow street. Wahab began to wonder how far he would be able to go. At last, Kheibah pointed to a decorative wooden door weathered by the sun. Entering, the four men paused at a staircase. "We must go up four floors. I will lead the way," Kheibah said, then raced up the stairs without looking back.

Two men took Wahab under the arms. They lifted his weight as the three took one step at a time.

They passed a confusing maze of high, bare-walled corridors and staircases. Wahab looked into a few sparsely furnished rooms, but saw no one. Kheibah stood waiting at the top of the staircase. "Come," he said, and led them to a room with large windows that faced east, toward Sayun.

"The doctor will be here," Kheibah said. "Lie down. Here is some water."

Wahab pulled off the *futa*. "I'll undress for him."

"As you like," Kheibah said, then motioned for the two men to leave with him.

Alone, Wahab looked around the almost bare room and eased onto a stool. He removed his shoes and found that blood had made its way into one sock. He let the sock drop and gazed out the window. The air was cool, but he felt faint. Closing his eyes, he wished to be somewhere else. The French Riviera came to mind.

Kheibah came back, followed by two men in Western dress. The older one wore rimless glasses, and Wahab assumed he was the doctor. A younger, pale-faced man carrying a black, old-style physician's bag accompanied him.

The doctor looked around the room. "I need a table. Bring a table. I cannot work on him without a table."

Kheibah and the blond-haired man returned, bumping a wood table against the wall. Once the table was positioned, they stood back and let the doctor and his assistant help Wahab lie face down.

"How much pain?" the doctor asked.

Before Wahab could answer, the doctor instructed the assistant to hand Wahab a sedative and shouted to Kheibah for water. "This will relax you. Maybe you will sleep," the doctor said, and then began scrubbing the area around the wound with alcohol.

The pale-faced assistant fumbled a blue pill from a container. Wahab wondered why the little man seemed nervous. He was not the one having a bullet removed from his ass. As the assistant handed him the pill and water, Wahab saw the assistant palm another pill-looking object. Something resembling an oversized grain of rice. Wahab swallowed the blue pill, laid his head on a cushion.

"Where did you go to medical school?" Wahab asked, eyes closed.

"Moscow." The doctor turned and instructed the young man to open the bag and set out the instruments. "Pay attention! You will never get to medical school unless you become more alert."

Wahab remained motionless as the doctor probed into the opening of the wound. Obviously, he thought, the man was a leftover from when the Marxists ran this part of Yemen. Fortunately, the blue pill began to work.

He wondered if the doctor had washed his hands. He opened his eyes and saw the nervous assistant. "Where do you want to go to medical school?" he asked.

The young man fidgeted and looked over at the doctor.

"He will be fortunate to go to Moscow for his training," the doctor said, now holding forceps. "If he has my recommendation."

Before Wahab lost consciousness, he wondered if the doctor had sanitized his instruments.

• • •

Sunset yellowed the landscape along the Wadi Hadhramaut, and in the far distance the buildings of Sayun sparkled white. The smell of mown alfalfa drifted in through the window. It had been noon when Wahab passed out. He now lay on his side with a cotton sheet covering him. Across the room, the blonde-haired man sat smoking a cigarette and looking out the window at the blue sky.

"May I have some water?" Wahab found his voice raspy, his throat raw.

The man got up and handed him a glass, then filled it with water from a large plastic jug.

"Thank you," Wahab said, turning and lifting his head to drink.

"The doctor instructed that you were not to move," the man said in a thickly accented voice.

"You are not Yemeni." Wahab took another swallow. The area around his right buttock hurt. "Where are you from?"

"Why do you ask, Saudi?" He went over to a small stand and picked up a small object. He came back and opened his hand. "They took this out of your ass. A 9 mm bullet. Not long ago, one like this was taken from my leg, but I did not need a pill." He let it drop on the table next to Wahab's face.

Wahab heard Russian inflections in the man's speech. His face had the look of those living on the Russian steppes. The man was a Muslim from Chechnya.

"Where are the others?" Wahab asked. "Is the doctor gone?"

"The doctor will stay here tonight." The man sounded bored and returned to the window.

A big plane flew low over the house and, after a minute, became visible through the window. "That Ilyushin is landing at Sayun airport," Wahab said.

The man said nothing, but studied the plane intently.

"An Ilyushin Il-86, I believe."

The man sneered. "It is a propjet, not a jet. An Ilyushin Il-114. I've flown them for the Russians." He kept looking at the plane as it began its descent, and then said to himself, "It has the newer engine."

Wahab laid his head down on the pillow and closed his eyes. This man was a Chechen Muslim and a pilot. How interesting.

• • •

SAYUN, YEMEN

A phone call from Mark Reilly interrupted the daydream Stone was having while he stared at the ceiling fan. He was lying on one of Sandra's beds, visualizing being with Lucinda, sailing on her yacht, *La Clare*. The Mediterranean air soft, the sea gentle.

Shouting over background noise, Reilly said he was in the team's helicopter heading for Sayun. "We'll meet you at the airport in an hour. The chopper has the mining company's logo on the sides."

"Where are you taking us?" Stone asked, sitting up, and speaking loud enough to wake Sandra.

"We're taking both of you to the Sana'a airport. I'll give you the details when we meet."

Sandra rose stiffly, looked down at her chest, and told Stone she had to change the dressing on her wound.

"While you're doing that, I'll go to my room, pack, and get us a ride to the airport. Then I'll come back and help you pack."

Sandra headed for the bathroom. "Lock my door after you. I don't want any more uninvited visitors."

• • •

The drive to the airport proved uneventful. The driver, Zaki, kept looking around at the other cars and drove faster than he had the day before. Stone assumed the man considered his two passengers to be trouble and didn't want to get caught in any crossfire. They arrived at the airport and made their way out onto the tarmac.

"General al-Wasi's jet is still here," Stone said. "Wonder if he knows we're leaving town?"

"He's probably sitting in the shack next to the plane watching us." Sandra eased herself down on her suitcase. "You know, Stone, I feel like shit."

"They'll get you to a hospital and see that cut's taken care of."

Sandra heaved a sigh. "And I'll have another session with

the psychiatrist." She looked up at Stone. "How is the leg, the arm, the finger, and *your* mind?"

Stone shrugged. He pointed west, down the wide wadi to the helicopter skimming over the palm trees. "There it is."

The helicopter landed, and Reilly jumped from the aircraft, took Sandra's bag, and motioned for them to get aboard. The pilot kept the engine running. When all were harnessed, the pilot lifted off and headed back in a westerly direction. Reilly handed Stone and Sandra a set of earphones. "Sandra, we're going to Sana'a airport, where you and another CIA officer will board a Lufthansa plane for Cairo. When you arrive in Cairo, CIA station people will meet you and have you checked out." He nudged Stone. "We're taking you in the chopper to the American embassy for a meeting with our chief of station."

Stone heard Sandra's voice. "Why isn't Stone coming with me? He's been injured."

"Colonel Frederick thinks his injuries can be tended to at the embassy," Reilly said, looking at Stone.

"Frederick said I was going to Asmara to meet him," Stone said. "Know what that's all about?"

Reilly shook his head. "We'll know more when we get to the embassy."

• • •

The American embassy compound, located in a residential area a few miles from the center of Sana'a and the old city, sat on twenty flat acres with a razor-wire-lined wall and fence surrounding the complex. Local guards manned the gates, and a marine security detachment protected the main embassy building.

Dust and dried grass billowed in the air as the helicopter set down on a vacant plot adjacent to the parking lot. Armed guards met them as they disembarked. After presenting identification, Stone and Reilly accompanied a woman dressed in a gray business suit across the grounds to the chancery, and then up to the CIA station.

After the heavy vault door closed behind them, the woman

identified herself as the assistant chief of station. "I'm Marie Hackett. The boss is in the SCIF having a secure powwow with our British and Canadian colleagues. Let's chat in my office."

Hackett's office was Spartan. Maps and charts covered the walls. A seven-foot long Yemeni rifle was propped in the corner.

"Sandra's flying to Cairo, and I understand I'm going to Asmara," Stone said. "When do I depart?"

Hackett studied him. "We'll get to that." She looked over to Reilly. "What's happening at the base camp?"

Reilly eased into a chair and eyed Stone. "We have Abdul Wahab located in Shibam. A doctor and our asset, a male nurse, extracted a bullet from his buttock."

Hackett threw a glare at Stone.

Reilly continued. "Our drone, the one that looks like a buzzard, has been floating over the tower houses. Shibam is a collection of tall tower buildings—"

"Been there," Hackett huffed. "Continue."

"Okay. Our asset placed the tracker capsule, Calypso, into Abdul Wahab's wound, and sewed it up. Now the only thing we have to do is activate it, and our people in Washington will be able to track Wahab real time anywhere he goes via the satellite, Polyphemus." Reilly smiled.

"Why don't we have a read on Abdul Wahab now?"

Reilly answered quickly. "First, he's still in that tower house with the terrorists. Probably until he recovers."

"And second?" Hackett twirled her gold pen in her fingers, looking impatient.

"Calypso, the small tracker inserted inside Wahab, has to be activated before our satellite, Polyphemus, is able to latch onto him."

"So." Hackett rubbed her forehead.

"We're waiting for Abdul Wahab to get out in the open, turn his ass in the direction of our drone, then we zap him and we'll know where he is at all times."

Hackett turned to Stone. "You fly to Asmara tonight, on our jet, and meet with Colonel Frederick."

Stone let a few seconds pass. "I never thought you'd answer my question."

Hackett rose from behind her desk. "You put one of our best officers in harm's way!"

"I don't have the authority to tell CIA case officers what to do," Stone said.

"She, like others, tends to follow your lead, which invariably ends in disaster."

Reilly spoke up. "Disaster? That's rather strong."

In the doorway, M.R.D. Houston, the CIA station chief, gave a slight cough, drawing attention. "I'd like to speak with Reilly, and to Stone before he flies off to Asmara," he said.

"Be my guest," Hackett said. "We're finished here."

Stone limped behind Reilly to Houston's office. Unpacked boxes, books, and maps cluttered the room. Stone had heard Houston had recently been promoted from base chief in Cape Town, South Africa to Yemen. He moved some files from a chair to sit down and take the weight off his aching leg.

Houston swiveled in his chair while checking his computer screen for messages. "Take Ms. Hackett with a grain of salt. She's only interested in catching spies, and thinks counterterrorism should be handed over to another agency." He tapped a key on the computer. "Like the FBI, for instance." His eyes left the computer and he leaned forward, elbows on his desk. "She thinks operatives like you, Stone, are cowboys who cause trouble."

Stone smiled. "She's right."

Reilly and Houston appeared to wait for the other one to laugh, and when both simultaneously did, Stone detected a hint of nervousness.

Houston looked at both of them. "The three of us did a good job in Africa, preventing that nuclear device from getting into the hands of the jihadists."

"Seems we have new problems here in Yemen," Stone said.

Houston nodded. "Just had a meeting with the Brits and the Canadians about Abdul Wahab and this terrorist group he's in contact with. They're perplexed about your gunfight with him. You were supposed to lure Wahab and his group out into the open so we could identify them. Killing Wahab was not in the plan."

"First, clarify the situation for me," Stone said. "Abdul Wahab has been recruited by us and the Canadians as a double agent. Correct?"

Reilly spoke up. "Hayden, you know the answer is yes and we know you disagreed with the operation." He held up his hand before Stone could respond. "We know that Wahab was responsible for the deaths of two CIA officers in the South of France and you believe we should have taken him out."

Stone took a deep breath. "If Wahab had killed two FBI agents, we wouldn't be having this discussion. It would have been handled." Stone paused a moment. "However, I've been told that's not necessarily the way things happen in the intelligence game."

Houston spoke in a careful voice. "Let's just say that the CIA conception of time differs from the FBI's, but the end result could be the same."

Stone let that comment sink in. "Second thing. Wahab is the one who's gunning for me. I'm finally getting a chance to hit back."

"Tell us more about that meeting this morning," Reilly said, as if to get the conversation on a new track. "Did the Brits or Canadians provide anything new on the operation?"

"The Brits think they know all there is to know about Yemen, the country having been their protectorate, but as usual they handed out useless tidbits of local gossip hoping to know what our technical coverage had learned."

"Which is what?" Stone asked.

"Little so far," Houston replied. "Reilly, how's our drone and asset coverage?

"Like I told Hackett, the male nurse who helped the doctor remove Stone's bullet out of Wahab's ass was able to insert the Calypso tracking device. We'll be able to use it when our drone activates it."

"Why didn't this nurse plant a listening device while he was there?" Stone asked.

Reilly shook his head. "The guy's scared shitless. If we'd given him two tasks to perform, he'd have screwed both up. We were lucky he put the Calypso in the right hole."

"Do we have any other options?" Houston asked. "Wahab could be staying in that mud brick skyscraper for weeks."

Reilly nodded. "We're trying to use the drone to launch a harpoon containing a microphone. So far, aiming the thing is a problem."

"Why?" Stone asked.

"We want to hit just outside the windows, maybe the roof. We want to send about five or six at the target. The harpoons are only three inches long, but have good electronics."

"So?" Houston said.

"It's when we fire them from the drone. So far, the closest we've come is within five feet." Reilly rubbed his face. "We've been practicing and…."

"And?" Stone said.

"This reminds me. I need a tranquilizer gun from the armory," Reilly said.

"Why?" Houston asked, impatiently.

"We were target practicing from the drone and we inadvertently hit a dog." Reilly began rushing through the story. "We located the dog because it was barking like hell and transmitting over the air. We took him back to the base camp, but he bit two of our guys in the process."

Stone and Houston looked at each other, shaking their heads.

"This dog just sits in the corner of one of our trailers and growls all the time. Won't let us near him. He only shuts up when we give him chunks of shish kebab." Reilly threw up his hands. "I'm sure he was mean as a junk yard dog to begin with, but now we need to put him to sleep so we can pull out the harpoon."

A moment passed, then Stone asked, "Any chance of improving your aim so we can get coverage before Abdul Wahab checks out of the building?"

"We can always hope," Reilly said.

Houston groaned. "Stone, about your meeting in Asmara.

Colonel Frederick is there with members of the Italian secret service. Also, Jacob will be there."

"Pick up any clues as to what they're up to?" Stone asked.

Houston frowned. "Something to do with a Saudi prince sitting in a yacht off the coast of Eritrea."

Stone thought a second. "Is the name of the yacht Red Scorpion?"

"Sounds right," Houston said.

Reilly spoke up. "That's the same yacht belonging to the Saudi prince who rented Contessa Lucinda's palace last spring for that al Qaeda big shot."

"You're right. Very interesting," Stone said. "Wonder how he figures in all this."

CHAPTER EIGHTEEN

ABOARD THE RED SCORPION, MASSAWA, ERITREA —OCTOBER 24, 2002

Prince Mohammed al Tabrizi took extra care trimming his beard. He had lost the pudginess gained by eating too well and not exercising enough. His new health regimen had proved helpful in fighting the pirates who had attacked his ship. In addition, rumors were now filtering back from the Saudi royal court about his exploits. One could always use good public relations.

He washed his face, toweled it dry. His valet handed him a red-checkered *kufiya* and adjusted the scarf over his head. His man dared only the slightest adjustment to the cloth. Satisfied with the way he looked, the prince mentally ran through the upcoming meeting today with the Westerners.

He'd chosen this *kufiya* to put Colonel Gustave Frederick at ease. It was the traditional color for Jordanians, and Colonel Frederick had good relations with the Hashemite royal house.

The prince's major domo entered the suite and waited deferentially.

The prince turned and asked, "Are we prepared to receive our guests, Jameel?"

Jameel bowed and advised that the seating had been set up on the ship's fantail. In addition, lunch would be served there.

"Just white linen. Do not set our best table, Jameel." The prince spoke in English. "We do not want to appear to be going overboard for these people." The prince smiled, but Jameel didn't catch the pun.

In fifteen minutes, his guests would arrive. The high-ranking CIA official Colonel Gustave Frederick, accompanied by Patience St. Jean Smythe of CSIS, the Canadian Security Intelligence Service, who resided in South Africa. His good friend Roberto Comacchi of the Italian Intelligence Service would be there. They would discuss al Qaeda and Saudi Arabia's support of the war against terrorism. Perhaps they might even mention the military buildup aimed at Iraq, but all this was secondary to more important personal issues.

He looked back at the mirror and fluffed out his gleaming white *thobe*, which fell from his shoulders to just above the floor. The servant handed him his Patek Philippe gold watch, his only display of extravagance.

. . .

The motorboat serving as a tender pulled alongside the anchored Red Scorpion and his three guests climbed aboard. As they stood on deck, the prince emerged from the ship's salon and greeted them.

"We have American soft drinks and, if you like, iced tea." He led them to the stern of the vessel. "I chose to sit out here today for the view of the sea and the mountains. The heat and humidity are not that uncomfortable." He waved his hand, suggesting his guests make themselves comfortable on the cushioned lounge chairs, shadowed beneath the white canvas tarpaulin.

Roberto Comacchi took the lead with expressions of thanks for his agreeing to meet with them. Only appropriate, thought the prince, since the two were on good terms. However, it was the colonel who, of the three, had the most authoritative stature, with his military bearing. Any subordinate of Colonel Frederick might admire or hate him, but the smart ones feared him. This was the prince's first face-to-face meeting with the colonel; their contact in April on the Riviera had been at arm's length.

After the prince exchanged pleasantries with Comacchi, Colonel Frederick said, "I believe I recall seeing the Red Scorpion anchored in Villefranche a few months ago."

"Of course, you did, Colonel," the prince said. "I enjoy the South of France as you do. So sorry we didn't meet at Contessa

Lucinda Avoscani's soirée that night. You know, the affair Abdul Wahab and Hayden Stone attended."

There was silence. The prince thought he might ease the delicate situation out into the open. The fact that none of his three guests showed any emotion at his mentioning Stone or Wahab impressed him. He looked toward St. Jean Smythe and said, "Speaking of the Contessa, please give her my regards. I understand the two of you flew in from Rome last night."

"I certainly will, Your Highness. She speaks well of you."

A cloud passed over the ship, and the dazzling light from the sun became less glaring. The prince removed his sunglasses. Patience St. John Smythe was all that he was told to expect. Stylish and proper, her raven hair slipping from beneath her beige head scarf. He wondered if the Contessa had helped her choose it back in Florence. Her voice had a soft English accent that masked the hard lines at the edges of her mouth. She was quite the match for the American ambassador, Marshall Bunting. His sources also advised that she and Hayden Stone had once been romantically involved. *That man Stone got around.*

Colonel Frederick crossed his legs and adjusted the crease on his cavalry-twilled pant legs. Without looking up, he said, "Prince Mohammed, we are here to learn about the terrorist situation in Yemen. Given that Yemen is a next-door neighbor to Saudi Arabia we know that the political situation there is crucial to your country's security."

The prince nodded. "I find it interesting, with all the problems in Afghanistan and now the impending attack on Iraq, that you should be concerned with the poor country of Yemen."

"Your Highness," St. John Smythe said, "we are concerned about the formation of terrorist groups in Yemen. We have solid reports that a group has already made moves to purchase arms and explosives." She looked to Comacchi and Frederick. "We suspect an attack to be directed against a target in Europe, the United States, or even Canada that could rival the attack on the World Trade Center."

The prince pulled out his prayer beads and began to finger them. "Any details?" he asked.

"We worry about Rome and its monuments, Your Highness," Comacchi said. "They not only have a high profile internationally, they also carry a religious significance."

"So far, religion has not entered into the equation," the prince said. "We are only dealing with cultural and, to a lesser degree, economic differences." He immediately wished he hadn't spoken so fast. Let his guests speak, and he would learn what they were thinking.

Colonel Frederick, who continued to maintain his military bearing, said, "We here do not subscribe to a religious connotation, but our sources have picked up some talk of that nature." He stopped and took a breath. "But we are here to ask some delicate questions of you, sir."

"Before we address these 'delicate issues,' shall we have lunch?" He clapped loudly, and the servant staff responded by going to the dining table and positioning themselves behind each of the four chairs.

When all were seated at the dining table, Colonel Frederick raised his water glass. "Thank you for your hospitality."

The prince signaled the waiters, and they brought platters of white fish, shrimp, chicken, and fresh fruit.

The prince had debated whether to offer them wine, as Eritrea was a liberal country, but thought better of it. Best not appear too gracious to his guests.

Roberto Comacchi had begun to show some discomfort. He had dabbed his forehead twice. True, the humidity had risen, but the unnatural reserve Comacchi had assumed since his arrival told the prince that the Italian feared a strain might be forthcoming in their relationship. Comacchi had been cultivating him as an intelligence contact for a number of years. Did he fear all his work was in vain with what his two companions were about to say?

As expected, the colonel broached the subject after sampling portions of white fish and shrimp. "Prince Mohammed. Your country is an important ally against terrorism, and you especially have been an ally and friend."

"We have common interests in maintaining the status quo."

At that, the prince signaled for his staff to leave them. When the last man had departed, he continued, "We may speak at ease."

Frederick hesitated, and then said, "Recently, your son-in-law, Abdul Wahab, agreed to help us in our cause."

How diplomatically put, the prince thought. This CIA man has savoir-faire, a little bit of the old school spy touch. "This comes as a surprise to me," the prince said. "Abdul did not mention this last week when he sailed with me."

St. John Symthe said, "Abdul Wahab is now in the Hadhramaut, meeting with members of a nascent terrorist group."

The prince resumed fingering his prayer beads. "I know he is traveling in Yemen." He watched Comacchi lower his fork and again dab his mouth with his napkin.

Colonel Frederick leaned back in his chair and traced the condensation along his ice water glass. He said softly, "Your son-in-law has been shot."

"I am aware." The prince looked out toward the sea. "You know that historically Massawa has been a shipyard for boats like that." He pointed. "It is, as I'm sure you know, a *dhow*. Such craft have been plying these waters for centuries."

Frederick continued, "It occurred under unfortunate circumstances."

Frederick's coolness impressed the prince. "That operative of yours, Hayden Stone, shot Abdul after my son-in-law attempted once again to kill him." His three guests sat up and waited for him to continue. "I understand Mr. Stone was also injured."

The three reactions interested the prince. Colonel Frederick shrugged, Roberto Comacchi's head tilted ever so slightly in sympathy, and Patience St. John Smythe, looking out to the ocean, registered concern. Fascinating.

The prince placed his napkin on the table, waited for dramatic effect, then announced, "This feud between these two men is really as you Americans say, out of our hands. Agree, Colonel? They must play it out for themselves."

St. John Symthe leaned forward, elbows on the table.

"Abdul Wahab is very important to us right now. We will restrain Hayden Stone." She hesitated a moment. "If you would, Your Highness, speak to Wahab and impress upon him the urgency to report to us. We've lost contact with him and are beginning to have doubts."

The sun broke through the cloud cover. The prince put on his sunglasses. He found himself departing from his planned script. "Abdul Wahab is a scholar of Middle English. I would not be surprised if someday he becomes a professor in England." He paused. "He is the husband of my favorite daughter." Now he found himself faltering, but took a deep breath. "And the father of three of my grandchildren."

"Yes, Your Highness," Robert Comacchi said.

The image returned of Abdul Wahab joining with him in combat against the pirates who had boarded the Red Scorpion. The fierceness in Wahab's eyes. These people believed they could control that man?

The lunch and the meeting having concluded, his guests waited for the prince to rise from the table. As he did, a strange fullness filled his chest, and he had to resume his seat momentarily. It was as if they had been talking about Abdul Wahab in the past tense.

CHAPTER NINETEEN

ASMARA, ERITREA—OCTOBER 24, 2002

A breeze made its way into the terrace of the SunShine Hotel, ruffling the tablecloth. "You told me you've traveled to Eritrea," Stone said. "What do you remember as your favorite breakfast?"

Contessa Lucinda, in an elegant cotton dress, studied the bill of fare. Stone guessed the slight puffiness under her eyes came from the long trip she and Patience St. John Symthe had made from Rome. On the other hand, perhaps it was due to his being too demanding the night before.

"Why do you have that big grin on your face?" Lucinda laid the menu down.

Stone let a few seconds pass, then whispered, "I forgot how much I missed you."

"You needn't whisper, Hayden. We are alone in the garden."

"Not quite alone." Stone motioned with his head to the well-dressed young man two tables away. "Your bodyguard over there."

Lucinda sighed. "My cousin Vicente insisted I have protection for the trip, so he had Roberto Comacchi assign one of his men to look after me. Marcello is a very nice fellow."

"I can protect you while you're here."

"Yes dear, but please humor the Italian intelligence people. Remember, Paolo helped you in Yemen."

Lucinda moved her chair closer. The two rested their elbows on the cotton tablecloth. They gazed at the flowering jacaranda tree. The garden glistened in the cool, thin air of the highlands plateau.

Stone saw the waiter approaching and whispered again, "This is a great R&R."

"You do have a certain glow this morning." She chuckled and picked up the menu again.

The waiter brought two coffees, and Stone asked him if the kitchen had any specials. He was told they had fresh grilled grouper.

"Too early for fish," Lucinda said.

Stone agreed and looked at the menu again and decided on *silsi*, a spicy fried tomato and onion stew, and fresh bread. "This dish can get pretty peppery, but I'll get some cheese and yogurt to cool it down."

Lucinda waved to the waiter. "I'll have the frittata, and tell the cook to be easy on the peppers."

The two sipped the dark, nutty coffee that the waiter told them had been roasted and ground in the kitchen that morning. Stone always enjoyed visiting Asmara.

"You appear at ease, dear," Lucinda said. "Is it because of me, by chance?"

"Of course it is." He laughed, and then sighed. "I like this country, and especially this town."

"It certainly has an Italian flavor from when it was a colony of Italy." Lucinda looked into her cup. "My parents brought me a number of times in the sixties. The Eritreans had just begun their thirty-year war of independence from Ethiopia. The country was poor. All the industrial plants the Italians had invested in the country before World War Two had been destroyed or removed by the British."

"But the city of Asmara and its art deco architecture remain."

Lucinda nodded. "And the restaurants still serve pasta dishes."

Their meals were served, and they enjoyed the quiet.

"When did you two arrange for the trip?" he asked.

"It was Patience's idea. Last week she passed by Florence and stayed at the villa. We talked about you and your mission in Yemen, and that you'd be traveling here for a meeting." Lucinda looked up at the jacaranda tree. "She suggested I join her, and of course, as you Americans say, I jumped at the chance."

Stone took another sip of coffee and wondered if he could

purchase these beans in Washington. Then the realization came that Lucinda had known he was going to Eritrea before he did.

"Paolo, the fellow your cousin Vicente sent to Yemen to look after me, came in handy. It was nice of you, but really, I don't need a babysitter."

She gestured with a nonchalant wave. "I knew you would not like it, but after the attack on us in Florence by Abdul Wahab's men, I deserve to be involved."

He took her hand. "As a matter of fact, Paolo helped me at a very critical moment."

"So, I have been told."

"You know a lot about what's going on." He thought for a moment. "Lucinda, back in France you were in league with French intelligence. Obviously, the same situation exists in Italy."

Lucinda looked at him and threw up her hands. "*Dio santo!* Hayden, good God, what is wrong with you? Of course I have connections with these people. My family is connected. It must be. To last as long as we have, my family has been part of, or friendly with those who know what is happening. Along with maintaining good bloodlines, it has kept the family intact."

"I see."

Lucinda touched his arm and squeezed. "Now we must go find Patience at the American embassy. She is there meeting with her lover." At this, she touched her cheek to his shoulder. "We will meet them and take a stroll around the city to see the beautiful buildings," she said. "How far is it from here?"

"Just around the block."

Stone charged the bill to their hotel room and when he looked up, Marcello had disappeared.

• • •

They found Ambassador Marshall Bunting at the embassy. The three of them had met just a few months before at Bunting's party in Cape Town. After some cordial chitchat, Bunting told them Patience would not return from a meeting in Massawa until late afternoon.

"She's with Colonel Frederick and Roberto Comacchi, and will want to rest when she gets back," Bunting said. "Let's get together tonight for dinner. Any ideas?"

"As a matter of fact, I know of a place about fifteen kilometers out of town," Stone said. "Very Eritrean in food and atmosphere. We'll probably be the only ones there speaking English."

"Just the ticket. We're at the same hotel as you two, so we'll buzz you when we're ready."

"Ambassador, I assume you're privy to why I'm here. When do we have this meeting with Frederick and Comacchi?"

"Probably this afternoon in the Sensitive Compartmented Information Facility." His face brightened. "After our little get together in the SCIF, we head out of town toward Keren, where the monasteries are."

Lucinda folded her arms on her chest. "Everyone?"

"No, just the four of us. As you know, Contessa, I'm a birder. We're going birding. Stay over for two nights in a farm or monastery, and then go searching for some birds."

"I'm sure we'll enjoy it," Stone said. "What does Colonel Frederick have on the meeting agenda?"

"He, Comacchi, and Patience are now with Prince Mohammed al-Tabrizi. We'll know when they return. I'm sure it'll prove interesting."

"Was there another man present, by the name of Jacob?" Stone asked.

"I heard he's in town, but no, he wasn't invited to the meeting with the prince."

Stone shook his head. "Doesn't surprise me."

• • •

Extra chairs had to be brought into the embassy's SCIF to accommodate the gathering. What Colonel Frederick had to say he didn't want leaked to foreign intelligence through electronic eavesdropping. Stone stepped aside to allow him to sit at the head of the table. Roberto Comacchi, Patience St. John Symthe, Jacob, and Stone took their seats in the cramped space.

Patience asked Colonel Frederick, "Are we not waiting for Ambassador Bunting to arrive before we begin?"

"I asked the ambassador to pass on the meeting," Frederick said. "Told him we were a bit cramped for space. I'll fill him in on the details later."

Stone eyed Patience, whose lips had tightened. She drummed a pen on the desktop, which annoyed Comacchi. Jacob, whom he hadn't had the chance to speak with in private before coming into the room, signaled "what's that all about" with a raised eyebrow.

Frederick hurried on, looking at his notes. "How are you feeling, Hayden? Wounds mending?"

"Just flesh wounds," Stone said. He remembered Bunting saying that he'd planned to attend and wondered what was really behind the change in plans. Then his thoughts went to his partner. "How is Sandra doing up in Cairo?"

"Complications," Frederick said. "For the information of all here, a few days ago in Yemen, Sandra Harrington was knifed by one of Abdul Wahab's thugs. Cut wasn't that deep, but she's picked up an infection from her stay at the Cairo medical facility."

"When will Ms. Harrington return to Yemen?" Jacob asked.

"Not immediately," Frederick said, then looking at Stone. "We'd like to send someone back with you, but—"

Stone spoke up. "I can team up with Mark Reilly. We worked together on the Riviera operation."

"I'd come with you, Hayden," Jacob said. "But I'd best not, for reasons I'll explain later."

Frederick again flipped through his handwritten notes, and then said, "The meeting with the prince went as well as could be expected. We told him we had an arrangement with his son-in-law, Abdul Wahab, who has failed to answer our messages as arranged before he left for Yemen. The prince got the message that he's out of control." He looked at Stone. "The prince is aware that Wahab was shot and probably believes we want him dead." He looked around the table. "I'm not sure the prince is aware that we want him alive so he can lead us to the terrorists we want to identify."

Comacchi spoke up. "I've had a man in Yemen." He stopped and stared at Stone. "He told me that Wahab seems more interested in killing Mr. Stone than organizing a terrorist cell. Why not keep Stone out of the country and let Wahab go about his business?"

Stone saw that Comacchi's remark didn't go over well with Frederick, but before the colonel could say anything, Jacob spoke up.

"Abdul Wahab has an old network out of Marseille," Jacob said. "They were into drugs, to finance his terrorist organization. Colonel Frederick and Mr. Stone disrupted them this past spring. However, he still has a sizeable group at his command."

"This is true," Frederick said. "In fact, members of Wahab's group recently attacked Sandra and Stone in Sicily."

"Other members attacked Hayden and Contessa Lucinda in Florence," Jacob added. "We captured them, and we're still getting information from them."

Stone felt it was time to say something. "All right, tell us. Where are Wahab's people now?"

Still clearly angry that Ambassador Bunting had been excluded from the assembly, Patience growled, "Two days ago, eight members of his gang flew to Aden. They're in contact with known members of the al Qaeda in the Arabian Peninsula, which we call AQAP."

"Yesterday five of Wahab's people flew from Naples to Sana'a," Comacchi added.

"That bolsters his organization," Stone said. "So far he hasn't recruited many local people in Yemen."

"And many of those he did have been put out of commission. Isn't that so, Hayden?" Jacob provided one of his rare smiles.

Frederick frowned at both of them. Again he juggled his notepapers. "One positive development to report. Mark Reilly cabled saying that the technical coverage on Abdul Wahab is now operational. We're tracking him wherever he goes."

"Where is he now?" Comacchi asked.

"Still in a tower house in Shibam," Frederick said. "Also, we can pick up some audio in his room. It's spotty, but something."

"Anything else?" Jacob asked. "Are they planning to gather somewhere? Are they talking about a target?"

"Nothing on those lines." Frederick paused. "We picked up a new piece of intelligence. A Chechen by the name of Dokka Zarov has moved into the tower house. Results of traces at headquarters give a possible match with a disgruntled Russian military pilot. He was cashiered over his politics, which were pro-Muslim."

The room became silent, and then Stone said, "Wahab or his buddy Kheibah may be planning another plane attack on a Western target."

"We have to keep all possibilities in mind," Frederick said. He put his notes away. "I hate to sound dismissive of this operation, but it has become a minor player in the intelligence world. We all know Afghanistan is hot, and now the big push is Iraq. We have few resources as far as time and material available." He rubbed his forehead. "Washington, Ottawa, Rome, and Tel Aviv don't want another terrorist headache here in Yemen. If this place goes, so will Somalia and everything across the Horn of Africa. Let's wrap this up and move on."

"What's the next move, Colonel?" Patience asked abruptly.

Frederick looked at the ceiling, as if thinking hard, and then turned to Stone. "Take a day or more to heal, return to Yemen, then you and Mark Reilly get together with our colleague General Ali al-Wasi and round up these terrorists."

• • •

When the meeting broke up, everyone filed out of the stuffy room. Jacob waved for Stone to follow him outside the chancery. They found shade under a Shibakha tree and settled themselves on an old concrete bench.

"I want to go with you to Yemen, but it's best I don't," Jacob said. "The situation is complicated."

"I understand," Stone said. "Have any words of wisdom for me?"

"Watch your ass." Jacob unfolded a blue traveler's sun hat and put it on his balding head. "My family is from Yemen. Lived there for centuries with other religious minorities, like you Christians. Regardless of the bullshit they give out, it's tough to live in a Muslim country as a non-Muslim."

"Did you live there?" Stone asked.

"When I was very young. In 1950 we moved to Israel during the mass exodus." Jacob studied the construction work being conducted at the far end of the embassy grounds. He let out a heavy sigh. "I don't want to go back there. Not now."

Stone thought it best to change the subject. "You said at the meeting you haven't gotten much information from those thugs we captured in Sicily and Florence. Any reason?"

Jacob straightened, as if his back ached. "We have come up with some information that you can use. These Arabs we picked up were criminals from Abdul Wahab's narcotics organization in Marseille. Of the six who are our unwilling guests, four were former drug users. Now all are clean and very religious. Two of them have relatives in Aden, Yemen. Doing some information analysis along with crosschecking their DNA, they are related to a couple of terrorists your people killed. Those terrorists were connected with the bombing of your destroyer, USS Cole, in Aden harbor."

Stone added. "Aden is where AQAP hangs out." He thought a moment, and then said, "Wahab is joining up with AQAP, which has a lot more going for it than Kheibah and his farm boys. He doesn't want to delay his plan, whatever it is."

Jacob leaned over and spoke in a low voice. "The AQAP is pledged to overturn the Saudi monarchy." He leaned back and smiled. "Interesting that Wahab wants to put King Saud and his father-in-law, the prince, out of commission. Why, I wonder?"

"As Shakespeare said of Gaius Cassius, 'He has a lean and hungry look.'"

• • •

THE NEXT DAY

An hour out of Asmara on the road to the monastery in Keren, Stone was sitting in the middle of the backseat of the SUV with Lucinda on one side and Patience on the other.

He watched the countryside roll past, and mused over the dinner the four of them had the night before. At first, Patience and Ambassador Marshall Bunting didn't add much to the conversation or pleasantness to the occasion. The tension wasn't a result of Stone's restaurant choice. To the contrary, as Lucinda exclaimed when they entered the place, "*Fantastico*! This is exactly how I remember Eritrea when I was a child."

The four of them shared plates of Arab and African dishes. Patience's and Bunting's stiffness melted by the time coffee was announced.

Stone thought he'd try to further ease the climate. "Ambassador, you didn't miss anything at the meeting. Really nothing new was brought up." From under the table he received a not-so-gentle kick from Lucinda.

Before he put his foot farther into his mouth, Patience saved him. "Your good chum Colonel Frederick is a big bastard. He deliberately excluded Marshall from the meeting, and there was new information discussed."

"I don't know what's going on," Stone said.

Bunting smiled for the first time that evening. "Hayden, let's have a little chat while we're birding." He sat back. "I'm looking forward to tomorrow. Right, love?" He placed his arm around Patience, who nodded.

. . .

In the morning, both Stone's stitched-up arm and leg ached, and one of the staff found a cane for him. Lucinda told him that they'd only bird-watch for an hour or two, then would let Patience and Bunting go off on their own.

"They need time for themselves," she said. "Besides, if you tell him you'll spend only a short time birding, he can plan his talk with you."

The four drove down from the farm into the fertile valley and exited the Land Rover in a field of maize.

"Perfect timing," Bunting announced. "Early morning is a good time. With this irrigation, birds fly miles to come and drink." He looked at Stone's leg. "Taking time to heal, I guess." He turned to the women. "We're going to check out that grove. We'll be back in a while. Hayden, ever do any birding?"

"No, can't say as I have." Stone thought it best not to mention to a birder that he was an upland game hunter who shot doves and quail.

Lucinda waved goodbye and then joined Patience, who had made herself comfortable on a concrete sluice gate. They had walked a few yards up to a tree with only a few leaves. Bunting had started to say something in a confidential tone when he quickly brought his binoculars up to his eyes. "Tell me what you see up there!" he said.

"What do you mean?" Stone asked, squinting against the sunlight.

"The marking on that bird. Up on the second branch from the top. On the left."

"Small. Gray."

"No, no. Color of the feet and beak. Markings on the face."

Stone told him what he saw, although he left the binoculars with Lucinda.

"That's a new one for me! Add that to my record. A Somali Wheatear." Bunting made a notation in his leather-bound notebook, and then faced Stone. "I want to talk something over with you."

"Fine."

"Over there. Let's sit on the log, get you off that leg." After they sat, he continued, "You and Colonel Frederick are good friends and you have worked for him for some time." He paused. "Frederick and I have a long relationship, strained as it may be. This has increased since I've agreed to take over a new center at CIA headquarters."

Stone had suspected Ambassador Bunting was CIA, and this statement confirmed it.

"Gus Frederick and I were vying for the same position, and it looks as if I've been picked for the job. Why I'm telling you this is because I'm gathering a cadre at Langley. The center will focus on Middle Eastern terrorism, and I need good men like you."

A birder and poacher, all in one.

"Hayden, when I go back to Washington, I hope that Patience will spend her time with me, although she may require some convincing to move to the States. She is a dedicated Canadian intelligence officer and all that. With you and Lucinda living in Virginia, just think of the four of us there together. It would work perfectly."

"Thanks Marshall. I'm flattered, but I signed on with Frederick and have to see this Yemen operation through."

Bunting tapped Stone on his good leg. "We'll chat after your mission is completed."

. . .

The four had an unremarkable dinner and retired soon after sunset.

"Do you plan to accept Marshall Bunting's offer?" Lucinda lay in the single bed, which squeaked when she moved. Stone lay in an equally noisy bed.

"He wants *us* to live in Washington and help him convince Patience to leave Cape Town and her career and move in with him full time."

"I am sure he values your talents," Lucinda said.

They lay quiet for a while, and then Stone asked, "What do you think about living in Washington?"

In the darkness, her serious voice came across. "I love your capital and Virginia. That is why I asked you not to sell your home there." A longer than normal time elapsed before she continued. "I do not like the arrangement where the four of us will be so close together."

Stone tried to digest that statement. Before he could, she went on. "What if something happened to Marshall and me and only you and Patience were left? You once loved her. Would you go back to her?"

What a loaded question? Stone knew he had to have the right answer. "I like Patience a lot, but you, I love."

"That is your answer?"

Stone thought of his immediate surroundings. "My answer is—and do not laugh—if you were not with me, I would probably become a monk and join a monastery like this."

"Hayden, my love, you are so full of shit."

. . .

When the four arrived back in Asmara, Stone found that both Colonel Frederick and Jacob had departed. Lucinda's bodyguard Marcello, however, still stood his post at the hotel. Lucinda said Comacchi had left a note telling her that if she needed him she could contact him at the Italian embassy.

Stone sent a secure cable to Frederick, who had flown to the embassy at Sana'a. He advised that he'd stay a few more days to recuperate and use the embassy's doctor to monitor his medical condition.

The following day, Ambassador Bunting returned to South Africa, and Patience to Canada.

Two mornings later, in their hotel room, with the windows open and a warm flower-scented breeze ruffling the curtains, Stone lay close to Lucinda. How many more mornings did he have in which to wake up and feel her warm, smooth skin next to his?

. . .

Later that day, Stone sat at the desk cleaning his Sig Sauer. Lucinda came up and placed her .25 caliber Berretta next to him.

"Forgot you were packing iron, my dear," Stone said. A wave of concern came over him. He had placed the woman he loved in harm's way.

"I've carried it since those gunmen assaulted us in Florence. Please clean it."

He fieldstripped the gun. "I'll have to go to Yemen soon."

"I know. When you do, I'll return to Florence, then fly to Nice and see how the repairs are going on the palace." She stood behind him and rubbed his shoulders with both hands.

"I have something for you to take back." Stone went to his travel bag and removed an object wrapped in a cloth laundry bag. "A Yemeni associate gave this to me." He removed a black stone bust from the bag and handed it to her.

"It is heavy and very lovely," she said, tracing her fingers across the face of the worn sculpture. "Oh, I see Christ written in Greek. It is very old."

"Probably third century AD, when Christians and Jews lived in the Arabian Peninsula. General Ali al-Wasi gave it to me as a gift, but more I think to keep it from being destroyed."

"I will place it with the villa's collection," she said. "This general must be fond of you."

"Perhaps. I guess you could call him a progressive. Today, a precarious position in Arabia."

He was about to say he wished he were returning to Italy with her when a hard rap sounded on the door. They looked at each other, and Stone slipped a magazine into his pistol.

"Mr. Stone. I'm from the embassy." The voice came from the other side of the door.

Stone opened the door cautiously and saw the freckled face of the new CIA case officer he'd met the day before. "Better read this," the young man said.

Stone invited him in the room and then read the cable the man handed to him.

> BASE CAMP IN HADHRAMAUT ATTACKED.
> TWO OFFICERS KILLED.
> REILLY WOUNDED.
> COME AT ONCE.
> FREDERICK

CHAPTER TWENTY

ABOARD THE RED SCORPION ANCHORED OFF
AL-HUDAYDA, YEMEN—OCTOBER 30, 2002

The morning humidity lifted like steam from the Red Sea. Prince Mohammed al-Tabrizi decided to entertain his guest in the air-conditioned comfort of the yacht's salon. He had asked his old friend Uthman to come from Sana'a and stay with him for a night. The man obliged, and arrived in the chauffeured car the prince provided. Two armed members of the prince's staff accompanied him for protection, both against hijacking on the road and harassment from the government's uniformed police.

"Welcome Uthman, peace be unto you." The prince met his guest at the head of the ship's accommodation ladder and led him up two deck levels to the glass-enclosed salon. Uthman appeared weary from his trip.

"How was your drive from Sana'a?" the prince asked, gesturing for his guest to make himself comfortable on an embroidered cushion.

"The distance was not far, but the road was busy." Uthman settled himself next to the low, round table that held plates of figs and fresh fruit. "Thank you, Your Highness, for sending a car and escort."

"My pleasure. The drive is a scenic one through the mountains," the prince said. "The Chinese engineers built a fine road."

"We were delayed for some time when an oil tanker hit two camels. The truck killed one camel and broke the leg of another. The camel with the broken leg had to be shot. Then the arguments started between the driver of the truck and the owners of the camels. More shots were fired. The police came, and of course that only aggravated the situation."

"Shootings and the police always complicate matters."

"Especially in Yemen," Uthman said.

The prince decided the two should sip their teas for a few moments before getting down to business. "I asked you to come because it is best we speak in person. The notes you sent me with respect to the person about whom I am concerned were most appreciated. However, the situation has become urgent. It is best if nothing of which we speak is written."

Uthman nodded and placed his cup in its saucer. His eyes stayed on the cup. "The person who is close to your family, and whose activities you are interested in, is… treading through a field of serpents."

The prince nodded, but remained silent. He would let Uthman speak and relate what he knew of Abdul Wahab.

"Your relative's father and my father were soldiers during the big war in Europe. This man requested assistance and, of course, I rendered it." Uthman looked directly at the prince. "This man—"

"You may speak his name to me, my friend."

Uthman took a deep breath. "Abdul Wahab bin Khalid is organizing a group to wage jihad. In doing so he is in league with a man named Kheibah, who is a fool but has many connections through marriage with the sheiks of Marib and the Hadhramaut. Wahab has also made contact with al Qaeda in Aden. These people are well organized and not fools." Uthman thought a moment. "I am told Wahab has brought some of his own people from France."

"May I interrupt, my friend?" the prince said. "I have heard that Abdul Wahab was shot. What is his condition?"

"He is still recovering."

The prince placed his teacup on the table, hesitated, then said, "I heard from a friend that Abdul Wahab and his people attacked the CIA."

"He left Shibam a few days ago to lead the attack against the Americans, whom I suspect were CIA. As we know, many of the Americans here are CIA. He now desires to leave the tower house in Shibam for Sana'a."

"Do you have details of the attack?" the prince asked.

"The story has many versions. The one that appears true is that Wahab, whom I have spoken with many times and, as you know, has been a guest at my home in Sana'a and in Marib, and who I believe to be a fine man, though at the present time the man is somewhat misguided.... Neither here nor there. My most reliable source is the sheik near Marib. An old friend, and I mean old in years."

"Sheik az-Zaddim," the prince added. "He has family in Saudi Arabia, and my family has helped him and his tribe on many occasions."

Uthman looked surprised. "Yes, Your Highness, of course." He readjusted himself on the cushions. "The story has it that Wahab is in negotiations with the AQAP, and wants to impress them with his organization and fervor for his cause. So, without consulting Sheik az-Zaddim, he attacked the CIA camped near the border of the Hadhramaut, in the sheik's territory."

"What happened?"

"Wahab's group killed two CIA people and captured two others before they were forced to retreat."

The prince removed his glasses and rubbed his eyes. "Continue, please."

"I am told the people from AQAP are very impressed. They want the prisoners, but so far Wahab refuses to hand them over." Uthman now appeared to search for the right words. "While the al Qaeda jihadists in Aden are considering working with Wahab, Sheik az-Zaddim is very displeased. For the moment, the sheik is obligated to the government officials in Sana'a, who are obligated, for the moment, to the Americans."

Moreover, the Sheik is obligated to me. "Where are the CIA prisoners?"

"In a village not far from Shabwah. The Sheik has sent a message to Wahab—I have spoken to the messenger—that he wants the prisoners turned over to him. Wahab has refused."

The prince clapped for the servant to bring lunch. He needed time to think.

The prince was pleased that Uthman enjoyed the food. The man would be very important to his plans to extricate Abdul Wahab from the mess he had made for himself. He insisted Uthman stay aboard the ship overnight and assured him he would be driven back to Sana'a the next day.

After the meal, and before retiring to his cabin, the prince asked Uthman one further question, "Do you know the exact location of these prisoners?"

"Yes, Your Highness. I also know certain people in the village. They raise bees, and are not happy with how Wahab and his people have disrupted their peaceful village. They resent foreigners pushing them around. They have complained to the Sheik."

. . .

The prince returned to his cabin and removed his Arab dress, put on khakis and a blue polo shirt, and then slipped into Italian-made loafers. He instructed his servant to leave and went to the hidden liquor compartment, selected a bottle, and poured a scotch on the rocks. Dropping into his leather armchair, he hoped the scotch would stop his oncoming headache.

Uthman was a fine man and a valuable asset, but the man, being a typical Yemeni, just circled around a topic. Americans could be annoying, but when conducting business they at least aimed for the heart of the matter and got to the point.

He allowed his mind to settle down and his thoughts to congeal into a pattern. He must sort out the problem of his son-in-law, Abdul Wahab. The ice in the glass slowly melted, and the scotch thinned to his liking. The prince sipped and pondered.

Uthman had provided additional details of the attack and Wahab's involvement. More so, the old man painted a picture of the world of double-dealing tribal politics, in which Wahab had become involved—or better put, entangled. Wahab also had that American, Hayden Stone, to contend with. The prince questioned if his son-in-law was up to the challenge.

The cousin in Riyadh told him the Saudi intelligence hierarchy considered the attack a major issue. Killing CIA officers did not make sense politically, especially if the murders were committed by Saudi nationals. "Many Americans remember Saudi nationals led the attack on the World Trade Center," the cousin said, and then concluded the conversation with the news that the file crossed the King's desk and it would be wise if the prince handled the matter, expeditiously.

He finished his drink. His watch showed two o'clock, and he decided to take a nap. He slipped off his shoes and lay down on the bed without removing the bedspread. The yacht rolled ever so slightly, he guessed in the wake of a passing ship.

Before his eyes closed, he thought about Uthman, with his connections in Sana'a, Marib, and the Hadhramaut. The man would be essential to his plan. As a reward for Uthman's help, he would allude to assisting Uthman's selection to the position of Sheik, when the ailing az-Zaddim passed on. Meantime, he would need the assistance of the old Sheik in gaining the release of the two CIA officers.

Most importantly, he mustn't forget to send the monthly stipend to General Ali al-Wasi of the Yemeni Political Security Organization. Without a doubt, Ali's cooperation would be essential.

He drifted into that space between consciousness and sleep and allowed his mind to return to the soirée on the Riviera given by Contessa Lucinda Avoscani. He watched a tall, dark-haired man in a tuxedo with a scar on his left cheek pass by. The man moved like a stalking cat and had the eyes of a hawk. The prince had asked a member of his retinue to learn the identity of this man. He was told his name was Hayden Stone, the Contessa's lover, and *bête noire* of Abdul Wahab.

His last image before falling into a deep sleep was of the Contessa gliding among her guests, her firm tanned breasts tucked into a low-cut black gown, below a dazzling emerald necklace.

. . .

SHIBAM—THE SAME DAY

"Abdul Wahab bin Khalid, you must feel very proud about your triumphant attack on the Satanic CIA." Dokka Zarov laughed, threw a leg over the armrest of his chair, and flicked the ash from his cigarette onto the floor.

Wahab leaned against the windowsill, looking down at the Hadhramaut from the tower house. He let the morning sun warm his back, which eased the pain. He had aggravated the bullet wound during the raid on the CIA base camp, but the success was well worth the throbbing. The CIA had experienced an embarrassing loss. He had showed the imbeciles gathered around him that he was a combat leader, not just a talker. A man to be reckoned with.

Zarov smirked as Wahab thought only a mixed-blood from Chechnya could. "What will you do with your CIA captives?" Zarov asked in his Chechen accent. "Sell them to the highest bidder?"

Wahab stared at the man, whose red beard looked tangled from remnants of his last meal. "What do you suggest, pilot?"

"Whatever you do, you should act fast. You have killed CIA people, and they don't like that."

"My sources tell me you have killed KGB agents, or now they are called SRV agents." Wahab looked out at the countryside. "I understand the Russians are looking for you. Is that why you fled to Yemen?"

"Perhaps. It appears the two of us have come to Yemen for our own reasons. I have come by way of Jordan. You have come from South Africa, or is it France?"

"Both." Wahab studied Zarov. "Can you fly a helicopter?"

"I have flown them." Zarov's eyes narrowed. "Do you want me to fly a Russian or American helicopter?"

"Russian."

"Is that why we go to Sana'a?" Zarov asked.

Wahab nodded. He was about to explain when voices came from outside the room.

"Two of your loyal followers have come to visit," Zarov said, scratching his beard.

Kheibah, along with a thin man clad in a gleaming white robe, whose name Wahab did not know, entered the room. Kheibah spoke using quick gestures. "Abdul Wahab. We have all gained a great victory against the Crusaders, and—"

Zarov interrupted. "And is there much rejoicing in the land and villages? And praise for your noble leader here?"

Kheibah looked confused. "Yes. No," he sputtered. "I do not know." He regained his composure, glaring at Zarov. "The question of the CIA prisoners. We have been conferring and believe we need to decide what to do with them."

"Who are we?" Wahab said in a low voice.

"I, and the leader of AQAP," Kheibah said. "Al Nasser, the eagle."

"Where is this Nasser?" Wahab asked and then, looking around, "and who is this boy?" Without waiting for an answer, he said, "All conferences are conducted with me in attendance. All decisions are made with my authority."

Kheibah looked down at the floor.

The young man stroked his wispy beard and glared at Wahab, and then looked at Zarov as if he were studying a strange object. The young man said in almost a whisper, "I am a member of al Qaeda. My leader is al Nasser."

Kheibah spoke slowly. "We have had a great victory, and you have led us, Abdul Wahab." He paused, as if letting the words settle in the small, bright room. "The prisoners are held in one of Sheik az-Zaddim's villages. The sheik is concerned that the village where the Americans are held will be attacked. He wants them moved, and he wants more money."

Wahab stood and paced the floor. "And what are the suggestions from your council of advisors? You have formed a council, no?"

"We have formed no official council, but we have met." Kheibah hesitated. "Al Nasser is talking with his al Qaeda people. He sent this young man as his messenger, but he will come soon to speak with you."

Wahab said, "Please, my friend Kheibah, tell me, what are some of your suggestions of what to do with the two CIA captives?"

"We want to ransom them for many millions to the Yemen government or to America. Think what we could do with the money. Buy guns, explosives, recruit fighters."

The young jihadist shouted, "No! Al Nasser wants to bring a film crew from Aden, cut off the prisoners' heads, and broadcast the act on *Al Jazeera* so that the world can see these infidels die."

"Why does that not surprise me?" Wahab shook his head.

"Not very original, these people," Zarov said, getting up and going over to the window. He flicked out his cigarette. He turned to Wahab and said, "At least these fools are trained fighters. They are good in combat."

The young man leaped from sitting on the floor and yelled at Wahab in a shrill voice, "We never see you pray!"

Startled, Wahab reached for his gun, but saw out of the corner of his eye that Zarov had already pulled out his automatic and aimed it at the young jihadist. Kheibah jumped up and cried, "No shooting, please! Peace."

"Who are you to question my faith?" Wahab kept his hand on his pistol. "Have you elected yourself as my *mullah*?" He knew that what he said and did now would be reported to everyone in the group: his own men from France, Kheibah's followers, and AQAP, the al Qaeda from Aden.

The young man continued to throw questions at Wahab. "When did you pray? Do you follow the dietary rules of *hallal*? Do you abide by *Shari'a* law? No, you don't. You sleep with an infidel whore!"

In measured tones, Wahab spoke. "My young fellow, have you met this man from Chechnya? His name is Dokka Zarov, and he is a pilot. Dokka, I believe this young man wishes to learn how to fly, like his wild words have just flown around this room."

"I had the same thought, my esteemed leader." Zarov slipped his pistol in his belt, walked over to the young man, and yanked him by his white robe toward Wahab.

Wahab stood aside and placed an armhold on the young jihadist, then shoved him toward the open window. "Look out there at the beautiful Yemeni landscape, my young, intense, and of course, very holy man."

"What are you doing to me? Remove your hands. My leader al Nasser will deal with you." The young man's eyes moved from Wahab to the scene of the Hadhramaut countryside, peaceful in the morning light.

Zarov bent down, took the man's ankles, and with Wahab's help threw him into the void.

As the young al Qaeda terrorist passed the halfway mark of his fall from the top floor of the eight-story tower house, Zarov remarked, "Look. He is waving his arms around as if he were a helicopter."

When the white-robed man landed in the corral below, a dust cloud puffed up. Something below held Wahab and Zarov's interest, and now Kheibah who joined them at the window ledge.

"*Ya ilahi!*" Kheibah cried, invoking God.

"Yes, dear God," Wahab said. "The man has surely fallen out the window."

"No. That is not what I mean."

After a moment, Zarov asked, "Have you never seen a man fall out a window?"

"That is not the problem," Kheibah whined. "That fool landed on my uncle's goat."

Another moment passed, and Zarov said, "I think the goat is dead."

Wahab murmured, "I must agree. The goat is dead." He patted Kheibah's back. "Tell your uncle we regret that the young fool threw himself out the window and killed his goat. I will pay for it."

Kheibah looked up into Wahab's eyes. "Thank you, *my esteemed leader.*"

Abdul Wahab turned away from the window and walked across the room to get a glass of tea. He called back to Kheibah, "Tell him, we want the goat for dinner tonight. I am certain its meat is well tenderized."

CHAPTER TWENTY-ONE

FLYING OVER YEMEN—OCTOBER 31, 2002

Hayden chose a seat in the front of the aircraft as two CIA executives in dark blue suits boarded. The glances directed at him suggested he had preempted their seating arrangement and, worse, that he wasn't wearing a coat and tie as a man of note would.

The men behind him had no sooner buckled in then the plane left the holding pad, found the runway, and took off. Stone had more on his mind than worrying about bureaucratic pecking orders. Mark Reilly was wounded—the extent of his injuries, Stone didn't know.

Abdul Wahab and his group must have launched the attack. Frederick would want Stone to end the problem. The station chief at Asmara said Sandra was still recuperating in Cairo. That bothered him. While he was off bird-watching and spending time with Lucinda in Asmara, Sandra was mending in Lord knew what kind of medical facility.

The CIA co-pilot came out from the flight deck in a brown leather jacket. Crouching under the low overhead, she held out a secure satellite phone.

"Have a call here," she shouted over the noise of the jets.

"I'll take it." The voice came from the back of the plane.

Ignoring him, the co-pilot said, "The call is for Hayden Stone."

"Thanks." Stone caught a whiff of floral scent and gave her a smile.

"Just knock on my door when you want to return the phone."

He took the phone. "Hayden Stone here," he said.

"Hi, Mr. Stone. My name is Elizabeth Kerr. I work here at Langley in the center John Matterhorn heads up."

Surprised, Stone asked, "How's John?"

"He's fine. He asked me to say hello. He would have called himself but he has a meeting with the brass on the seventh floor. You can imagine, with two of our officers dead and two in the hands of those bastards, there's a lot of tension here."

"I can imagine the turmoil." He told her he was on a plane headed for Sana'a to join Colonel Frederick.

"Mr. Stone, I guess I know more about you than the other way around. A few months ago I worked here on that African problem and know how you saved the situation."

"Ms. Kerr, first, I didn't get that nuclear weapon out of the hands of the jihadists by myself, and second, yes, I do know about your part in the operation. You discovered that the weapon had been stolen from the South African government and gave us the information that helped us retrieve it from the jihadists. John Matterhorn told me all about your involvement."

A second passed, then she said, "Well, John wanted me to pass this information on to you. Since the attack on the base camp in the Hadhramaut, and the loss of our technical capability on the ground there, our satellites have taken over coverage. As you know, in addition to the tracking device inserted in Abdul Wahab's body, we've had spotty audio coverage on his residence in Shibam. Wahab is on the move. He's left Shibam."

"Was he at the attack on the base camp?"

"We're pretty sure. We didn't take over technical control until twelve hours after the camp was overrun. At the time, Wahab was in that tower house in Shibam."

"Where's he now?" Stone asked.

"He's tracking outside the town of Marib. He stayed overnight there and is now on the road toward Sana'a."

"Any take on where he stayed? Do we have a hit on the residence?"

"He stayed at the compound owned by a man named Uthman."

"Do we have anything on this Uthman?"

"Yes."

The pause in the conversation told Stone that the agency had something on Uthman that was not necessary for him to know at this time. "Does Colonel Frederick know about all this?"

"We provided him with portions of past conversations at that tower house in Shibam."

Stone thought a moment, then asked, "Any take on Wahab's status with these groups he's trying to gather around him?"

"Wahab brought his personal gang in from Marseille. They're sort of his praetorian guard. A Yemeni by the name of Kheibah, who has his own following, seems to have come around to Wahab's thinking too."

"What about the al Qaeda people from Aden?"

"Don't know if Wahab's got them in line, but al Qaeda admires men with chutzpah. Anyway, here's why John wanted me to call you. The situation with the two CIA prisoners has become critical."

"Do we know where our people are being held?"

"In a mountain village a few miles from Marib."

"Do we have eyes on the location?"

"24/7. Something else: Since Wahab left Shibam, we haven't gotten any traffic from that tower house. However, we are getting some chatter from our al Qaeda coverage in Aden. There's personnel movement from southern Yemen, headed north toward Sana'a and Marib. We're covering both groups with our drones."

"We still have the drones working?"

"Langley took over control after the base camp was attacked. Three drones are operating from an amphibious ship in the Gulf of Aden. The one with the Hellfire missiles is over the village where our officers are being held captive."

"Thanks. I have a feeling I know where I'm headed. Give John my regards. If I need your assistance, will you be there?"

"We're here to help."

"Stay that way."

• • •

SANA'A AIRPORT, YEMEN

The jet taxied to a hanger set off from the main airport terminal. The soft, dusky evening sky served as a backdrop to the sharp flashing lights from utility vehicles, a departing Air Yemeni jet, and the airport control tower. The plane came to a halt, and Stone watched the two CIA managers in the back of the plane jump up and crowd the exit door.

The engines whined to a stop, and the door slid open. An authoritative voice boomed from outside, "Stand aside! I'm coming in."

Stone saw Colonel Frederick squeeze through the door and look around. He spied Stone sitting in the front of the aircraft. As he pushed past the two men, one of them gave a greeting using the colonel's name, Gus.

Frederick stopped, sized the two up, and then ordered, "I don't want you at the embassy. Go to the Sheraton Hotel. My people are waiting for you and will give you instructions." He looked at Stone and said, "Stay in your seat, we have to talk."

The two men silently disembarked. Frederick made his way up the aisle and sat in the seat across from Stone. Before Stone could say anything, the cockpit door opened, and the pilots came out.

"Sorry to tell you two, your day isn't over," Frederick said. "You're going to take Mr. Stone and another person to the airstrip in Marib. Do you have any problems landing there in the dark?"

"None," the pilot said. "We just received the orders, and were told we'll have a reception party with appropriate directional gear to guide us in. We're just checking on the fueling situation."

When the two pilots left, Stone said, "Well, I'm here as ordered. What do you want me to do? By the way, how's Mark Reilly?"

Frederick leaned forward, hands clasped. "Reilly was hit by shrapnel from an RPG. He isn't as good looking as he used to be, but hey, who is? He has ten people with him, five of them marines flown in from a ship lying offshore in the Gulf of

Aden. Reilly and his people are at a staging area about ten miles from where the jihadists are holding our people. They're waiting for the signal to move in on the village."

"Glad to hear Reilly's all right."

"This little sideshow in Yemen has grown out of proportion. The deaths of two CIA officers by terrorists has hit the evening news back home, and everyone from the White House down wants to know why it happened. Then there's the fact that these bastards are holding two of our people. Not good."

"I take it that you want me to go to Marib and rescue our people," Stone said.

"Yes, but you have some restrictions."

Stone stood, stretched his back, and then sat down again. "I don't understand."

"We suddenly have a lot of entities involved. The two parties you'll be concerned with are, as you know, Abdul Wahab and his gang. Then there's a new player, the local sheik, az-Zaddim. The village where our people are being held is in his jurisdiction. Even though he's a Sunni monarchist, he's on the Yemeni president's payroll."

"The president is not a Sunni and not a monarchist," Stone said. "And he's soon to be on our payroll."

"You do know Yemen, Stone. Az-Zaddim is making overtures that, for a price, he'll turn the prisoners over to us."

"But of course the sheik has already received funds from Wahab to keep our men locked up until Wahab decides what to do with them."

"Correct, but I failed to mention a third party you'll be concerned with. Al Qaeda." Frederick sighed. "Wahab is cozying up to the AQAP, al Qaeda in the Arabian Peninsula, the same crowd who blew up the USS Cole."

"And they're headed in the direction of Marib."

Frederick stiffened and shot Stone a hard look. "Are you guessing or have you been told this?"

"You know, being former FBI, I have good sources. To cut to the chase, what you're saying is that al Qaeda wants to grab the prisoners from Wahab and the sheik and do what they love to do with infidels: behead them. However, if that happens, Wahab will be pissed at losing his cards, and the Sheik, being a Bedouin, won't appreciate some effete Saudis coming onto his turf and telling him what to do and stealing his thunder."

"That's how it stands," Frederick said.

"There are more players than the three you handed me, right Gus?"

Frederick leaned back, checked his watch. "The White House, Langley, our State Department, the President of Yemen, the Royal House of Saud, and," he said, looking over at Stone, "our buddy, Prince Mohammed al-Tabrizi."

"All with different agendas, which change on a daily basis." Stone smiled. "Want to switch jobs?"

"Hayden. Do me a big favor. Just follow orders and don't go off half-cocked on this assignment."

Stone looked out the window of the plane and saw a car's headlights approaching. Finally, he said, "I'll try, Gus, but—"

Frederick's cellphone rang. He answered and gave the party on the other line an order to come aboard, then stared at the forward bulkhead for a few seconds. Stone heard the noise of someone clambering up the ladder and entering the plane. Frederick looked at him and smiled. "Your partner has arrived."

Stone turned around in his seat and saw Sandra Harrington throw a military-looking travel bag in a seat and move up the aisle toward them.

Stone jumped up and gave her a hug, making sure he didn't squeeze her injured chest. "What the hell's wrong with you, kid?" he asked. "You should be sitting in a sidewalk café in Paris. How's that injury?"

"Healing. Still have stitches, but catching that virus in Cairo was no fun."

She eased into the seat behind Stone and started to give Frederick a rundown on the latest information she'd learned at the CIA station in Sana'a. "Wahab has left the Marib area and is headed for Sana'a. Quick analysis at the station has it that he's abandoned the prisoners, or he feels comfortable that they're still in his control."

Stone spoke up. "Wahab must have a lot of trust in Sheik az-Zaddim to let him keep them under lock and key. Maybe he doesn't know about the AQAP thugs headed toward the village where our people are being held."

The two pilots filed in and asked Frederick when they should take off.

"Now," Frederick said, then to Stone and Sandra, "Get on-station as fast as possible. Take your lead from Mark Reilly. He's been handed the ticket on this, so listen to what he says, Stone, because he's getting his orders from me. Got it?" He paused a moment. "Even though he wasn't in charge of the base camp, he blames himself for what happened. Help him cope with the loss of his people."

"Understood," Stone said. "We'll see what we can do."

Frederick looked back at Sandra, but before he said anything, she told him not to worry, that they'd support Reilly.

As Frederick got up to leave, Stone said, "Colonel, have you ever had any problems with me taking orders?"

Behind him, Stone heard Sandra let out a forced cough, and then, without further word, Frederick rushed off the plane.

CHAPTER TWENTY-TWO

IN THE MOUNTAINS BETWEEN MARIB AND SHABWA, YEMEN—NOVEMBER 1, 2002

Hayden Stone woke with pain in his leg and arm. His back felt stiff from sleeping on the rocky ground. Even his wounded finger ached. "Get over it," he said to himself.

He unzipped the sleeping bag far enough to see a dark blue morning sky streaked with shafts of red and orange sunlight. One of the U.S. Marines had fired up a propane stove, and coffee bubbled in a pot. The smell mixed well with the crisp, earthy mountain air.

Stone raised his head and looked around. The CIA camp took advantage of the rocky terrain and elevation, making for a solid defensive position. However, nothing was permanent, and the CIA and Marine contingent could launch a quick attack on the village sitting ten miles away, on the other side of the valley. He made out twinkling lights from the adobe houses rising up the slope of a jagged mountain, where the CIA captives were held.

Stone's fellow operatives were dug in to ward off a surprise al Qaeda attack and, if necessary, disappear quickly into the mountain behind them. The tactical situation impressed Stone. The CIA's sit-and-wait-to-rescue-the-captive-Americans strategy didn't.

He watched Sandra go over to the coffee pot and take a little bit too long talking with a tall, good-looking gunnery sergeant. She looked back in his direction, made her way over, and sat on a nearby rock.

"How about a sip of that?" Stone asked.

"No."

"Thanks for nothing," Stone said with a grin.

"The guys are all watching for signs about our relationship." She repositioned herself on the rock to face in the same direction Stone looked. "Let's not give them fodder for gossip. We have enough on our plates."

"Point taken," Stone said. "Is the coffee good?"

"It's horrid." She took another sip. "So, we all want to know what your plans are for rescuing our people."

Apparently, everyone expected him to disregard Frederick's marching orders. "Talked with Mark last night," Stone said. "He's really hurting, and not just from that shrapnel wound on his face."

"How would you feel in a similar situation?"

"Yeah." Stone sat, leaning back with his weight on his arms. He studied the terrain across the valley and figured he could make it on foot, unnoticed, to within a thousand yards of the village. "Anyway, to change the subject, I didn't bring up my plan of attack."

"You didn't bring the plan of attack up with me, either."

"I'll get to that," Stone said impatiently. "Mark introduced me to Yassid. The Bedouin from that village."

"He's sweet."

"Yeah, real sweet. And right now he's our best buddy until someone else comes along with a better deal. While Yassid is our liaison with the village elders, he's also reporting to them and Sheik az-Zaddim on what we're up to."

"So what's new?"

"I'm going to have him take me up close to the house where our guys are being held," Stone said. "Reilly's not going to like it, but I'll convince him we need close coverage. Also, I'll learn how much support we can expect from the Bedouin tribesmen living there. I can call back and let you all know what's going on."

Sandra took a drink and made a face at the taste. "Mark Reilly won't buy that bullshit. He knows you, and knows you'll go in solo and try to free the captives. Doing so will jeopardize their lives. It's also against Frederick's orders." She threw the rest of her coffee on the ground. "Plus the fact that when you do go in, I'll be with you."

Stone thought a minute, then said, "Go find Reilly and work on some therapy on him. You may have more luck than me."

. . .

Later, Stone found Sandra and Reilly hunched over a pot of boiling tea. Both had ripped open MRE bags, and were making a breakfast out of a grilled chicken breast military ration.

"I found one you might like," she said, and tossed a chicken and rice packet to Stone.

"No ham and eggs?" he asked.

They ate without speaking. Other members of the contingent milled about the camp eating and policing the area. Stone searched through the brown MRE bag and found a chocolate brownie. He thought he might try to break the ice by offering to trade his brownie for one of their pound cakes.

Reilly shook his head, and then said, "Things are better with me." A fresh bandage covered most of the left side of his face.

Evidently, Sandra's mothering had helped. Stone nodded. "Good. Did Sandra tell you what I'd like to do?"

"She said you two want to take an advance position. Report the situation and be ready to move in, only if necessary." Reilly looked around. "I'd like to send two of the Marines with you."

Stone held back a response. Sandra had not only made it clear she was coming with him, but also that she was having a say in the mission plan.

She said, "Let's rethink the Marines. That's too many people to move up there without getting spotted, and we haven't had time to work with these men." Sandra handed her pound cake to Stone. "I'll take the brownie."

Stone handed it over. "I agree with Sandra."

"I'll think about it," Reilly said. "Don't know how much time we have. Frederick keeps saying to hold back. Meanwhile...."

"Meanwhile our people are probably being tortured," Stone said. "Any word about that al Qaeda group heading our way?"

"Reports from our satellite indicate they're parked twenty miles from here," Reilly said. "Frederick thinks they're being held back by Sheik az-Zaddim's people."

Stone stirred his chicken and rice. "What do you think, Sandra?"

She looked over, worried. Finally she said, "We should prepare to move in. I know it's risky because it's daylight, but twenty miles is not that long a drive, and if those terrorists head this way, we're screwed for time."

"Mark, when we go in we're going to find two men who need medical attention. Are there choppers available to get them to a medical facility?"

"There are two Blackhawks sitting on the other side of this mountain." Reilly motioned to the rise behind him. "Two of the Marines here are U.S. Navy corpsmen. They'll tend to the two men until the Blackhawks come."

"Time's wasting," Stone said. "Let's do it."

"Agreed," Reilly said. "I'm going to give the troops the word that you'll be moving toward the village and for us to stand by."

Sandra said to Stone, "I see they have the same Suzuki miniature motorcycles you and I used in Namibia. Perfect for this country."

Stone rose, placed the rest of his MRE in a black plastic garbage bag, and went over to where he stacked his gear. Sandra got up and followed. They passed a large boulder, and she tugged his sleeve.

"Hayden, anything bothering you?"

He smiled. "No. Just surprised things are moving along so fast."

"You didn't expect to go over there alone," she said, pointing to the village, "did you?"

He didn't answer.

"This is a team effort, Hayden. No solo stunts."

Stone felt his chest tighten. "Excuse me?"

"Solo stunts like going into that bathhouse in Tarim and having a shootout with Abdul Wahab." Sandra's eyes became fierce. "Nothing was accomplished from that exercise except that we both got injured. You didn't listen to me then when I advised holding back and not going into the baths. This time I'm taking an active part in the mission. You and I are partners. We work together."

Stone opened his arms. "Everything you've said is on target. I have to remember that we're partners."

She stared at him for a long time, and Stone became uncomfortable. Her eyes left his, looked around the camp, and then they returned. They had softened.

. . .

Yassid, a middle-aged Bedouin whose skin resembled dried bark, dropped Stone and Sandra off within a mile of the village. After jumping out of the pickup, they inched their way toward Yassid's village. When they reached a spot about a hundred yards away, they lay prone, using only rocks and leafless bushes for cover.

Flies and bees buzzed around them, and the sun warmed their backs as it rose overhead. They studied the windows and the only visible door to the one-story mud brick house. The structure sat a hundred yards down a slope from their position. Voices came from the house, but none in English. They identified three men coming and going: two with long beards, assumed to be al Qaeda, and a young man who hadn't shaved recently. On the phone Yassid told Stone that the young man was his relative.

For the past hour, while Stone had watched, Yassid wandered about his village with a cellphone to his ear, chatting and gesturing with his hands. He moved from the small town square to his own house farther up the hill, and then returned. His home was larger than the one commandeered by al Qaeda.

"I'm surprised you trust that guy," Sandra whispered.

Stone moved his binoculars to look at Yassid. He was now engaged in conversation with a man milking a camel. "I trust him for the time being," he whispered back.

She lowered her binoculars and rested her head on her arms. "My neck is stiff," she said. "Can't believe he's walking around with a cellphone. Won't that create suspicion on the part of those al Qaeda thugs?"

"Take a good look around at these people here. Everyone has a cellphone, and they all love to talk. Except for the assault rifles and the phones, we could be in biblical times." Stone lowered his head onto his arm. "I bet most of their clothing is from wool they've spun." He let a moment pass. "These people are like us and want to be left alone. Al Qaeda is another collection of thugs and bullies that, through the course of history, have been telling us how to live, work, and pray."

"We've been here an hour. When do we make our move?"

Stone checked his watch. "We can't wait forever."

"Can you be a little more specific?"

"Hang on." Stone keyed the phone headset he wore. He watched Yassid walk away from the man milking the camel. In Arabic, Stone whispered a few questions, then clicked off and said, "Shit."

"What?"

"I had an idea. In this country, around two o'clock the Yemenis go into *khat* time. People get moderately stoned from chewing the leaves from those bushes down there." He pointed to a tight grove of trees at the bottom of a gorge. "The *khat* leaf is a narcotic. I thought it would be the perfect time to attack when they're spaced-out. I asked Yassid when did the al Qaeda assholes usually chill out so we could make our move." Stone looked at her. "They don't. They're pure. They don't do such bad things."

"Figures."

"He did say that before we go in, he wants to get his relative out of there," Stone said. "He also wants to join in on the fun. Evidently, the al Qaeda guests have outlived their welcome."

"So when do we go in?"

At that a scream came from the house, followed by a cry in English.

"Now," Stone said, then phoned Yassid, and told him they were going in. He kept the line open to the Arab while saying to Sandra, "Call Reilly. Tell him we're going in. They're torturing our guys. Get here with the medical corpsmen."

Sandra made the call while he pulled a sound suppressor from his pack and attached it to his .45 caliber MK23 pistol. He rose to his knees and slung his M4 rifle over his shoulder as he watched Yassid hurry toward the house. Sandra knelt on one knee, ready to leap forward.

Yassid was twenty yards from the house when his kinsman emerged from the door looking back toward the screaming coming from inside. Yassid beckoned him to leave quickly.

Stone's body felt electric. The juices flowed. "Let's rock," Stone growled, and the two moved forward in a crouch.

The sandy ground was soft underfoot, and their boots crunched over dead twigs. The phone line to Yassid was still open, and Stone spoke into the speaker mic. "Ask your cousin how many al Qaeda terrorists are in the house." He was told five.

They stopped at a five-foot ledge that sloped down to the building's side door. Stone guessed the house had at most two rooms. A few feet to the right of the door, a ragged curtain hung out an open window. The yelling from inside the house ceased.

Stone nudged Sandra. "We slide down feetfirst. When we hit the ground, you cover the left side of the house."

Both slid down the gravel on their butts and, at the bottom as they gained their footing, a bearded man jumped out the door, alerted to the noise. Stone raised his pistol. Two spitting pops from his silencer hit the jihadist's midsection, and he buckled forward. Stone caught him before he fell and helped lower him to the ground. He removed the man's Beretta from his waistband and then, with the MK23, put a bullet in his head.

Sandra had moved to the left, M4 assault rifle at the ready, and stopped at the corner of the house. She looked around the building and then back at Stone. She signaled that there was another door on that side and asked if she should move on.

He waved a no, and indicated that he was going to the window to look in. He slipped past the door, seeing only one man with his back turned to him. As he reached the window, and was about to peer inside, he heard a man call out in Arabic from inside the house, calling Didi.

Stone looked back at the dead man. That was probably Didi.

Sandra caught his eye and both knew their element of surprise was about over. He took a quick look in the window, and then pulled back.

He hand-signaled that inside the room were three beards and two CIA. Then he motioned to the door. One beard.

Immediately after, a man came out the door and, looking away from Stone, shouted for Didi. The jihadist froze when he saw Sandra, and then reached for a gun.

Stone went, "Psst. Psst." The terrorist spun around, now gun in hand, but Stone fired twice, then two more times. Sandra ran forward and eased him to the ground.

Stone whispered in her ear, "We have to move fast. We go in, I take out one or two, using this." He patted the pistol. "You behind me. Control your fire—our two guys are taped to chairs in the middle of the room to the right side."

Stone removed the M4 slung over his back and grasped it in his right hand. The pistol with five remaining rounds was held in his left. He crouched low and moved fast through the door, Sandra behind him. She swept the left side of the room with her assault rifle while Stone took big steps to the right, toward the door leading into the room where the captives were held.

He pressed against the wall, looked past the doorframe, and peered inside. One captive was moaning, the other passed out.

Stone froze. Only two jihadists.

"We're missing one shithead!" he shouted back to Sandra, and dropped the pistol. With the M4, he opened up with short controlled bursts at the two terrorists in front of him.

Behind him he heard Sandra's M4 fire in three long bursts. They moved together until they stood back to back, both breathing heavily.

After a moment, she asked, "Did we get them all?"

"Let's count. Two outside. Three inside. Five."

"Hope your Bedouin friend can count," she said, took a

few more deep breaths. "We make sure these bastards are all dead, then we tend to our two guys. They don't look good."

"Roger that. Meanwhile, I'll phone Reilly to get here on the double."

The dead men were examined and their weapons removed. Stone dragged one jihadist away from the door so Sandra could go in and cut loose the CIA captives. As he did, the terrorist radio crackled, and he heard the faint voice of a man speaking Arabic.

"Yassid. Come in here."

The Bedouin appeared at the entrance door, his AK-47 raised. Stone waved him in and told him to listen to the radio and tell him what the man was saying, then joined Sandra in freeing the bound CIA captives.

The two men were covered in bruises and cuts. One had a welt over his left eye; otherwise their faces were untouched. Recognizable for television audiences. The men kept making comments like, "Thank God. Get me out of here. What took you so long?"

"We need that medical kit in one of the packs we left back where we were hiding," Sandra said. "These cuts are festering."

"*Ya Yassid, ya habbiti*," Stone yelled to the Bedouin in the other room, and asked him to run up the hill and bring back the gear they left behind.

Yassid came in with the radio pressed to his ear. "No good, Hayden Stone." He pointed to the phone. "Al Qaeda is coming! I go look."

"Shit," Stone said. "See if you can see them when you get the packs."

Yassid ran out of the house. "Stone, I need help here," Sandra yelled. "This one is becoming delirious. Splash water on his face." She opened the shirt of the other man and dabbed water along the edge of a long burn on his breast.

Stone found a cloth, soaked it in questionable-looking water, and patted it on the face of the man. He looked like he was in convulsions. It didn't help.

Stone called Reilly again. "Where are you, Mark? We need you, pronto."

Reilly came on the line. "We're mounted on our bikes and headed to the village. How are the men?"

"As expected, not good. We need those medics." Stone applied another wet cloth to the man's throat and chest. "Those al Qaeda bastards are headed this way. Do you see them on the road?"

"No, not on this road. Hold on." The line went silent and then, as Yassid came barging into the door with Stone's and Sandra's packs, yelling he saw two SUVs heading their way, Reilly came back on the line. "We've halted on a ridge. We've spotted two SUVS on the road coming in from the east, moving fast."

"Can you intercept them?" Stone asked.

"Negative. We both are coming from opposite directions. They should be there in less than eight minutes. The best we can do is ten."

"Damn it," Stone said. "What about those Blackhawks?"

"Airborne. Twenty minutes away. Sorry, we're back on the road going full speed," Reilly said, noise in the background. "You have to hold them off. How are you as far as your defensive position? How about ammo?"

Stone didn't answer. He thought of options. None came to mind. Reilly was of no immediate help. Two SUVs loaded with al Qaeda would be soon knocking on their door. Sandra looked over to him and mouthed, "What's going on?"

Stone held up a finger. He went back on the line with Reilly, "We have decent defense and enough ammo. Plus we have five AK-47s."

"Will the locals help you?"

Stone looked at Yassid. "We can count on one of them. I'll keep you advised." He rang off. Then he said low in Sandra's ear, "Shit's going to hit the fan. Two SUVs with those al Qaeda film crew murderers are headed this way."

"What about Reilly and his men?"

Stone said, "Reilly's going to be a little late, so we'll have to hold them off until they get here. Maybe five minutes."

"I don't like this at all."

"I'll be back." Stone motioned for Yassid to follow him

outside. He studied the village before him and tried to see a place where he could intercept the two vehicles. From above, the houses stepped down along the hill to the valley floor. Nothing he saw could be used as an ambush point. Yassid pulled at his sleeve and pointed at two fast-moving SUVs turning off the valley road and heading up the grade in their direction. The lead SUV flew a large black flag.

"I have to get back to the house," Stone said to Yassid. "They'll be here soon."

"We have a lot of shooting," Yassid laughed. He raised his AK-47 in the air.

"Us?" Stone said.

"You, me, and my cousins." For the first time Stone saw Yassid smile, showing teeth stained yellow from chewing *khat*. Amazing. The man was willing to give up his daily chew for the Americans.

Before Stone reached the house, a thought came to him. Why had it not occurred to him before? He stopped, turned around, and looked down in the valley at the approaching SUVs, then searched the sky.

He found the radio channel Elizabeth Kerr had used to call him the day before on the CIA plane. After the fifth ring, he was about to hang up, when he heard her voice.

"How are you, Mr. Stone?"

"We are in a very bad bind," Stone said quickly. "My partner and I have freed the two captives. But I'm looking at two Toyota SUVs with some real badasses headed our way. They'll be here before our backup gets here."

"We're looking at the situation now. Hold on," Kerr said.

She came back on. "From the drone we watched you two go into the house a half hour ago. Good work. We were in contact with Mark Reilly, but for some reason lost connection."

"That drone doesn't carry hellfire missiles does it?"

"Yes it does. And we can't fire them without National Security Council authority."

"Oh, that's just great." Stone wanted to rip off the headset. He was about to turn and head back to the house when he saw a fiery streak from the clouds come from above toward the two SUVs. A second later, the lead Toyota exploded. Stone and Yassid stared at the spectacle as another streak of flame shot down and the second SUV exploded, pinwheeling film equipment, pieces of SUV, a satellite dish, and assorted body parts into foaming black smoke.

"What did you think about that, Yassid? Pretty cool, eh?"

"*Jayyid jiddan.*"

"Yeah. Good, very good."

Into his microphone Stone said to Elizabeth Kerr, "I owe you one. How did you get the authority so quick?"

"Here at the center we have an inside track."

Stone said, "Now that's what you call a *deus ex machina.*"

• • •

Stone and Sandra climbed up the hill a few hundred feet to where they had lain concealed a few hours before, watching the house. Down below, Reilly and his men went from one dead terrorist to another taking DNA samples, photographs of faces, and fingerprints. All would be sent back to headquarters for entry into the CIA terrorist databases. They found a computer, which was also headed for analysis.

One Blackhawk carrying the two wounded CIA men had taken off and was now headed for a U.S. Navy vessel in the Gulf of Aden. The other helicopter sat on a flat piece of dirt up the hill waiting to extract the Marines, providing protective cover while the CIA people cleaned up.

Sandra remained quiet, sipping water from a plastic bottle. Letting herself wind down from the action, Stone assumed. He wanted to do the same, but he had to talk, say something.

"You know that stack of dollar bills we found down there? I gave it to Yassid. Thought he deserved it."

"Hmm." Then she looked away.

"From what I gather, according to the rules, he'll parcel out money to his family, some to the village chief, then some to

Sheik az-Zaddim. The rest he'll probably use to buy a Toyota truck or Land Cruiser."

"God, I hate the monotony of this landscape," Sandra said. "It's all dirt brown, gray, and black. Everything. Houses, hills, the valley."

"Remember this morning, at daybreak, the valley looked almost mystical," Stone said softly. "You pointed out the planet Venus up there, big and bright, and down in the valley to the horizon there was a pink-colored haze. And remember the stillness?"

She leaned back on her hands. "That was this morning. A long, long time ago."

His phone rang. Frederick was on the line. "Hayden. Good work. Is Sandra there?"

"She's sitting right next to me."

"Put us on speaker phone so I don't have to repeat myself." Frederick waited a second, then continued, "You two did well. Freeing our two people from the terrorists takes a lot of heat off the agency. Reason why I was holding back giving the okay to attack was Sheik az-Zaddim was supposed to have brokered a deal for their release. However, he and General Ali al-Wasi got in a pissing contest and things went south."

"Par for the course in Yemeni politics," Stone said.

"I want you two to head for Sana'a tomorrow," Frederick said. "We're getting chatter that an attack is planned against Westerners staying at the Sheraton Hotel."

"Is our target, Abdul Wahab, leading it?" Sandra asked.

"Yes. He and his gang, including members of al Qaeda from Aden. We plan to lure them in and—"

Stone interrupted. "And settle the matter with Abdul Wahab, once and for all."

CHAPTER TWENTY-THREE

ON THE OUTSKIRTS OF SANA'A, YEMEN
—NOVEMBER 2, 2002

At intervals, groups of trucks rumbled past the garage heading toward Sana'a, overloaded with crates and cargo, spilling black diesel smoke into the thin air. Abdul Wahab paced inside the building, watching the pigeons roosting in the twelve-foot ceiling. Arabic music blared on a radio while mechanics worked on vans. Wahab would have chosen another location for the meeting, but Kheibah assured him that this site was secure and the owner could be trusted.

Once again, Wahab checked the positions of two of his trusted men from Marseille. One stood at the far end of the garage looking out the open bay doors, while the other stood near Wahab, at a window. They watched the traffic coming from the east, the direction from which they expected al Nasser, the head of AQAP, to arrive.

Wahab had spread out his eight men and Kheibah's sixteen in their SUVs and pickup trucks. The two-lane road bisected the collection of shops, businesses, and houses that made up what resembled a town. His idea was to not draw undue attention to their presence. One never knew when the police would drop by, so he and his men had to stay alert. Also, al Qaeda could not be trusted.

Dokka came back in from walking around the building, crushed out a cigarette on the dirt floor with his shoe, and came up next to Wahab. "Let us speak outside and escape the noise and fumes in here."

Wahab led him through the back door, and they went out

into a wide yard. They searched for a clear place to stand. The workers used the back of the building as both a toilet and a dump for oil, grease, and motor parts that had no further possible value. As a conflicting backdrop to this toxic dump stood a chain of beautifully etched mountains topped by a thin line of white cumulus clouds.

"This is worse than inside," Wahab said in disgust. In an attempt to avoid attention from strangers and the police, he was in *mufti*: a black suit coat over a white *futa* and a wound, shawl-like *meshedda* on his head, one end of which dropped to his shoulder. Beneath his coat he wore a shoulder holster.

"I spotted the guys I think are al Nasser's advance people," Dokka said. "I would expect him to be arriving shortly."

"Are you certain the men you saw were al Qaeda?"

Dokka nodded. "They look too effete for ordinary locals."

"I expect al Nasser will make us wait for him, perhaps a half hour. He'll want us to think we're working for him. We will let him play his game."

"I do not trust al Qaeda. They betrayed my group in Chechnya." Dokka lit a cigarette, and asked, "Why do we put up with them?"

"We need him and his men. They will play a very important role in carrying out my plan."

Dokka looked away.

"I haven't told you everything, Dokka, not because I do not trust you. It is because the plan has only begun to come together in my mind. You have an essential role."

Dokka smiled. "Tell me Abdul Wahab, in this grand plan of yours, does a helicopter fit in?"

"Of course," Wahab said. "Let us go back in the garage. This place is depressing."

Kheibah ran up to Wahab. "Sheik az-Zaddim called me. The Americans have rescued the two CIA people. All the AQAP men who were guarding them are dead. The Sheik said that a column of vehicles filled with al Qaeda were also killed by American bombs."

Wahab looked at Dokka. "If al Nasser has heard, he and his men may not be coming."

Dokka shook his head. "Remember, that was the second column coming up from Aden. Al Nasser still has his group headed here."

"And he may not be aware of the setback." It had been wise that Wahab had withdrawn his people from guarding the CIA prisoners. The warnings from the Sheik and Uthman that the Americans were about to launch an attack had proved fortuitous.

"Do we tell al Nasser if he does not know?" Kheibah asked.

"We had best keep this to ourselves," Wahab said.

"One further thing, *sayyedi*," Kheibah said. "The Sheik said to give you a message from your benefactor, the prince, that it would behoove you to keep up contact with the people of the snow country."

Wahab's brow furrowed.

"I've repeated the Sheik's message word for word, *sayyedi*."

"Does that message have anything to do with your plan?" Dokka asked.

"I'm not sure." Wahab walked away and thought. The snow people the prince referred to had to be the Canadians. Had Patience St. John Smythe contacted his father-in-law?

One of Wahab's men burst in through the open bay doors and announced that an SUV with four armed men had pulled up.

Dokka signaled Wahab's two men to be alert, while he withdrew to the back of the building, his hand on his gun. Wahab and Kheibah advanced to the door to meet with the al Qaeda leader.

Al Nasser strode into the garage flanked by two bodyguards. He wore a common white *thobe*. Wahab noted the expensive jambiya at his belt.

"Peace be to you," Al Nasser said, sniffing as if he found the surroundings offensive.

Wahab fought back a sneer. He thought back to his Cambridge University days and his classmates' expression for such people, a supercilious twit.

"And peace to you. What an honor to meet you at last,"

Wahab said, returning a gesture of greeting. "What a blessed event this is that we combine our forces to fight the infidel."

Al Nasser smiled and said, "What fortune it is that you join me in our cause. We will be able to use you in our bold endeavor."

Wahab struggled to maintain control. This man talked in semi-proverbs, and he noted that every time he spoke, al Nasser's eyelids closed for a second. Was this an affectation, or was it some physical quirk?

"We cannot stay here long," Wahab said. "There are many eyes in Yemen."

Al Nasser moved farther into the garage, and his men hung close on either side. "The attack on the Sheraton Hotel will commence at dawn tomorrow. The exact time I will phone to you an hour before it is to occur." He folded his arms across his chest. "How many men will you provide me?"

"Fifteen." There was no need to give this man an accurate count of the strength of his forces. Out of the corner of his eye, Wahab saw Kheibah frown. He hoped Kheibah wouldn't correct him in his count. He didn't.

"You and your men will launch the attack at the entrance," al Nasser ordered. "You will move fast and kill everyone you see. Then hold your position."

"Where will you be?" Wahab asked.

"We will enter from the rear of the building, through the service entrance."

"And how many men do you have?"

"We have twenty-four." He opened his arms. "I know. We have more men, and you think we should lead the frontal assault. Trust me. We, the AQAP, the *Ansar al-Sharia*, are more experienced than you or your people in such matters. We have informants in the hotel and know the weaknesses of the building, and most importantly, the inadequacy of the security there."

Wahab smiled broadly. "I have the utmost confidence in you and your organization."

Al Nasser began to leave, then stopped. For once the placid, angelic face became serious. "What hear you of my people who guard the CIA captives?"

Wahab shrugged. "They are of no interest to me after you insisted on taking charge of them."

The al Qaeda leader thought a moment, and then said, "We have lost contact with the guards at the house where they are being held. Most strange. And we have lost contact with the detachment I sent there to make a film for the Arabic news stations."

"Would you like me to make inquiries?"

Al Nasser nodded, then turned to leave. "One of my men will be in contact with you with further instructions."

Wahab called after him, "I assure you that we are eager for the fight against the Crusaders. I myself will lead my men in the attack, as I know *you* will also lead your men in combat."

Al Nasser stopped and turned to him. "Of course, I will lead my men into b-b-battle."

"Please do not mistake me," Wahab said. "Your exploits in battle are legendary in Yemen. You are always at the front of your people during the attack."

Al Nasser looked uncomfortable and headed out of the building into the street, followed closely by his two guards.

Dokka joined Wahab and Kheibah, and the three watched al Nasser board a Toyota SUV after shooting a glare at Wahab.

"This will be a major battle, won't it?" Kheibah's voice quivered.

"Do not be concerned," Wahab said, and touched Kheibah's shoulder.

Kheibah appeared to relax. "I don't think that al Qaeda shit appreciated you tricking him into promising to lead his men into battle." All three laughed.

"The best thing was that you had him say he would do so in front of witnesses," Dokka added. "Those assholes with him have already told a dozen of al Nasser's men that their esteemed leader was going to lead the charge."

"He's in a corner now," Kheibah said. "His people won't move until he does."

Kheibah left to tell his men to start moving toward the next staging area. "I'll keep in contact with you by phone, *sayyedi*," he called back.

Now alone, Dokka said, "I know that pimp, al Nasser. He's one of your fellow Saudis. Don't you know him? His family is from Dhahran. The al-Manabis. Lots of money." Dokka put his face close to Wahab's. "Why do we take orders from that pig?"

"We don't," Wahab said.

"It sounded like we were. This man has a bad reputation. He is only good at killing unarmed women and children, not fighting men." Dokka moved away. "I do not like being under that shit's command."

Wahab smiled and patted him on the shoulder. "Do not worry. Please do me a favor. Walk over by the window and call me on your phone, and say, 'Where do we attack?' I will answer, 'At the back of the building, you fool. Don't call again.'"

Dokka looked puzzled, but when asked to do it again, made the call. When they had completed the routine, he returned and looked hard at Wahab.

"You wonder why I had you do that, don't you," Wahab said. "The CIA and the Yemeni intelligence must have listened in on our conversation. It won't take them long to figure out where and when the attack will come, and they will be ready. The killers we just met will be the killed."

Dokka's glare turned slowly into a smile.

"Exactly, my friend," Wahab said. "Everyone. Al Nasser and his al Qaeda will fall into a trap and end up like their comrades back in the mountains of Marib. The CIA and General Ali al-Wasi and his gang, they will be at the Sheraton Hotel, waiting. We will not be there."

"And where will we be, Abdul Wahab?"

"Flying in your helicopter, Dokka."

CHAPTER TWENTY-FOUR

THE NEXT DAY

Slumped in the back of the SUV, Stone was jarred from his dozing when they bounced from the gravel road onto the paved two-lane highway. The Yemen countryside morning parade zipped by as the CIA motor column increased speed. Arabs walked along the road with burlap-wrapped parcels on their shoulders, leading dusty donkeys laden with firewood. Their children worked herds of goats.

"We'll be at the Marib airport in a little less than an hour," Reilly yelled back over the road noise from the open windows to Stone and Sandra, both hanging on in the backseat.

Sandra pulled the buzzing satellite phone from her pocket, said "yes" a few times and "right" a few times, and then hung up.

Before she could say anything, Stone said, "Colonel Frederick is sending someone to meet us at the Sana'a airport. We're to be taken to wherever the command post is."

"Wow! You and Frederick are on the same wavelength." Sandra elbowed him. "Hope this operation completes our visit here."

"Agreed."

• • •

The windows of the CIA operations center had an unobstructed view of the Sheraton Hotel about a half mile away. The four-lane Sana'a Ring Road, filled with late-afternoon traffic, separated them from the hotel compound. Stone studied the back of the hotel with its swimming pool. He remarked to Sandra and Colonel Frederick, who were standing beside him, that the hotel sat on an isolated plot of ground, with roads on all sides providing a barrier from neighboring buildings.

"The hotel should be an ideal place to protect. Any idea when the attack is scheduled?" Stone asked Frederick.

"Ah, the benefits of good source coverage," Frederick said. "Live sources tell us to expect the attack to happen at daybreak tomorrow. The same informants tell us that Abdul Wahab and the AQAP leader from Aden have joined forces. That last part has us concerned. The head of this group, a man name al Nasser, has terrorist experience. He was involved with the al Qaeda attack on the USS Cole."

Sandra added, "Al Nasser is in the business of murdering Westerners, especially Americans."

"He's also responsible for the deaths of two of our people back there in the CIA camp." Frederick checked his watch. "By the way, you two did a great job freeing our two operatives." He looked back at the door. "I'm waiting for General Ali al-Wasi to arrive. The two of us have some tactics to work out before tomorrow."

"How many terrorists do you suspect will be in the attack group?" Stone asked.

"We estimate the combined force will be around thirty-five. It's a big concern. To counter such a force we could use up to one hundred people, but keeping them concealed in the hotel is tricky."

Stone said, "You have your hands full. The Americans have to work as equals with the local intelligence and security service, namely General al-Wasi. My past relationship might help in your dealings with the Yemeni general. What is the plan?"

"We want to lure them in and wipe them out," Frederick said.

"You don't want prisoners for interrogation purposes?" Sandra said.

"We have enough of them. Besides, they're a pain in the ass to keep captive."

"Could turn them over to General al-Wasi," Stone said.

Frederick sneered. "The Yemeni prisons have revolving doors."

"Back to the plan," Stone said. "What about the hotel guests?"

"Luckily, only a few visitors this time of year, and they were moved to other hotels. In fact, that was al-Wasi's idea, which was a good one."

"What about intercepting the terrorists before they get to the hotel?" Sandra asked.

Frederick sighed. "We will if we can, but the satellite is down, and we don't have a read on their location."

"What else do our sources tell us?"

"Abdul Wahab and his group will hit the front of the hotel while al Nasser and his assholes enter the rear of the building. Pun intended."

"That's pretty specific info," Sandra said. "Where did that come from, may I ask?"

"We overheard a telephone conversation between Abdul Wahab and one of his men, named Dokka Zarov, a Chechen terrorist."

Something didn't sound right to Stone. "Abdul Wahab talking on a clear phone line? Not like him to make such a mistake."

At that, General al-Wasi and his entourage entered the apartment. "We can discuss that later," Frederick said and he went over to greet al-Wasi.

The general's party filed through the door, and soon there was little room to move in the tight space. American embassy personnel and CIA operatives led a few of the Yemeni security people into the kitchen and offered them refreshments. Frederick waved Stone over to join him and al-Wasi. As expected, Stone found them at loggerheads on the next day's plan of operation.

"We will set up a perimeter of defense," al-Wasi insisted. "Perhaps we will bring in a tank."

Al-Wasi's demeanor surprised Stone. Years before, when this man had worked at the American embassy, he never demonstrated any strong force of personality. He did a competent job as a Foreign Service national, but never made any waves. Stone got to know him better when he acted as his official driver, even giving al-Wasi presents for his children on Muslim holidays.

Colonel Frederick stiffened his back, making the point that the element of surprise was essential. Their forces should lie in wait. "We can't scare them off. Your people shouldn't be in uniform. Have them in disguise."

"You tend to forget," al-Wasi said. "This is my country, and you are merely assisting us."

Frederick glanced at Stone as if to say he needed a little help.

"I agree, General," Stone said. "But we have the chance to round them up. It will give your country some time, maybe a year of breathing time, before another terrorist group rears its head."

Al-Wasi turned to Stone. "I see that you have returned from your expedition in the countryside. Your CIA compatriots are free, and the al Qaeda dead." He turned his attention back to Frederick. "I suppose you think you can unilaterally work the same way here."

So, that's his problem. His nose is out of joint. Stone interjected, "We were under the impression that you and Sheik az-Zaddim were in agreement on that operation. We acted not hastily nor without regard for your authority, but for the safety of our people."

Frederick continued to press al-Wasi. "We know that the attack will be two-pronged, one at the front of the hotel led by Abdul Wahab, and the second at the back by the al Qaeda group.

"Wahab's people have to pass the security line at the street," Frederick continued, "break through, and rush the entrance door. They'll probably be in SUVs." Frederick directed al-Wasi to the window to look over at the hotel. "At that time of the morning it should still be dark, and we can position people in those outbuildings." He pointed. "Then you can bring in your helicopters and land your people there. The terrorists will be in their vehicles and easy targets. The tough nut is the group coming in from the back. That action will be hand-to-hand. They'll come as singletons, doubles, and if they gain access they'll spread out in hallways, rooms. Some may already be in the hotel."

Al-Wasi nodded. "Our sources identified three workmen suspected to be al Qaeda. They will be in custody by midnight." He adjusted his uniform jacket. "The operation will be successful if we all work together."

Stone smiled. "It appears we're in agreement." As to what, Stone wasn't quite sure.

The Yemeni security people followed their leader, al-Wasi, out the door. Frederick turned to Stone as Sandra joined them. "What do you think? Gut feeling?"

Stone looked around the room. Not only CIA operatives crowded the room, but also the diplomatic security staff from the embassy, all prepared for combat. "It seems everyone from the embassy wants to be in on the show. We have a lot of people, not all of them trained for this type of action."

Sandra said, "To get everyone into position, our people and al-Wasi's, we have to come up with a gimmick. Al-Qaeda's sources in the hotel will be watching for anything suspicious. I suggest we bring in some of our people on a bus, as if they are visitors just arrived from the airport."

"Might work," Frederick said.

"The others, including al-Wasi's people, could just sneak in under cover of darkness. Stash them in hotel rooms," Stone added.

Frederick looked down, thinking.

"Again, we seem to have good informants. We know of an impending terrorist attack. We are aware of the players." Stone paused. "The assumption is that the Sheraton Hotel is the target. Do you see anything wrong with all that?"

Frederick looked impatient and moved away, saying, "All the dots seem to connect."

"Where do you want Sandra and me to be stationed?"

"I need you here at the command post."

Frederick left to confer with the communications technicians. Stone whispered to Sandra, "I think he wants to keep me under wraps."

"Do you blame him?" she asked. "He believes you have one

goal and that it is to nail Abdul Wahab. He thinks your obsession could complicate an already difficult operation."

"I'm more professional than that."

"I know."

Stone led her to the window. "Something doesn't add up."

"What's bothering you? The mix of CIA and the Yemenis? You do trust General al-Wasi, don't you?"

"Al-Wasi has proven himself as a professional and, I believe, as a friend." Stone moved close, touching his shoulder to hers. "We're getting a lot of source information on this attack. How reliable is it? I'm getting bad vibes. Are we in for a big surprise?"

CHAPTER TWENTY-FIVE

SANA'A, YEMEN—NOVEMBER 3, 2002

Uthman checked his wristwatch. It was exactly midnight. Uthman rose from the hard plastic chair and headed for the restaurant's front door.

Across the street, the Internet café still bustled with young men. The owners had left the door open to let out the thick cigarette smoke. Uthman watched a man wearing a white T-shirt, too young to have a beard, get up from a computer and settle his account with the owners. He paused at the doorway, looked over at Uthman, and gave him the hand sign they had agreed upon— the signal that Uthman's message had been sent. The young man then hurried down the crowded street.

As a precaution, Uthman used a cutout or proxy to send his messages. The police and the intelligence service closely watched Internet establishments. In addition, everyone believed the Americans, the British, the Russians, and the Iranians read the e-mail traffic coming from Sana'a. Coded messages were suspect, so Uthman hired poor men to send them. Men who did not know him.

A brief coded message had been sent to Prince Mohammed al-Tabrizi. The two had used this means of communication for a number of years. At first, Uthman objected to the system, saying a messenger was a much simpler method and that using a code would be difficult. The prince insisted on using the faster e-mails and said they had to use a code. Arabs have been using codes for years, the prince said. The famous tenth century *Adab al-Kuttab*, the Secretary's Manual, had sections on cryptology.

They agreed on a simple coding device. Both had out-of-print Arabic books on Middle Eastern birds, identical editions.

Each letter in the message text would be found in the book, by page, by paragraph, by line, then the first letter in the line. The message would be sent in numbers, 23-4-2, which would translate to page 23, paragraph 4, and line 2. The first letter of line two would be used for the first letter of the first word of the message. This was repeated for each letter until the full message was composed. It was a form of monoalphabetic substitution cipher, which was easy to manage and almost unbreakable.

Uthman had alerted the prince about Abdul Wahab's plans to attack the Sheraton Hotel. He had received this information from the old watchman at the Yemeni National Museum. This man worked for General Ali al-Wasi and not only provided information on the activities of al-Wasi's security service, but was also very useful in Uthman's fledgling antiquities trade.

The watchman confided that General al-Wasi intended to embark on a mission to counter a terrorist attack on the hotel. Abdul Wahab's name was mentioned a number of times, along with al Qaeda. The people surrounding the General kept repeating, "It will be a victorious battle."

Uthman hurried home. He'd had unexpected guests that afternoon, one of whom was Abdul Wahab. He might learn more information about this attack for the prince's benefit.

• • •

A little after midnight, Abdul Wahab gathered his two lieutenants on the top floor of Uthman's tower house. Dokka chain-smoked, and Kheibah let out small burps while rubbing his stomach. Wahab attempted to maintain a calm, commanding presence.

"We have only a few hours to prepare for our mission." Wahab laid a map and drawings on the round table. "Look at these. There has been a change in plans."

"What change?" Kheibah let out a loud belch. "When did this happen?"

"You will like it when I explain."

Dokka crushed out his cigarette and poured more tea for himself. He leaned over to Kheibah and said, "Be calm."

"Be calm? How can I be calm? How does this change in plans affect me and my men?" Kheibah looked around the room. "Are we safe here? Can we trust Uthman?"

Wahab hit the table with his fist. "Be quiet and listen! We are not attacking the Sheraton Hotel. Al Nasser and his fools will provide a diversion. We are attacking the American embassy."

Kheibah's eyes widened. Dokka let out a laugh and slapped him on the back. "Good news, don't you think?"

Wahab continued, "The plan I devised is a simple one, not complicated. We do not have time for complications." He adjusted the map and sketches, and then pointed to the north wall of the embassy. "We climb over the wall at this point. We scale the wall at daybreak when we hear gunshots coming from the direction of the Sheraton Hotel, which is only a little more than a mile away."

"Who are *we*? How high is the wall?"

"You, me, twelve of your men, and two of mine. A few men will stay behind with the escape vehicles," Wahab said. "The wall is the American standard height for security, eight feet."

"What about Dokka?"

"I will come to his role in a minute." Wahab pointed to a list. "This is the guard routine for making the rounds of the embassy compound. We must take the guard shift into account. Then we scale the wall and quietly approach the main chancery building. With such a large group, we must be disciplined in order to not alert the guards until the last possible moment."

Kheibah thought a moment while he looked at the map and drawings. "When they hear the gunshots coming from the hotel, they will sound the alarm."

"That is why we must move quickly to the chancery, which is connected to the ambassador's residence."

"What is our goal?"

Wahab took a deep breath. "Capture the American ambassador as she prepares to take her morning jog. Our source tells us that she runs with a security man and sometimes with a member of the CIA every morning at dawn. She spends a half hour stretching and exercising outside her residence before running."

Kheibah looked at Dokka, who nodded. "Do we kill everyone?"

"No!" Wahab spat. "We are not al Qaeda religious fanatics. This is not a suicide mission. This is a political act. We capture them and hold them until our demands are met."

"Some people will die," Dokka said, "but that is not the intent of this mission."

"And what do you do while we are fighting, Dokka?"

"Dokka flies in with the helicopter and takes the prisoners away. We expect that is when the shooting will become intense. The Marines stationed there will not sit back and allow that to happen without a fight. That is why speed and surprise will be essential. Once the helicopter leaves with the ambassador, we will fight our way back to the wall and escape."

The three remained silent as they each looked at the plans spread out on the table. Wahab drank some tea, and then asked Dokka for a cigarette. Kheibah had stopped massaging his stomach, and started to speak softly to himself as he studied and shuffled the papers.

Kheibah jerked his head up and looked at the two men. "Al Nasser knows nothing of this?"

Wahab and Dokka shook their heads.

"Al Nasser will be furious. He will come looking for revenge," Kheibah said. "He and his people are good at killing."

"I doubt very much that he will survive the attack at the hotel," Wahab said. "However, he will not have died in vain. He will have contributed to our cause."

"What is your goal, Abdul Wahab? It cannot be money. You have all you need."

Dokka spoke up. "A good question, Abdul. You never gave me a clear idea what we were up to."

Wahab thought a moment, and then said, "This country has no strong central authority. The president rules by issuing favors or threats. The mix of tribal allegiances changes daily."

"This is not news," Kheibah said.

"We will hold the American ambassador and whoever else is with her and fly her companions to a mountain village north of here. We will begin negotiations with the government to allow us to rule the eastern part of the country. Hear me out. Kheibah, you come from the eastern region. You do not speak Arabic the same way as these people here in Sana'a, or the people in Aden, or the mountain people in the far north. You are of Bedouin stock. Years ago your family and tribe spilled over from the Saudi desert. Saudi Arabia funnels money to the tribes and families from Tarim to Marib. There is a long, strong connection."

"And you, Abdul Wahab, are from Bedouin stock and a Saudi." Dokka smiled. "The obvious choice for leader. Tell me Abdul, have you let the Kingdom of Saudi Arabia in on your plan?"

"Not yet, but they will get the message soon."

Kheibah shook his head in disbelief. "You believe this will all work?"

Wahab gathered the map and drawings, and then stood, signaling their meeting was over and that the operation would commence. To Kheibah's question, he said, "*Insha'allah.*"

• • •

When Uthman returned, he found Abdul Wahab upstairs with two companions. He stayed in his study on the floor below and listened to their conversation through the air vents. Only the last few minutes of their conversation were heard before the three men gathered their belongings to depart. Because of the wind blowing down the vent, Uthman managed to hear portions of what they said and what they had planned.

On the way out, Wahab dropped by his room and thanked Uthman for his hospitality. They spoke for only a few moments, and then Wahab hurried off, racing down the stairs to the ground floor, followed by his two companions.

Uthman sank into his favorite armchair. How would he tell the prince what he had heard? The situation had become much more serious and what was to occur would happen in a few hours. It took more than an hour for him to code a message. Then he had to run to the Internet café and find someone to send it. Much too much time.

He looked at the phone on the end table next to him. With a shaky hand, he picked it up.

• • •

Prince Mohammed al-Tabrizi sat in the lounge of his yacht, the Red Scorpion, smoking a Cuban cigar. A half-full brandy glass sat out of sight, on the shelf of the table next to him.

A knock came at the door, followed by, "A message for you, Your Highness."

The prince beckoned the man and took the one-page memorandum. He read the contents of Uthman's message carefully, shaking his head. He had expected something like this to happen. He had hoped Abdul Wahab would eventually come to his senses. Now his son-in-law was in league with al Qaeda, and when one partnered with that group, the result was blood and needless violence. The Sheraton Hotel was a favorite of visiting Westerners, especially Americans. Wahab's involvement in this escapade, along with the killing and capture of the CIA people a week ago, would certainly keep him on America's hit list.

He tossed the sheet of paper on the table next to him. At that moment, another knock came at the door. "Telephone call, Your Highness, on the special phone."

When the prince answered, he found Uthman on the other end of the line.

"Sire, I had to call and speak with you," Uthman said." "Did you receive my message?"

"I just finished reading it."

"Something new, sire. I must tell you."

"Send a message," The prince said.

"It would take too long."

The prince remained silent.

"The object of interest is not the Sheraton Hotel," Uthman whispered over the line.

"You bloody fool! Send a message."

"It will be too late," Uthman insisted. "The object is very close to the hotel, but the same people will be—"

"Stop!" the prince shouted, and then tried to imagine what Uthman was saying. He visualized the hotel and the surrounding neighborhoods, and then realized what was near. *The American embassy.*

Uthman stayed on the line, saying nothing. Finally, the prince said, "So, to be sure of what you are saying, send me a message even if it is after the fact. Understand?"

"Yes, sire," Uthman said.

"Meanwhile, I will send a number of my people to Sana'a. They will go to your home. Take them in."

After Uthman agreed, the prince rang off, leaned forward in his chair, and rubbed his face hard. How to limit the damage was his only thought.

• • •

At four o'clock in the morning, Hayden Stone and Sandra Harrington followed Colonel Frederick into the command center in the Sheraton Hotel. For the past few years, the U.S. government had leased two floors of the hotel for Americans traveling to Yemen on official business. Now the floors were blocked off from the rest of the hotel, and the area resembled a combat zone. Stone recognized the RSO, the regional security officer, and the CIA station chief, M.R.D. Houston, talking with the head of the FBI task force investigating the USS Cole bombing.

Frederick went over to General al-Wasi and conferred about the positioning of his police and the CIA. Stone noted that the colonel no longer took an adversarial role, but now emphasized cooperation. *Time to man the barricades,* thought Stone. *Daybreak is only an hour or so away.*

"Any signs of an approach?" Frederick asked.

"None," General al-Wasi said. "No unusual traffic at the front gate. If a suspected attack vehicle or vehicles approach, they will be allowed to enter one hundred feet, then they will be stopped and surrounded at a second checkpoint. They will be eliminated."

Frederick nodded. "Let's double-check. My people are teamed with yours on the lower floors. Also, we have teams in the outbuildings, like the pool house, correct?"

"We're in radio contact with all stations," General al-Wasi said. "The terrorists should attack soon." Then as an afterthought, he added, "We not only picked up the three suspected jihadists working in the laundry, but also arrested five more employees who looked suspicious."

Sandra whispered, "Rounded up the usual suspects."

"Like the way they do things," Stone whispered back.

Both Stone and Sandra carried their sidearms and M4s, but Frederick still insisted they stay with him at the command post. He came over and asked them to come with him to the next room. They found the room darkened with people fixed at the windows, scanning the hotel grounds with night vision binoculars.

Frederick brought the two to a window. "When the terrorists attack the back of the hotel, they'll probably appear out of the woodwork."

"Abdul Wahab's frontal assault through the main entrance will be easy to stop," Stone said. "If General al-Wasi is correct, Abdul Wahab and his group will be toast. My job will be finished."

"Thank goodness," Sandra said. "This mutual vendetta between you and Wahab has lasted too long."

"I agree," Frederick said, "although, it has paid off."

"Excuse me?" Stone said.

"Oh, don't act surprised. You know we used the mutual animosity between you and Wahab to lead us to these terrorists." Frederick headed back to the other room.

Stone debated giving him a wisecrack, when shots came from somewhere below in the hotel. He looked back at the window and saw the first light of dawn.

"Here we go," Sandra said, heading for the window.

Stone held her back. "Bullets could come flying in, let's move away." At that, he felt his cellphone vibrate. Elizabeth Kerr's number appeared on the screen.

"Mr. Stone." Elizabeth Kerr skipped the formalities. "About four hours ago, our people picked up a phone conversation from Sana'a to Prince Mohammed al-Tabrizi, who is on a yacht anchored off the coast of Yemen."

"Who was he talking with?"

"Can't get a read on the Sana'a telephone number," she continued. "What pinged our net were the words 'Sheraton Hotel.' We did a quick translate and this is the analysis. Abdul Wahab is not attacking the hotel."

"You say he's standing off from the attack?"

"How far is the American embassy from where you are?"

"Around the block."

"That's his target."

"When?" Stone asked.

"From what we gather, at the same time the hotel will be hit."

Stone heard increased gunfire coming from the floors below and now shots from the pool area outside. "Thanks, Elizabeth, it appears the time is now."

Shoving his phone in his pocket, he called to Sandra and Frederick. "Wahab is attacking the embassy! Where are the station chief and the RSO? We need a ride."

CHAPTER TWENTY-SIX

SANA'A, YEMEN

Abdul Wahab and his men lay prone behind abandoned construction material twenty yards from the U.S. embassy wall. To the east, a glow formed on the hazy horizon. He caught the smell of the dry grass they crushed crawling to their positions. Off in the distance, birds began their morning calls.

Squirming next to him, Kheibah asked for the third time, "When?"

"It will not be long," Wahab whispered. He looked around and saw other men hugging the ground, dressed in black pants and jackets. Some wore balaclavas. A week before, Kheibah had proven himself when they attacked the CIA camp, but they'd had the tactical advantage. Today the assault was against a semi-fortified position, the kind that Wahab had faced numerous times in Afghanistan.

"How long will those lights stay on?" Kheibah asked, pointing to the halogen lamps positioned along the embassy's perimeter.

"The sunlight will automatically switch them off. I hope before al Nasser begins his assault on the Sheraton Hotel."

Wahab had devised a simple plan he hoped could be carried out by Kheibah and his men. They would lie in hiding until they heard gunshots in the distance from the attack on the hotel. At that time, no matter if the compound perimeter lights were on, they would take two ladders, run in columns to the wall, throw old mattresses over the razor wire on the top, and scale it.

"Remember," Wahab said. "Once over, we turn to the right and move quickly along the wall toward the ambassador's residence. If we encounter a guard, attempt to subdue him and leave him bound. They are fellow Yemenis. If he resists, a quiet knife will solve the problem. We must not alert the Marine security guard."

"If an alarm is sounded, what do we do?" Kheibah asked.

Wahab patted him on the back. "The alarm will sound. The Marines will come."

"Tell me again. What do we do then?"

Wahab closed his eyes. "There will be shooting and much confusion. People will not be where they should be. Some of our people will be shot."

Kheibah said, "Yes, that is what you have said."

"And what have I told you all to do?"

Kheibah spoke as if reciting a phrase. "Keep the objective in mind. Capture the ambassador. Hold off the Marines until the helicopter comes."

"Good man," Wahab said, and then added, more to himself than to Kheibah, "Before we go over the wall, I must call Dokka in the helicopter and tell him he has ten minutes."

"Is that long enough?" Kheibah asked.

"It may be too long." Wahab looked to his left and saw the horizon had become brighter.

The embassy compound's security lights hummed out. A few voices from the men were heard, and Kheibah signaled with his hand to be quiet.

Moments passed, and then in the distance shots were heard. Kheibah looked at Wahab. "Now?"

"Now," Wahab said. He radioed Dokka, said, "It has started." He checked the time on his watch.

Kheibah jumped to his feet and motioned to his men to bring the ladders forward.

Wahab was the first man up one of the ladders, followed by two of his trusted men from Marseille. At the top, he threw his legs over a mattress, and slipped down the eight-foot wall.

The only guard Wahab saw was a hundred yards off, walking in the opposite direction. He led the men forward in a jog close to the wall, until they neared the first series of buildings. These he was told were the outside cafeteria and automotive maintenance shops.

He stopped the team and listened. Intermittent gunfire continued to be heard in the distance. Shouts and a car siren came from across the compound outside the main gate.

"Are they coming for us?" Kheibah asked, out of breath.

Wahab shook his head. "I think the police detail is heading for the hotel." He signaled with his arm to move ahead.

They ran over grass and dirt patches until Wahab spotted two men exercising outside a two-story building. Their hair was shaved off along the sides. Marines.

The two Marines saw Wahab and his group, leaped up, and ran into the building. Wahab knew he had less than two minutes to get safely by what he knew was the Marine house. After that, Marines would come out shooting.

"Kheibah," Wahab shouted, and pointed. "When we pass this building, place your men over there to form a defensive line."

"Why?"

"Marines will be coming out, armed," Wahab said. "I'll take two of your men and continue to the ambassador's residence."

"Why?"

Wahab stopped and shook him. "Do as I say." At that, the second phone he carried rang. On the other line was the embassy guard who was their informant.

"Ambassador is outside her door warming up for her run."

"Anyone else with her?" he asked.

"She is with the deputy security officer and a CIA man."

"Good work." Wahab rang off.

"Where should we stand?" Kheibah pleaded. His men bumped into each other, confused.

"Not stand, you shit. Move up there, then position your people there, and there, behind that wall and the electrical box. The Marines will be out soon."

Kheibah motioned to two of his men to follow Wahab, then called after Wahab, "What should we do when the Marines come out?"

"Shoot them," Wahab yelled back, and as he did saw three Marines in white underwear, wearing flak jackets and bandoleers.

They carried shotguns and began firing. Two of Kheibah's men went down.

Wahab shouted to the seven men with him to hurry. They reached a small vegetable garden, turned left, and saw a woman in a blue workout outfit with two men dashing for the door of the ambassador's residence.

Wahab fired warning shots from his AK-47. The two American men pulled out pistols and faced Wahab.

"Don't shoot," Wahab hollered. "If you do, you die." He motioned to his men not to shoot. "We want you three alive, not dead."

As the two Americans hesitated, Wahab looked behind him and recognized the cracks of AK-47s interspersed with booms from shotguns. How long Kheibah could hold the Marines at bay was questionable.

"We don't have time to play games," Wahab yelled. "Drop the guns, or we kill you. We will still take the Ambassador."

The two Americans spoke to each other, then dropped their pistols and raised their hands. Wahab checked his watch and, as he did, he thought he heard in the distance the faint *thump, thump* of a helicopter's blades.

"Toward the tennis courts," he ordered, pushing the Ambassador hard so her glasses slipped off. His men bound the three with Max-Cuffs and pushed the captives ahead.

• • •

The armored SUV carrying Stone, Sandra, and M.R.D. Houston swerved into the American embassy's front gate. Another American SUV skidded to a halt behind them. Local guards and military police ran back and forth. No one appeared to be in command. Stone heard gunfire coming from the embassy compound.

The RSO radioed his security guards in the gatehouse to open the gates. "Open both gates! Don't leave us hanging in the sally port. Where the hell is my local guard chief?" the RSO barked into the radio microphone. "Where is Sameer?"

Sameer came on the radio. "Armed men have invaded the compound."

"No shit, Sherlock!" The RSO switched radio channels and called Marine Post One stationed inside the entrance of the embassy. They drove through the gate and hung a left, driving over the grassy picnic area. He stopped a hundred yards in front of the main entrance to the embassy.

Stone and Sandra leaped out and rested their M4s over the hood of the vehicle. "See any bad guys?" Stone asked.

"Negative," Sandra said.

Houston leaned against the hood next to them, trying to raise someone in the station's communication center.

The RSO called out the SUV window, "Post One says that terrorists are in the rear of the compound. The Marines have taken out at least seven, maybe eight. They're chasing the rest toward the far end."

"I hear shooting over in that direction," Stone said.

"Yeah. Damn, that's next to the ambassador's residence."

At that moment, a tightly knit group of people emerged from the walkway separating the chancery building and the ambassador's residence. It was light enough to discern their faces.

"They've got the Ambassador," the RSO said, his voice almost despondent.

Stone and Sandra said at the same time, "That's Abdul Wahab leading them."

They watched Wahab and at least ten others make their way toward the tennis courts. Stone broke the silence. "I think it's negotiation time." He looked back at the other SUV and yelled to the FBI agents, "Either of you an experienced hostage negotiator?"

"That would be me, boss."

Stone shook the agent's hand. "Let's get a plan together, pronto."

"Too late for that," the agent said. "Look. They're waving us over."

Stone went to the SUV window and asked the RSO, "Do you have a bullhorn adapter with the siren unit?"

"Yeah, but I've never used it."

"Flip a few switches, and let's talk to these assholes," Stone said.

The RSO found the right switch and tested the volume. "Now what?" he asked.

Sporadic gunfire continued, and Stone saw Abdul Wahab look back toward the direction his men and the prisoners had come. Then he searched the sky.

Stone told the FBI agent to start talking over the bullhorn. "The terrorist in charge is Abdul Wahab. Use his name. He speaks English."

The agent called Wahab and told him that his situation was hopeless. It was best to release the Americans, then begin talking about surrendering. Wahab's response was to send back machine gun fire.

Wahab shouted across the field, "Hayden Stone."

Stone took the bullhorn from the agent. "Looks like the end of the line, Wahab."

Wahab yelled back, "Stone. I want you and the blonde to come over here."

Stone looked over to Sandra. "What's he up to?" He looked up at the sky. "Do you hear a helicopter?"

She shrugged. "Let's stall Wahab. He's not going anywhere."

Wahab took both male prisoners by the arm and the three walked a few steps away from the group toward the SUVs. "I suggest a prisoner exchange, Mr. Stone. You two for these two men."

The FBI agent holding the bullhorn answered, "No deal, Wahab. Now let's get serious. It's time to surrender."

"Here is your deal," Wahab shouted. "Stone and the woman start walking toward me, or I shoot one of these men." Bursts from machine guns and blasts from shotguns erupted from behind the ambassador's residence. "As we argue, men are dying. This man will be just one more body."

Stone told everyone, "Let me go. They're not going anywhere. They're boxed in." Two more American SUVs skidded in next to them. "I'll buy us some time."

"Hayden, he wants both of us," Sandra said. "I'm going with you. No arguments."

Stone looked at the FBI agent. "Are you wearing an ankle holster?"

Without answering, he handed the bullhorn to the RSO and unstrapped the pistol and holster and handed it to Stone.

"Sandra, this is what we do. We both walk forward with our pistols in our belts. Wahab will order us to ditch them. I'll still have this one on my ankle. Hope they don't have time to search me."

The FBI agent cautioned, "Take your time walking over there. Don't piss them off. They're under a lot of stress."

"We'll make an effort to stay alive," Stone said, then to Sandra, "Let's go, pal."

As suggested by the agent, the two took their time moving across the grounds to the terrorists. Stone saw Wahab looking up at the sky. Was that an American Blackhawk Stone heard?

The shooting behind the embassy buildings stopped, and four black-clad jihadists ran from between the chancery and the ambassador's residence toward Wahab. Marines in riot gear came out the front door of the embassy and took positions that pinned Wahab and his men to the far end of the compound next to the embassy tennis courts.

"Nowhere to go," Stone called as he and Sandra approached. "You made your point. You're a mastermind at insurgency. Time to negotiate."

When they were ten feet away, Wahab motioned for his men to seize Stone and Sandra and take their guns. "Bind them, then call the escape team. Have it meet you with their vehicles on the other side of that wall."

"What wall? Where?" the man cried.

"Kheibah, get ahold of yourself!" Wahab said. "Tell them the northwest corner."

The thumping sound of a helicopter's rotors grew louder. Stone whispered to Sandra, "That doesn't sound like a Blackhawk."

Wahab hit Stone on the side of his head with a glancing blow from with his pistol. "Be quiet!"

Kheibah's face froze. "Am I not going with you?"

"Go behind that vegetable garden over there. Find the steel exit door. Break the lock. Go out into the street and meet the escape team."

"But—"

"Go, and take your men. Join me at the place we talked about. Go!"

The sound of the helicopter grew louder. Stone watched Kheibah, along with four men, hurry toward the garden a hundred yards away. The Marines readjusted their positions and moved forward cautiously.

"Tell those people to back off," Wahab yelled.

The ambassador came up to Wahab eye-to-eye, and cried, "Stop. We can negotiate. We can work things out."

The Marines stopped and held tight. The FBI agent called over the bullhorn for Wahab and his men to lay down their arms. A huge gray machine appeared over the trees, emitting a roar and blowing loose debris across the compound.

"That's not one of ours," Sandra yelled.

"It's a Russian Mi-24. They call it the 'flying tank.'"

"We are going for a ride, Mr. Stone," Wahab shouted.

CHAPTER TWENTY-SEVEN

A MOUNTAIN VILLAGE, NORTH OF SANA'A
—NOVEMBER 4, 2002

Hayden Stone had a hard time believing Abdul Wahab's men had failed to discover he was wearing a gun on the inside of his left ankle. They'd searched him a number of times, but always rubbed down the outside of his legs, not the inside. Chalk it up to poor training, he reasoned.

The three of them were confined to a room with dark granite floor and walls. Only the ceiling lent a softening touch with planking and timbers. From the odor, the room had quartered animals at one time.

Stone and Sandra sat on a wooden bench, but the ambassador reclined on a pile of colorful cushions in the opposite corner of the room. Rank had its privileges, Stone remarked to Ambassador Manfred, who failed to see the humor.

The hands of the three were bound with fresh sets of plastic restrainers, Manfred's hands in front of her, Stone's and Sandra's behind them. In addition to extra security precautions ordered by Wahab, Stone had received a number of well-placed kicks to the body and blows to the head. He concentrated on the defensive rules of leaning away from the hits and kept his breathing steady, keeping his blood flowing.

One of Kheibah's men sat next to the door on a stool, smoking a cigarette. His right hand held a Beretta pistol. On the right sleeve of his blue suit jacket, the sales tag was still attached. Stone knew this to be a custom among the tribesmen in this region. Like showing off a designer label.

The man watched Stone, who had pushed his back against

the wall. When the guard looked away, he slowly rubbed the nylon plastic cord against a rough section of granite.

They had been in the room for close to three hours. The trip from Sana'a to this mountain village of Kawkaban had taken almost twenty-four hours of constant movement. The Mi-24 helicopter had dropped onto the American embassy's tennis courts, taken them aboard, and lumbered off. Dokka was at the controls and first flew east, probably as a diversion, Stone thought, then banked the helicopter to the left and roared northwest, full throttle. The craft shook so hard Stone wondered if its rivets would hold.

An hour later they landed in a field, climbed out, and went into a hut alongside a dirt road. Dokka flew off, leaving them in the silence of the countryside. By dusk, Kheibah showed up with his men in two SUVs and a van and after a few arguments—Wahab cursed him for taking his time to get there—the convoy headed north into the Kawkaban Mountains and arrived at the village the next morning. The entire time they traveled, Wahab never spoke to Stone or Sandra, but talked privately with Ambassador Manfred.

The room was quiet, the only noise coming from the guard's rickety stool. Stone looked over at Manfred and asked what she and Wahab had talked about on the way there. She glared and told him that under the circumstances he need not know.

Sandra shouted, "What's with you, Ambassador? We're all in this together."

Manfred arched her back. "You may not realize it, but I may be able to convince these people to release us. So, be quiet."

Their conversation made the guard edgy, so Stone called over in English, "My friend, you are wearing a very nice jacket."

The guard made no sign of understanding. Stone winked at Sandra. "How tight are your restraints?"

Sandra looked at the ceiling. "They're coming loose."

"Make no attempt to escape," Manfred ordered. "I can handle this matter diplomatically."

"Why not try to escape?" Stone asked, rubbing harder against the rock wall and feeling the plastic cords fray.

"You're Hayden Stone," Manfred stated. "Your presence in Yemen has been problematic from the moment you arrived. You only create problems."

Stone looked at Sandra. "Whatever that means."

The door opened, and the guard jumped to attention. Abdul Wahab rushed in. "Ambassador, come with me."

Wahab looked down at Stone's feet, and then pushed Manfred out the door, into the hands of a waiting terrorist. He told the guard to assist him and came across the room to Stone, lifted his foot, pulled the pant leg up, and ripped off the Velcro-fastened holster off his ankle.

"Before you slug me," Stone said, "chew out your men for not finding it."

Wahab had raised the holster and gun to whip Stone, but stopped. "That wouldn't be sporting now, would it?"

Wahab hurried out the room and slammed the door behind him. The guard carefully took his seat, this time watching Stone as if he was some form of caged tiger.

Sandra said, "We've got to get out of here. Sooner the better."

"Yeah." Stone felt the cord on his right wrist snap.

He looked away from the guard and to the lone open window. "I'm free. How about you?"

"Just about to slip out of both, but they're bleeding."

In Arabic, the guard ordered them to shut up. *Iskeeta!*

"I think our friend is getting nervous."

The guard snarled. He rushed over, put his face next to Stone's, and began to shout at him in Arabic. Stone held back until the guard's head was in the right position.

"Hands free," Sandra called over.

Stone grasped the guard's beard and gave him a head butt across the nose. A second blow crunched the man's front teeth, spraying blood. Stone snatched the guard's jambiya, and then kicked him off. He cut the zip ties loose from his feet.

While the guard squirmed on the floor holding his mouth, Stone freed Sandra's feet. The guard staggered to his feet, but

Stone kneed him in the head, sending him across the room where he hit the wall. He lay still, empty eyes pointed toward the ceiling.

Sandra now held the guard's Beretta pistol. "Go through his pockets and look for more magazines," she said. "We're going to need extra ammo."

"Got them," Stone said. "Now let's get out of here and find Wahab."

Stone eased open the door and was greeted by the bandaged face of Mark Reilly. His friend motioned to be quiet, and he and the CIA driver, Mohammed, dragged the bodies of two more terrorists inside the room.

"That's three jihadists down," Sandra said.

"We just got here," Reilly whispered. "Follow us."

They raced along deserted, trash-filled alleys. Twice Stone stumbled on the uneven pavement, before they halted in front of the patched wooden door of a building that looked as if it were about to collapse. Reilly looked both ways, and then went through the door.

Stone and Sandra followed through the abandoned building, crossed a litter-strewn yard, and entered another house. There they stopped and caught their breath.

"Damn, Hayden, this town is made of rock," Sandra whispered.

"Used to be a fortress. For centuries, villagers would hole up here in time of war."

Reilly motioned for them to enter the next room, and Stone found three armed CIA operatives in from Sana'a, dressed in local garb. They were setting up telecommunications equipment and computers. An Arab, whom Stone recognized as one of General al-Wasi's lieutenants, sat in the corner smoking.

Reilly brought out a medical kit and bandaged Sandra's wrists and asked Stone if he wanted the gash on his forehead tended to.

"You'd better put some antiseptic on it," Stone said. "I cut it on the guard's teeth."

The CIA operatives started typing on the computers while speaking into their headphones. "Our two people are with us.

They're free. No reaction from terrorists so far. When will you move in?"

Stone moved close to Reilly. "What's the situation? Where are the rest of our people?"

"Sheraton Hotel is secure. None of the al Qaeda made it out alive. Wahab lost eight men at the embassy and only one Marine got hit, in the leg." Reilly smiled. "Here in Kawkaban, we have an interesting development. Colonel Frederick, General al-Wasi, and assorted members of the Yemeni government, are all sitting outside the city gate anxious to get in and rock."

"What about Wahab and the Ambassador?" Sandra asked.

"That's where it gets interesting." Reilly paused as he gathered his thoughts. "Abdul Wahab is negotiating with the President of Yemen, and his offer is for the release of the American ambassador. He wants to share control of the eastern part of Yemen with the Yemen president. He wants to be some kind of viceroy."

"And the President of Yemen has told him to take a hike?" Stone said.

Reilly laughed and shook his head. "Wahab has a few tricks up his sleeve. An emissary from the Kingdom of Saudi Arabia is now with the President. Intercepts reveal that Saudi Arabia is willing to provide Yemen with two frigates and a hundred million dollars if they accept Wahab's deal."

Stone looked at Sandra. "Wonder how involved Ambassador Manfred is in all this?"

"Interesting that you say that," Reilly said. "The official U.S. position is that such an arrangement would foster democratic progress for Yemen."

"That would explain her attitude," Sandra added.

Reilly continued, "As befitting this interesting, convoluted scheme, a certain party doesn't go along with all this."

"My buddy, Colonel Frederick," Stone said.

Reilly looked at Mohammed. "Did you hear that noise outside?"

When Mohammed and al-Wasi's lieutenant slipped out the door to investigate, Reilly said quickly, "Correct. Frederick says we're not going to have Wahab set up a legitimate state to house and train terrorists. So we need a fast-moving game plan."

"Let's keep it simple." Stone rose and went over to a table and picked up an M4 with a sound suppressor. He asked Cosgrove, the CIA operative, "Mind if I borrow this?"

"Bring it back empty," he said, and went back to his computer.

CHAPTER TWENTY-EIGHT

The CIA operatives had locked on to the tracking device inserted in Abdul Wahab's backside. He was on the third floor of a tower house two hundred yards away. A listening device in the building, along with aerial drone surveillance, confirmed Wahab's group consisted of nine men, three stationed out front.

Reilly said, "Sorry, we don't have more firearms for you."

"We'll pick some up from dead terrorists on the way," Stone said.

"We can't take the streets or alleys," Reilly said. "They'll spot us."

"Let's go," Sandra said. "It won't be long before they discover we've escaped."

The four crisscrossed a passageway, and then ran through a yard, scattering chickens and goats. They went through an empty kitchen, crossed another alley, then stopped and hugged a wall. At the far end of the walkway, sixty yards away, they spotted a sentinel on top of a three-story building.

"That's the place," Reilly whispered.

"Where are the townspeople?" Sandra asked.

Reilly looked up. "They're peering out their windows, waiting for the action to start. Better than TV."

"Let's give them something to look at," Stone said, raising his rifle and aiming up at the man.

"Be my guest."

Stone fired once and missed. He guessed the sound suppressor at the end of the barrel of the M4 had been knocked off kilter, throwing off the bullet's trajectory. His target now looked around him as if looking for a passing bee. Stone made an adjustment, and his second shot was accurate. The man bent over and did a somersault down onto the pavement below.

When his body hit the ground with a thud, and his rifle clanked along the gutter, two other terrorists rushed out of the tower house and ran over to the body.

"Let's move," Stone said, and they ran toward the men.

The two men leaning over their dead comrade only had time to look up and sling off their AK-47s before Stone and Reilly used their M4s. Stone recovered one AK-47 and a bandoleer of ammo. He handed the M4 to Sandra.

As Stone checked the Kalashnikov, he said, "We'll meet opposition on each floor. Does Wahab have an escape route from the third floor?"

"He can take the roof of that building there," Reilly pointed, "and make his way down to the street."

"Mohammed. Best you watch from out here. Better still, cover the door of the house the terrorists might use to escape," Stone said. The man nodded and hurried away.

"Better move fast," Sandra said.

The three carefully entered the first floor of the tower house and found no one. Evidently, the two men lying on the street were the first-floor guards. Voices came from the floor above. The only access to the upstairs was a flight of steps. Stone asked for the M4 from Sandra, who showed her displeasure, but he whispered in her ear, "Let me go first. I'm younger than you." He didn't get a return smile.

"Control your fire," Reilly warned. "We don't want to hit the Ambassador."

Sandra now smiled. "What happens, happens."

Stone carefully made his way up the staircase, his companions close behind. As he neared the top he saw the heads of two men. With his rifle raised, he reached the top before they saw him.

The two men shouted, and one pulled a pistol from his belt. Stone dropped him with one shot. The other ran to a table, picked up a machine gun, and as he turned back, Stone downed him.

Shouts came from above, then the door at the top of the

third floor slammed shut, and Stone heard the pounding of footsteps on the wooden ceiling. Sandra and Reilly checked the two men on the floor and took their guns. One man was still alive, and Stone knelt next to him and asked in Arabic how many people were upstairs. The man spit in his face.

"Abdul Wahab! Surrender!" Reilly shouted toward the ceiling.

The door at the top of the stairs opened, and a burst from an AK-47 sent Stone and the others to the far side of the room. Sandra ran to the middle of the room, pointed her Kalashnikov at the ceiling, and emptied its magazine.

Stone heard people running above them toward the far end of the building. "They're taking the escape exit," he said.

Reilly made a move to ascend the stairs, but Stone held him back. He whispered, "Wahab will leave one or two of his men behind to cover him. We'll fire a few more shots, then head off Wahab when he exits the other building."

As they crept down the stairs, Sandra paused and emptied another magazine at the door. Then they raced downstairs, went out onto the street, and spied Mohammed, who told them three men and a woman had come out and run toward the square.

They went in the same direction Mohammed indicated, and arrived at the square, but found it empty.

"Where do you think they went?" Reilly asked Mohammed.

The man thought a moment. "Perhaps toward the edge of the town."

"Show us," Stone said.

They jogged past abandoned buildings that had been destroyed. Stone slowed them down as they checked the area.

"They could be using any of these structures for an ambush," he said.

"Looks like the place was bombed," Reilly remarked.

"They were—in the civil war in the sixties." Stone stopped them and said to Mohammed, "I remember the cliff is nearby. Which direction is it?"

Mohammed pointed. "Over there."

They ran to a five-foot wall and looked over. They came

under fire. Reilly motioned for them to go to the left toward a collapsed block building.

Inside the ruins, Stone looked through a window frame that was still in one piece. From there he watched Wahab shove Ambassador Manfred behind a boulder, and then yell to two men to take positions behind what resembled an outhouse.

At the same time, from behind them, gunshots came from the direction of old Wahab's hideout. Reilly spoke into his headphone, saying, "That's a roger. We've cornered our subjects at the edge of town." A pause. "Sounds good."

"What's up?" Stone asked.

Reilly said, "General al-Wasi and his men, along with Colonel Frederick, were allowed through the gate. They're at the house where Wahab held up and they're having a little dust-up with the men Wahab left behind."

Stone removed the silencer from the M4, reloaded, and got himself in a comfortable position at the window. Wahab had hidden himself behind the same boulder as the ambassador. Beyond the terrorists, a rock-strewn plain sloped gently toward the edge of a cliff.

A man's head appeared from behind the outhouse, but before Stone could pull the trigger, Reilly got off a shot. The man's *ghutra*, his colorful headdress, popped into the air.

"We're down to Wahab and one other man," Stone said, looking over his sights at the same spot.

Stone asked Sandra to rake the area with machine gun fire. A man Stone remembered Wahab calling Kheibah leaped from behind the building and headed toward the cliff.

Wahab cursed him, then followed his henchman, using the outhouse as partial cover.

"Let's go!" Stone shouted.

The three jumped the wall and ran after the two men. As they passed the ambassador, her hands still bound, she screamed, "You idiots! I just had Abdul agree to a truce."

They ignored her and continued running, avoiding the jagged rocks, until Wahab and Kheibah came to about fifty feet from the cliff edge. They stopped, climbed behind a pile of rubble, and opened fire.

Taking cover, Stone fired a few rounds, and then said, "They've no place to go." He turned and saw Mohammed crouched a hundred yards away, and behind him a small army forming, consisting of General al-Wasi's men and CIA operatives.

Reilly was on his phone and, when finished, said, "That was Frederick. It's simple, and yet not simple." A bullet hit nearby and spattered them with pieces of rock. "General al-Wasi is holding back for word from the Yemeni president, who is trying to get more millions from the Saudis. Wahab may still get everything he wants. Meantime, al-Wasi considers this still to be an antiterrorist operation. If anyone takes out Wahab, it must be us. Al-Wasi is covering his ass in case the situation reverses."

"What?" Sandra asked.

"We can nail Wahab, but make it fast."

At that a loud noise came from the cliff, and Stone saw the Russian Mi-24 helicopter gunship rise from the valley. It maneuvered toward Wahab and Kheibah, then a rope ladder dropped from the open side door. The pilot inched his aircraft toward Wahab.

The team of CIA operatives moved forward and opened fire. Bullets bounced off the helicopter's armored plates. That was why Russian soldiers call it a flying tank, Stone thought, firing a few rounds in the direction of Wahab, who was reaching for the ladder.

The helicopter hovered above Wahab and Kheibah, taking heavy fire. At the door, two terrorists appeared and raked the ground around Stone with machine guns. They all dove behind a boulder as bullets cracked the rocks around them.

Stone saw the CIA operatives who had been shooting at the helicopter duck for cover.

"Wahab is escaping!" Sandra shouted.

"No goddamned way!" Stone jumped up and ran toward the helicopter. The engines howled and blew a cloud of dirt and pebbles into Stone's face.

Wahab hung with both hands from the ladder and was

being pulled up by the men in the Mi-24. The aircraft banked and headed down toward the valley a thousand feet below.

Stone emptied his pistol in its direction, while Wahab, now inside the craft, turned and waved.

Sandra and Reilly stood next to him and watched Kheibah see his leader fly away. He turned and dropped his gun. He appeared despondent.

CHAPTER TWENTY-NINE

KAWKABAN, YEMEN

Stepping in from the alley, Colonel Gustave Frederick looked around the CIA command post and saw his men packing up their communication equipment. Cosgrove, the team leader, handed equipment to a woman, who placed the gear in a backpack. One laptop computer still remained active.

"We have to get out of here before one of the Yemeni big shots changes course and decides to harass us." Frederick sat before a laptop with a blinking cursor. "What did this thing monitor? The audio and video device in Wahab's hiding place?"

Cosgrove's mahogany skin glistened with sweat. "No, sir. That's the monitor for the beacon Calypso that was inserted in Wahab's ass."

"How did it work?"

"Not so good with all the rock walls around here, but we were able to track him to the edge of the cliff and follow him when he flew away in that helicopter. Our satellite lost him down in the valley."

Frederick rose and told the three operatives to get a move on. "I'll meet you by the city gate."

The laptop was the last to go into the backpack, and as Cosgrove sat down to turn off the machine, he saw the signature belonging to the beacon inside Abdul Wahab blip. The faint signal came from a mountain area in the far north, near the Saudi Arabian border. The pulse lasted a few seconds, moving slightly, and then disappeared. He waited another minute and, when nothing reappeared on the screen, he shut down the computer.

• • •

The SUV moved smoothly along the newly paved blacktop highway toward Sana'a. Stone and Sandra watched silently from the backseat as the vast, empty countryside, marked by the occasional green-terraced hillside, passed on both sides of the highway.

"What are those for?" Sandra pointed to a pile of rocks that stood four to five stones high.

"Cairns. You see them up here in the hill country. I've been told some are boundary markers, some shrines to spirits. The *djinn*."

"These people believe in genies?" Sandra leaned close to the window to get a better look.

"So I'm told."

Their convoy reached a straight section of the road and sped up. Sandra leaned over and asked, "How do you feel about the outcome?"

"I wanted to see Abdul Wahab's dead body," Stone whispered. He patted her hand. "Colonel Frederick told me that General al-Wasi and his men would try to search north Yemen, but not to expect miracles. That section of the country is in semi-rebellion and not under the government's full control."

"I can't believe the bastard managed to survive," Sandra said.

"Do you still plan to take a sabbatical?" Stone asked as the SUV slowed to pass a camel train.

"I've told Colonel Frederick I needed some time off," Sandra said, touching her side where she'd been stabbed. "He said he'd make some phone calls for me. How about you?"

"Heading for Tuscany. A little warmer than the south of France this time of year," Stone looked at her, with her blonde hair pulled back in a ponytail. How she managed to look so clean after all the dirt and grime they put up with was a mystery.

"I still plan to go open up my apartment in Paris. It needs a painting. And I'll probably volunteer for the community liaison office at our embassy."

Stone thought about the archaeological excavation Lucinda showed him on her villa and told Sandra he might get involved in the Etruscan dig. "Also, I want to start cooking again. Haven't done any for about a year. Did I ever tell you I once thought of opening a café on a beach north of LA?"

"I'm going to remodel the kitchen in my apartment."

"The one thing that always appealed to me was the wall color on many Parisian apartments. Not the dead white you find in the States, but that crème fraîche, yellow-white that goes so well with the Paris light."

She laughed. "Where do you come up with stuff like that? Hayden, you constantly amaze me."

"What?'

She shook her head, and then whispered, "We've had some interesting times together."

"The best."

THE RED SEA—NOVEMBER 6, 2002

Prince Mohammed al-Tabrizi met with Uthman and the emissary from the Saudi intelligence agency. The emissary had flown in that morning from Riyadh. They sat under an awning on the open fantail of the anchored Red Scorpion for an hour exchanging pleasantries.

Finally, the intelligence agent addressed the delicate subject of Abdul Wahab. "My apologies for my agency's detainment of your son-in-law."

The prince noted the man wore a Western pinstripe suit and sported Italian sunglasses. His heavy gold watch kept clanging on the armrest, which annoyed him.

"*Malish*," the prince replied. "So be it."

"I am here to advise you of the latest developments." The man removed his sunglasses, which seemed to accentuate his beak-like nose. "The President of Yemen has agreed to accept one hundred million dollars in aid. We suggested half in foodstuffs for his people, but he wanted all cash placed in a Swiss bank in a special account."

"Interesting," the prince noted. "Perhaps the renewed trouble in the south of Yemen has him worried."

"Cautious, I would say. How did he put it recently? 'Governing Yemen is like dancing on the heads of snakes.'"

"What do we get in return?" The prince began fingering his prayer beads.

"A great deal of influence in Yemen. We were to have Abdul Wahab be the governor of the eastern provinces, but now...."

"A leading figure in Marib is the old gentleman, Sheik az-Zaddim, but I have a suggestion for a younger, more reliable candidate," the prince said. He looked over and gestured toward Uthman.

The emissary replaced his sunglasses and smiled broadly, "A wise choice."

The prince looked toward the cloud-covered mountains of Yemen and sighed. He already missed the company of Abdul Wahab.

TUSCANY, ITALY—NOVEMBER 7, 2002

Hayden Stone enjoyed his negroni, relaxing before the flagstone fireplace. Burning logs crackled, sending stray sparks onto the brick hearth extension. Curled up next to him, Lucinda sipped her Campari. They had inspected the Etruscan excavation and come inside as the sun was about to set. Stone looked forward to a good Italian meal, and took in the mixed-herb aromas drifting in from the kitchen. Lucinda had an ornery cook. He wondered if she would object to him trying out the kitchen. Probably.

Lucinda nudged his shoulder with her cheek. "I appreciate you working with my consigliore, Philippe. Your suggestions on my bond portfolio and the real estate holdings surprised him. I did not know you were so well-versed in finance."

"They taught me a few things at NYU."

"Tomorrow morning, please give me the clothes you are wearing," Lucinda said. "I will throw them out with the rest you brought back from Yemen."

He gave her a quizzical look.

"They are filthy and they reek from Lord knows what. I've

bought you some new clothes." She put her glass down on the end table. "Would you like to try them on?"

"Now?"

"After dinner." She rested her head on his shoulder. "We will have a fashion show."

. . .

Stone stood in front of the mirror. Lucinda pretended to be miffed when he said the shoes she had selected were too Italian and the colors of the tight turtlenecks too extreme.

"My wardrobe tends to be American conservative," he said. "My tailor in Washington would consider these shirts a bit much."

"I suppose you are right. They would look better on a younger man."

That was when he tackled her and they fell on the bed. All his new clothes soon lay scattered on the floor.

. . .

The next morning, after cappuccinos and bowls of muesli, she announced she had a surprise for him in the garage. They walked from the main house to the garage and he spied an impeccable, French blue, nineteen-sixties Citroën DS.

"That's some surprise," he said.

"No dear, that is mine. This is your new car."

She led him to a new Porsche Carrera.

"I chose a blue color close to the Citroën. What do you think?"

He embraced her. "You certainly know how to please a man."

. . .

A day later, under a sky spotted with white clouds and alone at the wheel of the Porsche, he pushed it hard on the sharp turns of the Tuscan back roads. Eventually, he slowed and pulled off on the crest of a hill. He turned off the motor. The autumn colors of Italy spread before him. A chill breeze crossed over from a fallow field. Before him stood a tall, almost leafless oak bending over the road. High up in the branches, he spied a goshawk.

The bird repeatedly turned its head in different directions and shifted its weight on the branch. Stone noted its golden eyes and feet. Black teardrops marked its breast.

"The most difficult hawk to train," he mused.

As if finally making up its mind, and now knowing where it wanted to go, the bird pushed off. Stone watched the hawk until it disappeared into the distance.

Hayden Stone turned the ignition key and listened to the sound of the motor. How soon would he respond to that urge to fly away?

THE END

ACKNOWLEDGEMENTS

At the date of publication, the country of Yemen was in the thralls of a religious war and terrorist attacks. The few tourists, scholars, and archaeologists I met during my travels from 1996 to 2008 are no longer seen visiting the countryside. I wonder how my faithful driver, or Mustafa, the son of the Sultan in the Hadhramaut, or other fascinating Yemenis I knew have fared during this turmoil. Perhaps in time this land will return to being the *Arabia Felix* of antiquity.

I want to thank my writing group members, especially Betty Webb, Deb Ledford, Virginia Nosky, Sharon Magee, Eileen Brady, Louise Signorelli, Bill Butler, and Pascal Marco, who read and critiqued my manuscript.

Thanks to my publisher, Diversion Books, in particular Mary Cummings, Sarah Masterson Hally, Chris Mahon, and especially my editor, Randall Klein, whose patience and assistance with the manuscript was invaluable.

My associates in the Desert Sleuths chapter of Sisters in Crime, Society of Southwestern Authors, and the International Thriller Writers have been most supportive of my writing. Special thanks to the author Eric Hansen who helped me on Yemen history, Bill Vanderpool who kept me straight on firearms, and the support of Doug Hopkins of the Society of Former Agents of the FBI and Elizabeth Bancroft of the Association of Former Intelligence Officers.

Of course, thanks to my agent Elizabeth Kracht of Kimberley Cameron & Associates, who works so hard on my behalf.

Finally, I want to express my gratitude to my wife, Donna, for her support.

ACKNOWLEDGEMENTS